THE DEMON BAQASH

OTHER BOOKS BY THOM REESE

CHASING KELVIN
DEAD MAN'S FIRE
13 BODIES

THE DEMON BAQASH

THOM REESE

SPEAKING VOLUMES, LLC

NAPLES, FLORIDA

2011

THE DEMON BAQASH

ISBN 978-1-61232-009-0

Library of Congress Control Number: 2010942879

For Kathy
The author of all that's good in my life

Acknowledgments

Writing a book can be a solitary process, but it's never done alone. Thank you to all of you who have encouraged me, read my drafts, and put up with me along the way. In particular, special thanks to my amazing wife and best friend, Kathy, who has read – and honestly critiqued – nearly every word I've written. I'd accomplish nothing in life without you. To my wonderful girls, Trista, Amy, and Brittany, you have no idea how each of you, in your own way, brightens and encourages me. To my "constant reader," Jeff Granstrom – more manuscripts for you to read coming down the pike! To Randall Dunn for wading through so much of my (mostly dreadful) early writing. To Kirk Bechtold – the printer's still kicking out manuscript pages. To Kurt Mueller at Speaking Volumes, for his confidence in me and his support. And to all the others who have been there for me along the way.

CHAPTER 1

Kim Troxel's sleep was restless, punctuated with bizarre half-dreams and images. There was a dark figure, not a man, something different, with wings – six of them – moving independently, like tentacles slithering, reaching, grabbing. The creature had four faces, each directed to a different point. One laughed, while another cried. One ranted, the last smirked. Even through the mist of dream, Kim felt tense, felt her stomach twist, her skin go cold. The faces were not right. A hollow moldy cheek opposite a chubby infantile counterpart. A large uneven eye adjacent a torn and empty socket. The man-thing was somewhere else, someplace far away.

So very close.

A fire crackled and glowed. The smell of burning flesh assailed Kim's nostrils. The non-man was before her now, grinning, though, in truth, Kim could make out none of the features. But they were familiar, so familiar. Yet… faded, incomplete. The man, the thing, entity – whatever! - it was holding a phone – handing it to her.

Kim's eyes fluttered as she rolled over to face the annoyance. "Alright, alright. I'm coming." She stretched, extending her arm as if she could will it to be longer. Why did the phone have to be on Trent's side of the bed when he was never home from work until three A.M.? "Uhuggh, hello," she managed in a dry midnight growl.

"Good morning, Kim."

"Trent?"

"I've got a surprise for you."

Kim squinted at the blurry alarm clock. Why did it seem the numerals faded as if fleeing some unseen menace?

"Trent, what time is it?"

"Late, Kim. Terribly late. But, someone is coming to see you."

*****

The deliveryman was tall. Taller even than the six-foot six Trent. Pro basketball tall. Wide-shouldered and statuesque. Kim fumbled to wipe the sleep from her eyes, attempting to bring the face into focus. Somehow it seemed the man had multiple features, each fading and then reemerging in subtle parody of itself. He seemed so inconsequential, as if he might simply evaporate on the cool evening breeze. Kim blinked again and then again. The man was solid. Of course he was solid. How could he be otherwise? Strangely, at the sight of him, Kim felt a warm rush, a kind of electric hum or vibration, both comforting and unnerving, familiar yet alien. It was almost sexual but simultaneously horrifying. Strange. Why should she feel anything at all?

Something in this man's face was familiar. Intimately so. But how? She'd never seen him before. One would remember a six-foot eight-inch deliveryman with deep multi-colored eyes.

"Mrs. Troxel?"

The strangely accented voice brought Kim back around. "Yes. I'm sorry. I'm still half asleep."

"Undoubtedly," he agreed. "I assume your husband informed you of this delivery."

"He did," she said, rubbing her eyes. "It's just late." Then, pausing, she ventured, "And since when are deliveries made at this hour?"

The man smiled. It was somehow inviting, beckoning her to come to him, to wrap her arms about him, to engulf him and...

What was she thinking?

"Distributions of the highest priority can be delivered around the clock, ma'am." He extended the clipboard for her to sign. Those strange eyes – so knowing, as if he knew her every impulse.

Kim's mind was fuzzy, unclear, still flirting with those horrible dreams. How was it that this man's face seemed so ill-defined? She closed her eyes tight, and then opened them wide. She was simply tired. His face was fine. Wacky dreams.

"Would you care to come in?" she asked.

*****

"Reggie," said Kim to her live-in brother-in-law. "What's that?"

The sound of someone shaking the front door flooded the tiny home. Kim and Reggie were seated at a table in the small, sparsely decorated kitchen, sipping a sweet herbal tea as Kim jotted ideas for a new poem. Writing poetry normally comforted her, separated her from the day-to-day drudge. But tonight her thoughts were scattered, her lines lacked meter, her meaning remained unclear. The deliveryman had left only fifteen minutes prior – three A.M. – and Kim had decided against climbing back into the oh-so-inviting bed. Now, she felt this might have been a mistake.

Reggie brushed his dark matted bangs from his eyes. "It's Trent, I think. The door must be stuck again. He sounds kinda excited. Maybe he needs to use the bathroom." Turning toward the door Reggie hollered, "I'm coming, Trent. I'm coming." He rose gracelessly from the chair, his pear-like form sluggish as he hiked his lagging pajama bottoms with his left hand. "That door needs a new handle. It needs a new handle."

Kim took another sip of tea. Reggie was probably right. It most likely was Trent, but Kim doubted his urgency had anything to do with bodily functions. The pounding and shaking of the door sounded like someone panicked.

Four faces.

Panicked.

Six wings.

The midnight fog cleared from Kim's brain like the lingering sound of a marching band. Something was wrong. Terribly wrong.

"Hey Trent," said Reggie as he pulled the door open with a forceful twist and a sharp tug. "We've got some tea. I can fix you some tea. It's good. You can go to the bathroom first. I'll just start…"

"Kimmie," said Trent as he brushed roughly past his brother causing the smaller man to shuffle backward, nearly tripping over a nearby crate.

Four faces.

"Trent?" Kim nearly screamed at the sight of him. His sandy red hair was disheveled, his face flushed and sweaty, his right hand was wrapped in

3

something red, and his eyes. Trent had strange eyes to begin with, one green, one blue. But this. There was something in Trent's dual-colored eyes. Something she'd never seen, not when he was dismissed from the church in disgrace, not even when he'd watched Ashley emerge red and slimy from her body. It was fear. Real fear. Deep down in the soul fear. The kind one expected to find in the eyes of a man who'd just learned that the cancer had spread, that he had five weeks to live. "Trent, what happened?"

Six wings.

"Extraordinary," he muttered, then paused as if somewhere between bewildered and flustered. "No, horrifying," he added, wiping a hand on his corduroy leg. "Yes, horrifying is better. Did he come here?"

Kim stared up into her husband's face and saw tears. "Trent, what happened?"

"Was he here, Goober?" asked Trent, using the pet name he'd given Kim when she'd been pregnant and craving peanuts. "I tried to call. Couldn't get through. He was here. Of course, he was here."

"Who, Trent? What's this about?"

It was then that Trent noticed the boxes, twenty-seven of them, coarse wooden crates crowded into each corner, behind and under the not-quite-antique furniture, in the open closet, beside Trent's upright bass. How Trent had missed them was beyond her. But undoubtedly he had. There he stood, jaw prepped to catch flies, golf ball eyes, and his head cocked like a cocker spaniel. If it hadn't been so tragic, it would have been hysterical.

Kim stepped forward, embraced her husband in a fierce hug, brushed her lips wistfully across his, and then buried her head in his chest. The strangest, most horrifying thought came to her then.

Four faces.

Six wings.

Kim Troxel began to cry.

CHAPTER 2

It had been Trent Troxel's own nature which dulled him to the internal alarms screaming at his very core. Trent was dangerously inquisitive, approaching life with a playful curiosity which bordered on recklessness. Despite his height, natural athleticism, and aggression, Trent often came off as a pseudo-intellectual, tossing about multi-syllabic responses to mundane inquiries and delving into matters better left undisturbed. It was this playful nature which blinded Trent to the dangers of the stranger who had confronted him that Tuesday night as he sat alone in a booth huddled over his nightly paperwork more than an hour after closing.

He'd ignored the electric impulse racing through his limbs, that fight-flight instinct, that survival instinct.

He'd dismissed the sudden turn of his stomach, the sudden chill in his spine.

He'd subdued the intellect on which he prided himself, dismissed the illogic of the situation, considered it mere childish emotions still trapped within the clutter of his subconscious.

There had been a monogram on the royal blue cuff, the letter "B." It stood for "Baqash," though Trent had no idea how he knew this. The movement, the manner in which the stranger held himself as he slid into the booth, seemed inappropriate for someone of his age, late twenties or early thirties. There was an economy of movement, a subtle elegance. It almost seemed the way an elderly man might move had he the agility and stamina of a well-toned twenty year-old.

"You do recognize me," assumed the stranger.

Suppressing the irrational urge to flee, Trent gazed into the sharp angular face, which, though distinct, also hinted at near feminine softness. The skin was dark, but not as that of an African or even a Hispanic. It was more of a golden hue, nearly iridescent in the dimly lit room. Trent wished the man would remove his dark designer sunglasses and allow him to search his eyes for intent.

"You were at the church – that day," Trent ventured, his voice animated in anticipation of an enigma resolved.

"Yes. That day. Nearly a year now." He leaned back in the booth, gazing past Trent to a black and white photograph of Al Capone. "You virtually manage this establishment single-handedly. Your father-in-law grants you great authority, and even a modicum of trust. You have recovered well from your difficulties."

How well Trent had recovered was open to speculation. After leaving the church in disgrace, he'd remained unemployed for nearly three months before finally fleeing rural Kentucky in favor of the big city. Chicago had welcomed the Troxels, or rather, Trent's father-in-law had welcomed them, hiring Trent as assistant manager in one of his four Irish pubs. The income was steady, but not spectacular. Kim had been forced to take up substitute teaching after a nearly ten-year hiatus from the classroom.

"I have been with you other times as well," said the stranger. "Though you may not have noticed." The man spoke with an ever-so-slight accent. At once it was European, yet Middle-Eastern, and yet – Texan? "You are, I suppose, wondering who I am."

"Baqash," said Trent without thinking.

"Yes, Baqash. Yet the pronunciation is closer to 'Bah-kah-sh'. Allow the 'ah' to sustain."

Trent narrowed his gaze, an intrigued grin creasing his lips. "How did I know that? There's the monogram, but it's only a 'B.' I've never heard the name Baqash before."

Baqash shrugged. "Perhaps you recall my name from previous encounters; from that discreet little 'counseling session' with Mrs. Phelps. Or maybe from the time your accountant – what was his name? Kennelly. Perhaps from the time Kennelly suggested that 'creative' use of figures on your tax return. Could it have been then?"

Despite his irrepressible curiosity, Trent Troxel went hollow inside. Those had been private meetings, only the participants present. "In heaven's name, who are you?"

Baqash leaned back in the padded vinyl seat, hands folded lazily across his taut belly. "In heaven's name, I am no one. Here, I am Baqash."

Trent leaned forward on his elbows, his natural curiosity overriding blaring internal alarms. "How did you know about those meetings at the church?" Trent paused. "And as to Debbie Phelps – nothing happened."

Baqash smiled. "I suppose that depends on your definition of 'nothing.' Wouldn't you agree – pastor?"

Trent cocked his head and smiled. "Are you trying to goad me, Mr. Baqash? You know I'm no longer a pastor."

Baqash ignored Trent's comment. "As for my absence in those rooms, simply because you do not see something, does not mean it is absent." A pause. "Pastor, you believe in God – the invisible. I suppose you believe in Satan as well. The supernatural is your business, your life's work. Why are you so astonished to encounter it?"

Trent contemplated the strange man for a moment, and then laughed. "Ah! I get it. You think you're God. Or, at least, you want me to think that you think you're God."

Baqash roared in astounded mirth. "God? God! Certainly not. Try again."

"Satan, then."

No. Though we are acquainted."

"A demon."

Baqash shrugged. "I really prefer the term, retired angel – or perhaps, heaven-impaired host. That has such a nice ring to it."

Trent stared at the stranger. "A demon? Manifested in human form? Tell me, have you spent much time in Elgin, the state mental hospital?"

Baqash sighed, "Oh, wicked and perverse generation which seeks a sign." Slowly, purposefully, the stranger removed the charcoal-black glasses from his long indistinct face. His eyes had the appearance of constant motion, of infinite depth. One color rolled into another, and yet another supplanted that. The shades merged, stretched, retreated, all within the tiny orbs. The effect was disconcerting, nearly trance inducing.

Abruptly Baqash leaned forward, his face inches from Trent's, his eyes green, then orange. "Name a Language," said Baqash.

"Excuse me?"

"A language, Pastor. Name a language."

"Umm… Spanish. French, German – pick one." Trent could barely think of anything but those eyes modulating before him like some satanic lava lamp. He felt his skin begin to crawl, his stomach to grind. Trent closed his eyes, breathing deeply, calming himself. When he opened them again, Baqash was speaking.

"*Como esta usted*? *Parlez-vous Franceis*? *Sprechen sie Deutsch*? Please tell me you are not that simple-minded." Baqash sat upright snapping his fingers twice. "Something difficult. Ancient Greek, Hebrew, the language of the Amorites. It's actually quite lyrical. Don't you agree?"

Baqash proceeded to spew verbiage in one tongue, then another, and another. It seemed nearly an endless current, consonants and vowels rising and falling, ebbing and flowing, rhythms abruptly changing as the man sifted through dialects. Trent was tempted to deny the reality. Anyone could approximate the sound of a foreign tongue. But as he listened, as he focused on the meter, he could tell by the enunciation, by the flow, the very essence that these were actual vernaculars.

And then it seemed the very breath was snatched from his mouth. Trent actually comprehended the words. He was hearing them in foreign tongues, yes, but his mind quickly translated. Or at least, he assumed it was his mind. In some ways it seemed more that the translations were whispered into his ear.

And the words spoken – Genesis. Baqash was quoting Genesis verbatim: creation, the fall of man, the Nephilim, the flood. He flowed seamlessly from one ancient dialect to another. Some languages seemed scarcely human, others nearly familiar.

Baqash stopped as suddenly as he had begun. "Tell me, Pastor, what temperature is my hand?" His arm lashed out catching Trent's right hand, pulling it toward him, squeezing. "What temperature? Tell me."

The hand was cool, nearly icy. Then without warning it became – hot! Dangerously hot. Trent ripped his hand free with a wail as his seared flesh sizzled like Sunday morning bacon, popping and blistering, clear liquid dribbling across his reddened palm.

Baqash stared at him, appearing almost hurt, perhaps even fearful. "I've injured you," he said, removing the scarlet kerchief from his breast pocket. "Wrap your hand in this."

Trent eyed the cloth warily like an abused mutt might contemplate a treat from a stranger. "Take it," coaxed Baqash, his face taut with concern, whether real or feigned. "It is harmless, I assure you. The injury was unintentional. I sought only to provide evidence of my claims." He leaned forward. "We shall be allies, you and I."

Baqash offered the fabric once again, his calm demeanor flushed with burden. But Trent sensed the concern was not for him, but rather, that the demon – yes, demon, he couldn't deny the fact just then – may have bungled whatever he had hoped to achieve through this encounter.

Cautiously, Trent accepted the kerchief and wrapped his throbbing hand. The two stared at one another, neither speaking, neither so much as blinking. He studied the demon, gazing into, and then willfully avoiding, the powerful beckoning eyes, wondering if he was about to die, if this monster had come to collect his soul.

Finally, regarding his wrapped hand with a wince, Trent said. "You've been with me for some time."

Baqash nodded. "On a regular basis, nearly ten years, less in your youth."

Ten years, this monster had been in his life. Through all those years of ministry, throughout his marriage – the birth of precious little Ashley. Through the months of climbing back, correcting past wrongs, the months of rebuilding, a demon had been by his side – or worse. Far worse. "You're saying I've been possessed," the words were barely a whisper.

Baqash laughed, his bizarre eyes squinting into pulsating slits. "Possessed? No. I provided opportunity and perhaps a modicum of motivation, nothing more. Your fall from grace was entirely of your own volition."

Baqash paused, his strange face shifting, as if he sought a particular yet evasive expression. "Pastor, I believe we may aid one another toward a common goal."

Trent closed his fist tightly about the red kerchief. "What common goal could we possibly share?"

"Redemption, pastor. We both seek redemption."

"What makes you think I seek redemption?"

"Really, Pastor. Is that any way to speak to a lost soul in need of guidance?"

"Guidance?" Trent nearly laughed. "How is a fallible man to guide a being condemned since the earliest days of the earth?"

"The answer to that question, Pastor, will become clear when you arrive home."

"No," said Trent with sudden conviction. "You will go nowhere near my family. You will stay away. Leave them alone. Taunt me, I've earned it, but I will not have my family involved in your evil." Trent did not know where the strength had come from. By all rights he should have been fleeing for his life and sanity. Perhaps it was that Baqash had assumed the form of a man. Tall, yes. Unusual in color, with the bizarre eyes and ill-defined features, yet here he sat as a man, wearing a designer suit – Prada, Armani, whatever – sporting a diamond stud earring, with his hair pulled back in a tight ponytail. A demon yes, but packaged for humanity.

Baqash angled his head as if perplexed. "How can you be sure that I'm entirely evil? Satan harbors the greater darkness, deceiving the fallen as well as humans. You're a man of God. Do you have no desire to defeat this monster?"

"The only monster I see is you."

"Ah," smiled the demon. "So, if you do not see the evil, it does not exist."

"Oh, it exists. No doubt, there. And since you've mentioned it, yes, I do believe that you are evil."

"A shame, really. I had hoped you'd be more enlightened."

"Lies," said Trent. "You say you seek redemption, yet you admit to prodding me toward my own destruction. That seems rather inconsistent, Baqash."

"Entirely inconsistent," agreed the demon. "Simply put, I have traded my allegiance. As I manipulated you toward your ruin, I served the Satan. Now, I seek redemption and the devil's ruin."

"Ah," said Trent. "You see, there's the rub. You're a fallen angel – a demon. What possibly could you do to be redeemed?"

Baqash smiled, the picture of twisted dignity. "Why, defeat Satan, of course."

"Your nose is growing, Baqash." Trent had scooted to his left, meaning to leave the booth. "Now, go," he'd said. "The last thing I need is more lies in my life."

The face hadn't so much changed as split, separated, overlapped into multiple features – fierce features. The swimming, lava lamp eyes had betrayed the very landscape of hell, the voice was that of a train wreck. And for a moment, only a moment, Trent believed he'd seen six serpentine wings. "I will deliver secrets to your hovel," said the demon now only inches from Trent's face. "Treasures no human eyes have ever seen, no human hands held. You will study them. You will learn of me, as I am, as I was. After which, I will instruct you further. If you value your family, you will not betray me."

CHAPTER 3

Kim needed a new husband – or at least a lobotomy for the one she had. Trent was simply losing it. He'd called her in the middle of the night, had the mysterious crates delivered, showed up injured and ranting, spent hours pacing back and forth, eyeing the crates, running his good hand through his hair; yet, here they sat: every crate, unopened, untouched.

Trent hadn't revealed the contents of the crates to Kim. He'd acted as if he didn't know himself. But he did know. Or, at least, he knew where they had come from, why they were here. He had never been a great communicator – except in front of his congregation, there he'd been brilliant – but this was an all-time low. How could she live with this? For all she knew, her fallen pastor was drug-running or dealing in illegal weapons.

What had become of her man? Time was when Trent had been so spiritually attuned that she swore he strolled straight into heaven and sat chatting with God over manna, lettuce, and tomato sandwiches. But Trent had shifted his focus from God to… What? What road was he riding, and to where?

At some level, Kim had been strangely relieved by this turn. Trent had always taken his religion too seriously. In some ways, this had created a strange attraction, almost a fixation. Still, in others, this same trait had nearly driven her away. Kim had not been a spiritual person. She'd learned to become one specifically to win Trent. Why he'd been such a prize, she couldn't be sure.

That wasn't true.

She knew exactly what had drawn her – what still drew her. It simply came down to who he was: to his quirky personality, his strange mix of academic, athlete, and jazz musician, his sweet sense of offbeat romance, and his intense, nearly manic drive, all packaged in the guise of an evangelical pastor. But now her husband, her lover, was into something else, something frightening, probably illegal.

Reggie was deep into a nap, Ashley wasn't yet home from school, and Trent was out for an afternoon run along Oak Street Beach. Clearing his mind, he'd said.

If that was the case, it could be a long run.

Kim glared at the offending crates. There was opportunity.

Locating a hammer kept in a nearby closet, she began prying the boards of the nearest crate.

Four faces.

Nails squeaked in protest, wood snapped as Kim strained in determination.

Six wings.

Kim blinked. Why the sudden shudder? It seemed a near-maddening vibration seeped into her very bones.

Disregarding the strange sensation, Kim moved left, inserted the hammer claw between two boards, and pried. This portion relented with less of a struggle. Why did her hands tremble so violently? She was doing what she must, taking control of a dicey situation. Why was she so unnerved?

Four faces.

One more corner, and she was able to pull the top back with a creaking groan worthy of Dracula's coffin. Styrofoam peanuts spilled onto the floor with the sound of a thousand miniature footsteps as Kim dropped the hammer and gingerly sifted through packaging in search of – what?

Did she really want to know? Could she dare to know? What if there were narcotics? What if there were guns? Could she turn in her own husband? And if she did, wouldn't this endanger the family? Wouldn't the drug lords or whoever had sent these come seeking their merchandise? Wouldn't they retaliate against the meddling wife?

No. She had to pursue this. There really was no choice in the matter.

Several handfuls of peanuts later Kim discovered something solid, about eight inches tall, five in diameter, and carefully concealed in bubble wrap. The weight was surprisingly heavy for the small size. Kim lifted it gently from the crate. This was not cocaine, nor did it appear to be a weapon. Slowly, she unwrapped the object. A soft sigh escaped her lips.

"Oh... How beautiful."

*****

Trent hadn't meant to hit her. He'd never struck Kim before. Yelled, sometimes. Hollered, yes. Pestered, constantly. But hit, never. He'd always been careful to release his intense inner rage through sports: football when he'd been younger – he'd actually been scouted by the Packers – basketball, swimming, and triathlons as he'd moved into true adulthood. Though strangely lanky, he'd excelled in each event, bringing a near unnatural intensity to each sport.

But this time there'd been no sport, no outlet. He'd hit Kim, his fist connecting just behind the right ear, causing her to scream and falter. It was surprising how easy it had been. The circumstances were just right – or wrong, he supposed: the room full of demonic Christmas gifts, his scarred and enflamed right hand, Baqash's threats. But it was the challis that had triggered it.

There she'd been, sitting beside an open crate, in her hand a jeweled challis. Trent had not known what the boxes contained; though insanely curious, he'd forced himself to refrain. Still, if he had guessed, it would have been something darker, more sinister, something hideous, harboring the stench of death. Nothing beautiful. Nothing precious. He thought of these things later, of course. At the time, all he knew was rage.

His fist had come down hard and had immediately risen to strike again. Kim's arms had come up as Trent's arm descended. Reggie appeared from nowhere. It was probably the only time the guy had ever moved faster than a drunken tortoise. The surprise body block knocked Trent from his feet and onto the coarse carpet.

Now, two hours later, Trent sat on the couch – alone, absently thumping out diatonic scales on his old blond double bass. Kim had slipped crying into their bedroom, emerging ten minutes later with her purse and jacket, stating simply that she and Ashley would be out for the evening. With that, she was gone. Trent figured she'd intercepted Ashley on her way home from school and taken her out for dinner and a movie. He just hoped Kim could forgive him.

How could he have done that? What madness had possessed him? He loved Kim, nearly worshiped her. She was his soul mate. All that was good about Trent originated with Kim. And yet he'd lashed out as if she'd meant nothing, as if she'd been nothing more than an obstacle.

Trent eyed the challis, now situated on the coffee table, and set his instrument aside. Lifting the relic tenderly, as if it might explode, he turned it slowly before his eyes, examining the elaborate engraving, feeling the weight of the precious metal in his hands. He gazed at the symbols etched around the rim. It was Hebrew, he knew, recognizing the language from his long-past seminary days.

"Nice cup." Reggie's voice caught Trent off guard.

"Oh, Reg. Yeah, nice."

"Sorry about the, you know, the tackle thing. You're bigger than Kim. You could hurt her. You're bigger."

"I know, Reg. You did right."

Reggie studied Trent, his brown eyes squinting, his large lower lip curling under his upper teeth. "You've been acting weird. Why do you keep looking at that cup?"

"It's a challis. Kind of a fancy cup. It's… I'm looking at it because the challis is part of the problem."

"Uh, Trent, you hit Kim. I think hitting Kim is the problem."

Trent looked at his brother and chuckled. "You got me there, Reg. Still, I need to figure this out."

"Figure what out?"

"That, I don't know." Trent hefted the jeweled challis again, ran his fingers across the Hebrew symbols as if they were Braille, and then rose from the couch. "But it's time I find out. Where did you put the boxes containing my pastoral library?"

"In the attic, Trent. In the attic."

Twelve minutes later Trent was seated at his desk thumbing through a Hebrew Lexicon and jotting notes on a dog-eared legal pad. Lifting the challis, he examined the lettering, amazed at how much he remembered, disheartened at how much he'd forgotten. Ten minutes later, all of the characters had been copied. Trent went over it twice more, ensuring that he'd copied each correctly.

Next came the tedious task of translation. First, he interpreted any words he already recognized, four in all: king, perfect, Lord, and wise. He wrote each English word directly below the Hebrew characters on the page. As well, he identified two names: David and Solomon.

It took over thirty minutes for him to translate the rest, flipping through dusty pages, reexamining the challis, flipping again. Finally, when the phrase was complete, he rewrote it into a proper English sentence and hollered for his brother. "Reg, get in here. This is incredible."

"Okay, Trent. I've got some stew on. It'll be good stew."

The shorter, rounder man ambled into the living room as Trent leaned back in his chair and read aloud. "David, king of Israel, to Solomon, my son and future king. The law of the Lord is perfect. It restores the soul. The testimony of the Lord is sure, making wise the simple."

Trent pulled open another drawer and removed a Bible, an item he'd not handled in nearly a year. Flipping pages furiously, he landed in Psalms, scanned through, paused, and then gazed up at Reggie. "Reg, do you grasp the significance? This writing is from Psalm nineteen – a psalm written by King David of the Old Testament. If this relic is authentic…" He stared at the challis, his eyes glinting, his grin distorting his face. "A challis inscribed from David to his son Solomon, containing a portion of a psalm. Reg, what if this is an original writing? Even if not… It's most likely not. It's only a portion of the psalm, but a psalm of David on a challis given to Solomon."

"Is that good, Trent?"

"Oh, yes." Trent held the gleaming artifact before him, turning it in the light, allowing the many and varied gemstones to come alive in vibrant gleaming: rubies, emeralds, sapphires, even seven diamonds, all set in beautiful gold filigree.

And then the gleaming stones took on different aspects, not physically, but close. This thing, this deceptive treasure, had come from Baqash – a demon. Nothing pure could come from it. The rubies became the blood of innocents, the emeralds, infectious puss encasing unsuspecting souls, the sapphires, cold flames burning into the hearts of the damned, and the diamonds, a clear and perfect trap, a beautiful cage for the foolish and gullible.

"No. Reggie," he retracted. "It's not good. It may be real, may be worth a fortune, but it's not good." He placed the challis on the desk and gazed about the room full of crates: large crates, each capable of holding ten maybe even twenty artifacts of this size. If the rest of these contained treasures half as valuable, Trent would be a multi-millionaire, perhaps even a billionaire.

Of all the lousy things to happen to a guy.

*****

"Daddy." The voice was tiny, precious.

Trent blinked and readjusted himself on the sagging couch. Kim had not demanded that he sleep in the living room, but he'd known that he must. Call it his penance.

"Ashley? Honey it's…" Trent peeked at his Timex, "After four in the morning. Why are you awake, sweetie?"

"Daddy, I need you."

Trent blinked again, bringing his eyes into focus.

"Daddy, please."

Trent scanned the shadowed room. Empty. He peeked behind the couch, thinking the girl might be playing some sort of midnight hide-n-seek. Nothing. His daughter was not there. How was it he heard her voice so clearly?

Rolling into a sitting position he glanced down the short hallway toward Ashley's room and shivered. The temperature must have dropped forty degrees in the past thirty seconds.

Trent's stomach went hollow. Moving quickly, he rose from the couch and marched toward his daughter's bedroom. There was frost on the door-frame: white, crystalline, nearly an inch thick. Using his shirttail as a barrier between the cold metal handle and his flesh, Trent opened the door. What he saw sucked the breath from his lungs.

She was there, Ashley, precious little Ashley, naked, suspended perhaps six inches from the floor, her arms outstretched in some bizarre parody of crucifixion. Nothing held her there – nothing visible at least – she simply floated in the midst of her frost-covered room. "Dear, God," whispered Trent as he moved to her. Slowly. So, slowly. And cautious. Though his every instinct was to scream, to deny this reality, to thrash about, seeking to destroy this demon, this Baqash, he forced himself to remain calm – for Ashley. He must maintain his composure for Ashley. The thought drove home like an ice pick in the heart. This is real. This is all real. Despite all that had happened before, despite the near irrefutable evidence, it was now that this simple truth finally took hold. There was no denying the demon. He was here, and Trent would need to deal with him.

"Daddy," she said. How was it she seemed so tranquil, so detached? "Daddy."

"I'm here, sweetie. I'm here."

The room. Everything about this so familiar room was slightly altered. The stuffed animals now bore knowing eyes and glistening teeth. They drooled and shuffled in place as if eagerly awaiting tender flesh to devour. The walls, pink, they had been pink, were a deep frost-covered crimson and seemed nearly to ooze, to flow, perhaps reaching out for the girl, seeking, grasping. The bed, a simple metal framed bed, seemed to inch closer, to purr like a cat, or perhaps like a lioness on the prowl; a low rumble emitted from somewhere within the mattress. And Ashley, naked, white, so white, but peaceful, sedate. How could any of this be?

Trent was at a loss. Should he try to move her? Should he spout scriptures like some horror flick priest, try to scare the demon away?

No. The scriptures would be meaningless. Trent had no faith to speak of. Any efforts of a spiritual sort would be laughable. Instead, he moved to her, hugged her. "I'm here, sweetie. It's going to be alright."

Ashley nodded, glassy eyed, strangely serene. Trent began to wonder if she was even conscious, if she even knew what was happening to her.

"Baqash," said Trent, the word nearly catching in his throat. "Baqash, I know you're here. Release my daughter. I'll do as you instruct." Even in his own ears, his voice sounded desperate, pleading.

Nothing. Not a sound.

"Baqash!" he nearly screamed this time. "What do you want from me?"

Again silence. And then…

Ashley's scream nearly knocked Trent from his feet.

"My tummy, Daddy! My tummy!" And she screamed again. And again. Heartbreaking agony in every tone. How was it that Kim and Reggie were not rushing into the room? Surly the entire neighborhood could hear the commotion?

"What, honey? What do you mean?"

"My tummy!"

Trent stepped back, reading the words now appearing on his daughters flesh. The words: perfect script. Flawless except that they were composed of bright red welts on his daughter's skin. And with each stroke Ashley screamed again, her voice hoarse, tears streaming down her cheeks, her body shuddering in pain.

And now Trent screamed. "Damn you, Baqash! Damn you! Leave my daughter alone! Leave my home! Leave us!"

Trent grabbed Ashley, pulled her forcefully forward, cradling her in his arms.

And immediately everything was as it should be.

The stuffed animals were stuffed animals again. The bed was just that, a simple bed with no predatory disposition. The walls were pink, perfect. And it was suddenly an uncomfortable seventy-eight degrees.

Ashley was sound asleep in his arms: peaceful, undisturbed, as if nothing had happened. Even the words were gone, evaporated from his daughter's belly. But they were not really gone, for though Ashley would remember none of this, the words were burned forever upon Trent's mind.

You have been given the tools. Be about your task. Read. Learn. Perhaps then, your daughter might be spared.

CHAPTER 4

Eldon Troxel found himself in Turkey again. There he was, standing amidst crumbling ruins, his special prize, the object of his obsession, tucked tightly beneath his right arm. His younger brother Trent was there too, arguing with a winged beast, screaming, crying, beating on the thing as the creature cocked its head revealing multiple faces. Trent stepped to his left, granting Eldon a better view. The monster was holding a small girl dressed only in a white over-sized T-shirt. Her golden hair spilled over the thing's blistered and festering arms as her wide blue eyes locked with those of the beast. If eyes the creature had at all. For, they seemed more the emptiness of space consumed by the fires of hell than actual orbs.

The creature turned, moving away from Trent who seemed somehow unable to pursue. Eldon now noticed a fire. He could taste the rancid smoke, could hear the pops and crackles of flames devouring flesh. A great blaze was raging among the ruins, stretching into the starless midnight sky, erupting in plumes of orange and red. The beast stepped toward the inferno, hefting the child above his head as if to heave her tiny form into the raging holocaust.

"The time has come, Eldon Troxel," said a familiar voice, the dream voice that had once led him to this same chamber, to the object he now clenched with white knuckles.

"No. I don't know what it means."

"The time has come. You will know what to do."

"But I..."

And now Eldon was sitting upright in his bed, sweat rolling down his cool white face. His covers had somehow made it to the far side of the room; city lights peeked in from behind the blinds, and it seemed frost bordered the windows on this steamy May evening. Still, the thought that pressed upon him was of the mundane sort. Why had he dreamed of Trent? He hadn't seen the jerk in years.

*****

Trent was in his cool dank basement. The cracked cinderblock walls seemed to embrace the twenty-seven crates; the stale and dusty air tickled the back of his throat. The beast had attacked his daughter – abused her. Marked her. Trent had no choice but to comply with the demon's demands. The beast had defiled Ashley. Pure, sweet Ashley. Never. Never could he allow that to happen again, no matter what the consequences to him personally.

Trent lifted a crowbar and began ripping into the containers.

And what he uncovered. Archeological treasures in such scope and abundance as to make the famous Field Museum of Chicago seem like an also-ran. Ancient figurines, swords, coinage, pottery, religious pieces, he was no expert, but these things appeared to span centuries as well as the globe: a six-inch statuette of ancient Egyptian design, the dented and bloodied warrior's helmet of a Roman centurion, a Renaissance painting, an Aztec calendar. Under other circumstances Trent would have been enthralled by the treasures, would have inspected every piece, sought to discover their origins, their history. He half wondered what his older brother Eldon – an archeologist – would make of this all, but dismissed the idea. That just wasn't going to happen.

It wasn't until Trent pulled open the seventh crate that he found what might be the first real piece to the puzzle. The contents were unlike those of the others. Instead of artifacts, he found writings: parchments, scrolls, clay tablets, and other unknown surfaces. Each was wrapped in a thin leather-like material and numbered sequentially. Trent removed these gingerly, placing them in numerical order – twenty-one through thirty-five – on a strip of green and yellow carpet remnant he'd found rolled up in a corner.

The eighth crate offered eleven similar documents; the ninth provided seven. But Trent hadn't opened the crates in any particular order. Within each container, the numbered documents were sequential, but there were huge gaps in numbering from one crate to the next. The highest number found in these first crates was eighty-four. "How many of these things are there?" he wondered aloud.

Two more crates and he was onto something: documents one through seven. As Trent pulled each from its sheath, he found that they were inscribed on a peculiar substance, not parchment, nor papyrus, but something much softer. There was a strange element to the foreign lettering. They seemed in appearance almost three dimensional, as if carved deep into the material. But as Trent slid his fingertips across the cool gray surface he felt no indentations. The substance was perfectly smooth, as if nothing had been written at all. The fabric was thin, almost that of onion paper, but sturdy. It would take some strength to tear it. Trent turned the first document over, noting how cold it seemed. Though incredibly thin, there was no evidence of the writing from the front side: no dimples, no bulges.

Trent set this mystery aside, for not only did he possess these documents, but reams of handwritten paper as well – English translations, each with a number corresponding to the original manuscript. Trent's bandaged hand quivered as he gaped at the first translation.

From the journal of Baqash, angel of the order of Cherubim.

CHAPTER 5

From the journal of Baqash, angel of the order of Cherubim

The question of where to begin has plagued me for some time. It seems a simple question, I suppose. But it is one that could set the tone for the remainder of my writings, and thus, I must choose carefully. Proceed from the beginning, one might say. But my response would be, and is, the beginning of what? Of my existence? I do not remember my own emergence. It seems to me that I have always been. Perhaps the beginning of the universe. I could tell of the cold black emptiness beyond the farthest rim of the glorious realm, of the sudden burst of matter, of substance exploding into the formerly empty void, of swirling gases: blues, greens, reds, yellows, oranges darting and dancing amid great pillars of sparkling cloud. Perhaps I could detail the coming together of the sphere known as earth, of how indigo, scarlet, and emerald vapors swirled tighter, tighter, tighter forming a gaseous ball, solidifying into a luminous globe, initially hot and fiery, but cooling rapidly. The thing is of such immense beauty, of such boundless potential.

I could detail my hesitation in coming to this swirling blue globe, of how I feared leaving the realm, and of how I longed to remain with The Ancient of Days, my creator, my Lord. Of how my spirit cried to seek new adventure, new experience, of how the decision was finally made.

Still, perhaps it is best that I begin as I am now, experiencing my first days here on earth. This seems a logical beginning. It is, I suppose, where my own story truly commences. Yes, I believe this would be the most pleasing, the least audacious means to start.

The radiant heat of the sun is so alien, so unlike the glory of the golden realm. But earth is a wondrous place, filled with leafy vegetation and scurrying beasts, so unlike any I could imagine. Even the small buzzing creatures, the insects, are so wonderfully designed, with shimmering greens, reds and blues as well as deep midnight black. Some have numerous eyes collecting images from multiple perspectives; others have fur-like hair, soft and delicate to the touch. O, the joy of this place. Each moment is a new discovery, a new adventure. We hosts live in awe as we acclimate to this fresh and beautiful sphere.

This day I spent gazing into the eyes of an ape, admiring it, assessing it.

"Ho, friend Baqash," called my dear companion, Michael. He inquired as to why I stared so at the creature.

"The face. The hands," I replied. "They are so like us, yet there is no spirit, nothing eternal within the flesh. Still, there is some rudimentary intelligence."

By way of explanation, I bolted away, collecting five fruits and placing them before the beast. Initially, the creature fled, hiding behind the fan-like limbs of leafy vegetation, for with eyes of flesh it could not see me, a spirit being, and thus the fruit appeared to float of its own accord. Again, I rushed off, returning with five more fruits of a different breed, and placing them aside the others. Then we waited, I remaining with the fruit, Michael seated on an uneven stone of red and gray.

It was not long before the ape moved forward to inspect the fruit. First peering at these with suspicion, but soon moving closer. It began to knock these about with its large black hands. With each strike it retreated as if anticipating a counterattack from the fruit. Still, I sat patiently watching.

Next the creature leaned forward on its powerful arms, its massive head nearly to the ground, and sniffed at the air about the fruits. Finally satisfied that these were safe, it lifted one of the green fruits to its mouth and bit into it with large white teeth. Glistening juices ran from its lips and into its gray beard.

"Baqash," cried Michael. "This is not intelligence we witness, but mere hunger."

I turned, requesting patience of my companion.

The ape, now finished with the first fruit, then reached for one of the red fruits, but as it did so, I reached out and struck its hand. The ape drew back, cocked its head, sniffed at the air, and reached again for the same fruit. Again, I struck.

24

This time the creature let out a hoot of frustration and pounded its palms on the ground causing dust to billow into the air. Then, sniffing cautiously, it once again approached the enticing treats, choosing a green piece. I allowed it to do so. The ape eyed the red fruits suspiciously while quickly devouring the green with grunts and gulps. Upon finishing this, it slowly moved to where the fruits lay, gathered the remaining greens, and moved away leaving the reds untouched.

"See!" I cried. "In that short span it learned not to reach for the red fruits."

"And my guess is it will never desire the red fruit again," laughed Michael. "But I still do not see any keen intuition, rather mere survival instinct."

"Perhaps, but I find it truly fascinating. These creatures are magnificent."

"It seems a wasted exercise," came a musical voice from just beyond the tree line. Helel's voice. The most beautiful of the hosts. The most glorious. He glided into the clearing, settling just before Michael. At his side was my frequent companion, Pereh, deemed the wild one for his continuous exuberance. "Why do you waste your time with these tiresome creatures?" asked Helel, his golden hair gleaming in the yellow sunlight.

"It is nothing but sport," replied Michael. "A simple diversion."

Helel's golden eyes narrowed, his gleaming face darkened. "A diversion. It seems one such as you would not have time for such petty dalliances."

"Your meaning?" asked Michael, the jocularity now leaving his voice.

"You met with the Ancient One today."

"That is not unusual."

"It is said he gave you a position."

"He did."

"A position of power and prominence."

Michael rose from his perch on the rock. "It is the Ancient's right to dispense positions as he sees fit."

Helel smiled a taut, forced smile. "Of course it is. Congratulations, Michael. Undoubtedly, you are the best choice."

With that, he loosed his wings, lifting into the blue sky beyond. Curious, the behavior of hosts in the place. I cannot imagine a conversation such as this having occurred within the realm. Curious.

CHAPTER 6

Kim was surprised to find only one other occupant in the teacher's lounge, Sam Melter, a slight man of perhaps sixty, with salt-and-pepper hair, bushy red eyebrows, and a red walrus mustache. Kim knew Sam from several past meetings. He'd taught fifth grade for nearly forty years, and had from time to time taught the children of his earlier students. He was as much a fixture in the school as the walls themselves. Regular staff members often wondered if he'd ever retire, or just continue for all eternity, teaching grandchildren, and great grandchildren of his earlier classes.

Today he sat hunched over a book, his rolled back conforming readily to his reading posture. He wore a brown tweed sport jacket with patches on the elbows and a well-worn pair of green corduroy slacks. To complete the scholarly look, a large bowled pipe hung from the corner of his mouth. Turning a page, he grunted, and emitted a cloud of blue smoke.

Kim set her brown bag at the opposite end of the long folding table, and purchased a bottle of cola from the soda-pop dispenser. Her plan was to eat in relative seclusion and work on her latest poem. Sam looked up as Kim sat down. "Well," he said, "You look as though you've had a bit of a day already. The little buggers running you through the typical substitute teacher mayhem?"

Kim opened her sack and removed a turkey and Swiss sandwich carefully wrapped, by Reggie, in cellophane. "No," she smiled. "I just have a few things on my mind. What I really need is a good night's sleep."

"Well, don't trouble your pretty little head, Dearie. You haven't even seen real trouble yet." He smiled a knowing smile, took another long drag on his pipe, and stared intently at Kim, the intensity of the gaze catching her off guard.

She took a bite of her sandwich, and then removed a small spiral-bound pad from her purse. The little man continued to stare, smiling, unblinking, unmoving.

She took another bite. He continued to gaze. She picked up her pen. He gazed.

There seemed a movement from the corner of her eye. Perhaps a shadow; or maybe even a person. But when she turned to see, it had disappeared.

"Well, I'm surprised that none of the other teachers are here," she said, her voice nearly as tight as a tuned guitar string.

Sam Melter lost his grin and said, "They do not need to be here."

"Excuse me?"

He shrugged. "They need to be with the children, or perhaps in the ladies room. That is a popular place."

"Well, I'm sure they *all* don't need to be someplace else." Kim took another quick bite. This guy might be an institution in the school, but the kindly old gentleman was in full creep mode. She would make it a quick lunch.

Someone bumped into her causing her hand to jerk as she drew sandwich to mouth. She turned, expecting to see a fellow teacher squeezing past between the wall and Kim's chair. No one was there. But, she was certain that… That someone… She sighed, rubbing her temples in a gesture that reminded her of Trent. Was she that jittery that she was now imagining things? It seemed Trent had really messed with her mind this time.

Sam Melter returned to his book as Kim took a bite of turkey and Swiss. The man was staring at his book, but didn't have the countenance of someone reading: no eye movement, no concentration. Taking another bite, Kim focused her attention ahead to the yellow block wall opposite her, reading a poster outlining emergency evacuation procedures – anything to avoid eye contact with the little man.

"It doesn't make sense, does it?" said Melter.

"What?" asked Kim, but only to avoid appearing rude.

"This," he said, holding up the black bound book, a Bible. "It doesn't add up."

"What are you talking about?" asked Kim as the man's gaze bore into her, his strange eyes transfixing her.

The shadow appeared again – there and then gone. Kim blinked, shook her head.

28

The old man laughed, placing the closed Bible on the table and patting it amiably. "I wonder about the walls of Jericho, the parting of the Red Sea, angels and demons, the resurrection of Christ. Why who wou…"

"Stop it!" she blurted, cutting him off mid-sentence. "Please, just stop." She dropped her sandwich on the table and hid her trembling hands in her lap. She really didn't need this just now.

"Well," he said, "We're a bit touchy." Then, leaning toward her with a crocodile grin, he asked, "Is there a problem?"

Kim desperately wanted to flee the room, but felt unable to move, glued to her seat like a gaper on the highway, staring at the carnage of an accident, sickened by it, yet unable to turn away. "No problem," she heard herself say. "I'm just a little unnerved these days. Finances, that type of thing."

"Seems it might be more than that," said Sam. "Seems I hit a nerve. These questions, they don't bother you, don't tug at something inside, make you squirm just a little bit?"

Kim sat transfixed by his eyes. It took her a moment to respond, and when she did, her voice was as tiny as a desert stream. "No… No, there's no problem. Everything's just fine."

CHAPTER 7

The decision to visit his older brother, Eldon, was not an easy one for Trent. The two had been estranged for nearly two decades, only seeing each other once in that time – their father's funeral – and never corresponding via phone or email. Trent had no real desire to renew their relationship – he'd given up on those attempts years ago – and was certain Eldon was even less inclined toward a reunion than he.

But he needed Eldon now. Not emotionally, not in any familial capacity, but professionally. Eldon had been an archeologist – a good one. He'd spent most of his adult life traipsing about the Middle East uncovering treasures of the past. Treasures quite similar to the ones now littering Trent's basement. Eldon had left the field a few years prior, and now lived only miles from Trent.

Eldon stared out at Trent through the glass door of his shop named, "I'm History." The brown eyes were the same as Trent remembered, but tired, less vibrant. The dark brown hair was mostly covered with a Cubs baseball cap, the round face older, more defined, with the first lines of middle age etching narrow troughs about the eyes.

An electric charge ran through Trent as Eldon opened the door and stared up at him, registering no surprise at seeing him after all these years. "I was on the phone, placing a bet," he said retreating down the aisle and allowing Trent to follow. "You interrupted me."

The electric sensation danced about Trent's limbs, distracting him for a moment, and then evaporated with the subtle lakeside breeze. "The door was locked. I had to knock. How do you attract any business?" asked Trent as he hefted the two satchels he'd brought with him and stepped through the door, his eyes darting about the cluttered and dusty room, his nose immediately itching from the musty odor.

"Yeah, well, I run the shop by myself. Gotta take precautions." He paused, glancing at Trent. "By the way, my arm healed fine."

"Your arm?"

"The one you broke."

"Yeah, yeah," said Trent, pretending he'd just remembered the incident. "Right after you'd relieved me of my fiancé. How is Maggie these days? I heard you two had a son, what, fifteen, sixteen years ago?"

Eldon ignored the question. "You seen Ma since you've been back in town?"

Trent shook his head. "Only once. She tends to respond to me with hostility. I haven't wanted to aggravate her condition."

"That's pretty fancy rationalizing, there, brother." Eldon paused. "Heard you were in the ministry. You weren't a religious guy growing up. What happened?"

Trent shrugged. "Things changed. Now they've changed again. What is this place?" he asked, gazing in wonder about the dusty and cluttered space, his eyes bright with curiosity. "You've got artifacts everywhere. Ancient swords, daggers, tribal masks, pottery, I can barely even walk through this mess. It's wonderful!" Trent grinned, noting a suit of armor situated toward the back of the store and adorned with a Chicago Bears football jersey, number 54. The thing was autographed by Dick Butkus. An old seventeen-inch television set sat on the counter to the right of it, a Chicago Cubs banner hanging limply from the antenna. Typical Eldon: One part academic, two parts bleacher bum.

Eldon held his arms wide saying, "Welcome to the common man's door to ancient civilizations."

Trent's lips curled upward as he studied an ancient terra cotta lamp. The lines were subtle, elegant, the piece encircled with ancient script. "Meaning?"

"Meaning, archaeologists unearth thousands of unspectacular pieces every year. Common stuff: oil lamps, vases, small idols, whatever. Well, these things are no big deal to hotshot eggheads deciphering the scrolls of King Shalmaneser, but to the average guy they're pretty neat. Give a five thousand year-old sword to a twelve year-old and he's hooked for life."

"Give a sword of any kind to a twelve year-old and he's got a short life," grinned Trent. Eldon shrugged but didn't laugh at the attempted humor. Trent allowed an awkward moment to pass, and then said, "So, you gave up life as a true archeologist to do this?"

"Call it my mission," said Eldon; a guarded look crossed his face. "Besides, the Cubs don't make it to the mid-east very often." Eldon walked behind the east counter and rested his elbows on cracked and dusty glass. "Now," he said. "What's your mission?"

"Excuse me?"

"Come on, Trent. Unless those sacks are full of past-due Christmas presents, you're here for a reason. What do you need?"

Trent hefted one of the two satchels onto the counter top. "Take a look," he said. Then, noticing Eldon's cautious expression, added, "Good grief, El, it's not a bomb."

Eldon unzipped the dirty blue bag, reached in, and pulled out an eight-inch wad of bubble wrap. The archaeologist's eyebrows rose in surprise as he unrolled the wrap revealing an Egyptian statuette. Lifting the relic, he turned it slowly, touching the eight horizontal lines of hieroglyphics down the front, admiring the rich copper color, examining a slight crack at the base. "An Ushabti," he whispered.

"English is my preferred language, El."

"Ushabti. An Egyptian servant of the dead. They were put in the tombs of the ancient Egyptian jet-set to serve them in the afterlife. I'd say this pup dates back to about 600 B.C.E., the twenty-sixth dynasty." Eldon glanced down at the satchel, obviously noting the numerous other artifacts. "Trent, where did you get these?"

Trent looked down, breaking eye contact. "Ah, they were given to me by an acquaintance, someone who wanted me to have an extravagant amount of really old stuff."

Eldon stared up, his eyes narrow. "An acquaintance, huh? And how much of this 'really old stuff' do you have?"

"Over twenty cases." Trent paused. "Probably upwards of four hundred pieces."

"An acquaintance?"

Trent nodded.

"Let me see something else."

Trent reached into the sack and pulled out another item, a folded document wrapped with coarse string and sealed with a daub of clay. There were seven Hebrew letters visible on the exposed surface.

"Why exactly are you here?" asked Eldon.

"I need to know if these are authentic. Also, the majority of the pieces are ancient documents. I'd like to have them translated."

"Twenty-plus cases? That's a pretty tall order."

"True, but it's important."

"I thought these were gifts. What's the big deal?"

Trent paused, searching Eldon's eyes. "Eldon, listen, you think I'm a low-life. I can live with that. Honestly, about now, my wife would agree with you. And no, I haven't told you everything. But this is extremely important, and you're the only archaeologist I know, definitely the only one I can trust."

Eldon lowered his eyes to the document. "This is the endorsement, or title," he said with a sigh. "It tells what the manuscript is: a document of wifehood – a marriage contract."

Eldon removed the string and seal with precise delicacy, then, carefully testing the flexibility of the folds, lifted the top and pulled the right side back. What they now had was a long flat surface similar to a rolled newspaper. "This is in remarkable condition," he said. "Normally I would treat it, but I think we're okay without that."

Eldon slowly rolled back the folds revealing a large document of about thirty inches by twenty. The portion that had been exposed while folded was a dark, rich, golden brown, while the inner folds were more of a marbled tan. Eldon gazed at it reverently, touching it lightly, feeling for texture, looking for flaws or defects. "This is wonderful, Trent. Look at the detail here in the lettering."

"Can you translate it?"

"Yeah, yeah, let's see here. 'Document of wifehood which Tanon wrote for Damal. Damal being a slave. Egyptian of Meshullam. Damal brings to Tanon in her hand silver, three karsh, ten shekels. Gold. Five pieces. One cow.' It goes on, listing the price of the bride. Apparently there was some haggling over her worth, whether or not she'd remain a slave, would her children be slave or free, that kind of thing. It would take me some time to give you a complete word-for-word translation, but that's the gist of it."

"You're pretty quick with the translation," said Trent, "Obviously, you've progressed beyond Klingon."

"Funny. I'm okay with general content, but I read too many languages to be an expert at any – and I don't do Klingon."

Trent bent down and opened the second satchel. He hesitated, glanced at Eldon, scratched his nose.

Did he really want to take this next step?

Did he really have any choice?

"Take a stab at this," said Trent, handing Eldon the gold and jeweled challis of David.

Once again Eldon's experienced fingers went to work, running lightly over the relic. He caressed the fine filigree, turning the piece, allowing the gemstones to flicker in the light. Cupping his hand around the bowl, he hefted it, getting an accurate idea as to the weight. Then he placed it on the counter, examining the ancient script with practiced eyes.

"What the hell?" With a grunt, he stood upright, irreverently tossing the challis to Trent, who, caught off guard, fumbled it before cradling it tightly to his gut. "'David king of Israel, to Solomon, my son and future king.' What kinda crap are you tryin' to feed me?"

"You're saying it's a forgery?" Could this be a hoax? Could someone have staged the whole thing, the demon, the relics? No, that didn't make sense. Too much had happened. Baqash was real; there could be no doubt of that. Logically, his relics should be authentic as well.

Eldon leaned forward, placing both hands palm down on the glass counter. "Okay, brother. Time to put your cards on the table. I know that you're out of the ministry. I know *why* you're out of the ministry. Reg still writes. I've got the dope on you. Eighteen years since I've seen you and you waltz in here with this crazy story about a generous acquaintance who left you a fortune in ancient artifacts. You show me a piece that's pretty common; then you pull out what appears to be a legitimate marriage document dating to about 700 B.C.E. I'm getting curious. How does my long lost brother and defrocked pastor come into possession of such a piece? Now you pull out this challis, 'David, king of Israel, to Solomon.'" Eldon leaned into Trent's taut and solemn face. "Do you have any idea the kind of press coverage a find like that would cause? What do you think would happen if it ended up missing or stolen? So I ask you again, what the hell are you trying to pull?"

Trent set the challis roughly on the counter. "I am trying to verify the authenticity of these relics. I *need* to verify the authenticity." He paused, searching for words. "I understand your position. Now understand mine. Someone I do not trust forced these pieces into my possession. I desperately need to know if they are authentic. Now, please, is this challis real?"

It was long moments before Eldon spoke. "I suggest you pick up your goodies and go directly to the nearest police station. I don't know if that challis originated with King David of the Old Testament. I'd be amazed if it did. But the gems appear real, the handiwork consistent with the period. My first guess is that the challis is truly from that era, but the inscription was added later. Either way, it's probably stolen. Now," he said, pointing at the door. "Get out of here before I call the police myself."

CHAPTER 8

From the journal of Michael, archangel

Such an amazing experience, this new world: to bound down the mountainsides abreast the rams, to splash about the shallow waters with the mastodons, to soar beneath the clouds beside the eagle. Still, I long for the golden realm, to walk the glistening streets, to gaze at the crystal spires.

Yet, a glimpse of the realm has come to this world. And its source is one most unexpected. In an act of selfless initiative, Helel, whose stunning countenance and charming wit have gained him respect beyond that owed his rank and intelligence, has determined that those serving on earth should have a home, a base local, a reminder of the glorious realm. His choice of sites is a place he calls Pergamos or Fortress, a peculiar name to be sure, but apt as it lies some 666 cubits in height, upon rocky ground. Not the most inviting local on the planet, yet suitable for our needs.

The hosts have labored hard in erecting this stunning palace. Invisible to the fleshly creatures, its golden spires are accented with stones of many hues, creating beautiful rays of color as the sun illumines them. The halls bare wonderful tapestries depicting various earth locals: royal blue oceans, purple mountains, emerald valleys and pastures, each woven meticulously by hosts skilled in such arts. The ceiling reaches sixteen stories in height and is adorned with gemstones: rubies, amethysts, diamonds, sapphires. The floor and walls are of fine marble, and inlaid with the purest of gold. Great columns of polished granite stretch from floor to ceiling. Chimes of the finest crystal hang suspended from the ceiling, sending glorious ribbons of dancing color about the vast space and tinkling joyously in the gentle breeze. The entire scene is most magnificent to behold.

One additional detail deserves attention, as it is a feature of the palace which surprised even me. At the center of the great hall sits a great throne, a replica of the one situated at the pinnacle of the realm. Helel personally directed the construction of this, and pestered the poor workers to near exasperation, his tone often becoming sharp, his demeanor severe. I admit that at first I was quite taken aback by this, for I had not been aware of any such commissioning. When I questioned Helel concerning the matter, Helel replied simply, "All for the glory of the Ancient of Days."

Indeed.

CHAPTER 9

It was six-thirty A.M. and Kim stood watching the little stick in her firm unwavering hand, wondering if it would remain white or gradually turn to pink. Minutes crept by one second at a time, stretching seemingly into hours and then days. She stared at the thing, finally noting the test result, and wondering what emotions she should feel. Eventually she took the test indicator and flushed it.

Five hours later, Kim entered the teacher's lounge to find that once again, the elderly Sam Melter was the only other occupant. He sat in the same seat, smoking the same pipe, and wearing what appeared to be the same tweed jacket and corduroy pants as he had two days prior. Hunched over a book, he acted as though he didn't see her, though Kim caught a quick glimpse of his vibrant eyes flash in her direction.

Kim, you can sit here.

It seemed there was a voice. But, no.

Right here, Kim.

Is there something wrong?

Had she heard something? Was she actually hearing these sounds?

How? Who? No one was here but Melter.

Hoping to avoid conversation, Kim found a seat at the far end of the table and on the same side as he, the idea being to avoid eye contact. Perhaps she could even angle away slightly, gaze out at the distorted view through the block window, send some non-verbal cues.

The maneuvering proved useless. Melter simply picked up his book, ambled around the table to the place just opposite Kim and seated himself, his deep rolling eyes staring intently at her. Kim dropped her head and stared at her sandwich. "Hi Sam," she said with no enthusiasm.

How are the kids behaving today, Kim?

Kim glanced about, left then right. There was no voice. Of course there was no voice.

"Afternoon Kimmie," said Melter, startling her slightly. Trent was the only one who referred to her as "Kimmie". "How are things in the Troxel household this day?"

"Oh, just fine," she said before biting into her suddenly-tasteless tuna sandwich. There was something about this guy, something – wrong.

"Now, I know better than that," said Melter.

"Excuse me?"

"I've seen enough depression in my time to recognize it. The stuff's seeping from your pours, oozing from your pretty little eyes. There's no disguising it." He paused, puffing on his pipe and squinting his bushy eyebrows into one wavy red streak above his piercing eyes. "Is the problem with the husband or the kid?" he continued. "Which one? The husband or the kid?"

Kim remained silent as her fingers tightened about her sandwich, causing tuna to creep out from between the bread slices and to gracelessly plop onto the wax paper below.

"Husband, huh? Running around on you, is he? Running around?"

"No!" blurted Kim, further squeezing her sandwich into a Picasso replica.

"You sure?" pressed Melter. "We do all know what happened when he was a minister." His suddenly fierce eyes bore into her, anticipating her reaction.

"How did you..."

"Know about that?" Melter chuckled, emitting wafts of blue pipe smoke from his nostrils. "I've been around a long time. In a town this size, I hear things."

"A town this size? Chicago!"

"I hear things," he repeated, then stared fixedly at her, his wavering eyes nearly mesmerizing her.

It took Kim a moment to pull her gaze away, to seize her thoughts. But when she did, she was furious. How dare this man suggest these things? How dare he probe into her personal affairs? How dare he so blatantly accuse Trent without evidence or reason? She rose silently, bundled her mutilated sandwich in the brown sack, and tossed it across the table, past Melter, and into a trashcan as she marched out of the room.

Kim? Mrs. Troxel? Is everything alright?

Melter took a long drag on his pipe and smiled.

*****

Kim sat before the cluttered desk of Principal Diane Grady wondering why she'd been summoned. The children had worn on her, Sam Melter had unnerved her, and now all she wanted was a hot relaxing bath and a lobotomy. Diane Grady, a slender black woman of about forty, entered the room, smiled, greeted Kim, and seated herself opposite the substitute teacher. "I know you have a child at home, so I won't keep you. But I do need a couple of moments."

"That's fine," said Kim, attempting unsuccessfully to appear upbeat.

"I've had very good reports on your abilities. The teachers tell me you're competent and that, unlike with many substitute teachers, the children actually keep pace with scheduled lessons when you're in the classroom. Thank you for your efforts."

Kim smiled. Well, this wasn't so bad. "Thank you, Mrs. Grady. That means a lot to me."

"My pleasure, Mrs. Troxel," she smiled. "But that's not the only reason I've summoned you. I was hoping that you'd be willing to commit to teaching a fifth grade class for the next three weeks to finish off the school year."

The thought of regular income, even for a few weeks, heartened Kim. The family needed every penny it could scrounge. "Which class? Did a teacher leave suddenly?"

Diane Grady's smile faded. "I'm sorry. I thought everyone knew. It's Sam Melter's class. He passed last week, a stroke."

Kim's stomach contorted as the pink rushed from her face. "Last week?" she said in a mouse-like squeak. "I just had lunch with him today." Her pale hands clutched the arms of the old Early American chair on which she sat.

The principal gazed at her quizzically, probably thinking Kim had lost her mind. "You must be thinking of another day, Kim. He passed last week."

"No. I'm sure it was today. I sat down in the teacher's lounge. He was the only one there; he came over, sat by me."

Diane Grady, to her credit, tried to be as comforting as possible. But to Kim it was still poison-tipped verbal arrows. "Kim, I do apologize for contradicting you, but I and several others were in the teacher's lounge today. You sat at the far end of the table by yourself. Several of us spoke to you, but you seemed preoccupied. Five minutes later, you got up and left without finishing your sandwich. Sam Melter was not there."

CHAPTER 10

Trent's mind was on another world as he descended the five concrete steps and entered Baldwin's Refuge. The Smells of shepherds pie and Guinness tickled his senses, yet still his thoughts were of angels who would soon be demons, of the earliest deceptions, of devotion and deceit. He'd thought of calling off work, but needed the money. Despite the current weirdness of his life, bills must still be paid.

Trent felt the cool fingers of unease creep across his spine as Curt Baldwin, his boss and father-in-law, called him into the tiny office – barely more than a closet – at the far end of the establishment. At first, Baldwin seemed at a loss for words, hesitating as he decided whether to sit or to stand, averting Trent's bemused gaze and curious grin. Finally he seated himself behind the narrow card table situated in the corner of the room. "Trent, um, listen, we thought you would be good for Kim. You took your religion a bit too seriously, but otherwise you were a decent man. Besides, our daughter seemed to love you." Trent's mind jumped immediately to Kim. Had she enlisted her father's aid in uncovering his secret?

Baldwin ran his fingers through his salt and pepper hair and then looked down at the table before him. "Then there was that fiasco at the church. It was a disgrace. You really hurt Kim. And frankly, well, she remained with you only at my urgings." He sighed, ran his fingers through his hair yet again. "We encouraged you to return to Chicago, near to us, near to your own family. I'd hoped you would put your life back on track."

Trent pulled a chair from against the wall and seated himself across from Baldwin. "Excuse me, Curt, but where are you going with this?"

It was then that Curt Baldwin turned. He could be a weak man, averting a gaze, fiddling with his buttons, wriggling around for an hour before finally getting to a point. But he could also be a stern man, an opinionated man, fierce and determined, nearly irrational in his pursuit of strange little goals. Trent noticed the change. Where Baldwin had sat hunched and nervous, he now straightened, met Trent's gaze, even offering a grim smile of sorts. Trent had witnessed this transformation many times before. He supposed Baldwin must use some sort of self-help technique or some such nonsense to give him the courage needed for confrontation and difficult business decisions. He also knew that when Baldwin slipped into this mode, it was rarely a pleasant meeting.

The older man gazed intently at Trent. "I am your employer, am I not?"

Trent nodded. "Obviously." Why was it suddenly cold in this room?

"I am your father-in-law."

"I'm fully aware of your status in my life."

"So, you would steal from both family and employer."

Trent felt a sudden twist in his gut. "Curt, with all due respect, are you delusional?"

Baldwin leaned back in his molded plastic chair, crossing his legs, and laying his hands casually on his belly, all appearance of apprehension lost to the mists of memory. "Carlos, the busboy, saw you pocketing money from the nightly deposits."

"Curt... I... He's mistaken. I never..."

The man leaned forward, apparently enjoying Trent's unease. "He is certain of it, having witnessed this on three separate occasions."

"Well, he saw wrong." Trent knew his protestations rang hollow. Any real thief would protest innocence in the same manner. But Trent *was* innocent. What else could he say that would be more convincing?

Baldwin shook his head slowly, his eyes narrow and unsympathetic. It seemed the temperature in the room dropped fifteen degrees. "Fact is, we've experienced a dip in receipts lately. And your reputation..." Baldwin shrugged.

Trent scratched his nose and inched forward in his seat. "I would not steal from you, Curt – from anyone. I've made mistakes in the past, trounced on people's trust. But that *is* in the past."

It seemed Baldwin almost smiled. "I do not believe you. Not with your history."

"Okay," said Trent, realizing Baldwin had made an irrevocable decision. "You're judge and jury. What now?"

"Obviously, I cannot maintain your employment." He shrugged. "I will not press charges, of course. That, I could not do to Kimberly's husband."

Trent was out of his chair, pacing the confined space, three steps, turn, three steps, turn. "But you're willing to dismiss me, no opportunity to confront my accuser?" Trent paused. "No, that doesn't matter to you. How am I supposed to support your daughter and granddaughter, Curt – have you thought of that? No employer's going to hire a man fired for stealing. Have you given this even a moment's thought?"

Baldwin shrugged. "I suppose you'll need to find an alternate source of income."

CHAPTER 11

Kim Troxel left the house and didn't know when, or if, she planned to return. She was already unsettled after the pregnancy test that morning, and had become a walking twitch after the Sam Melter is-he-or-isn't-he-a-ghost thing. But when she'd arrived home to find her mother sitting in her tiny living room, waiting to tell her that Kim's father was in the process of firing her husband, well, suddenly the concept of exile to a foreign land sounded quite appealing.

Still, no matter how Kim tried to concentrate on her problems at home, her mind kept creeping back to Sam Melter, that obnoxious, belittling, nosey, yellow-toothed, old coot who, though dead a week, had still found some means of joining her for lunch – twice in three days. Despite the adamant protests of Diane Grady to the contrary, Kim knew beyond doubt that yes, it had been today, and yes, Sam Melter had been real. She could still smell the lingering pipe smoke on her blouse.

Now she sat in a dingy dive. A classic rock station blared Led Zeppelin's "Black Dog" on the overhead speakers; Robert Plant's screaming vocals soaring over the driving guitar. College kids hooted and howled at video games, which bleeped and blurped in response. A thick layer of bluish gray smoke hung suspended five feet above the floor. The clinks and clacks of dishes mingled with the driving chaotic symphony of sounds. "*Oh yeah*! *Oh yeah*!" bellowed Plant.

Kim's hand trembled violently as she took a sip of lukewarm coffee. Brown liquid dribbled over the rim and onto her lap. She chose not to notice, sipped at the cup, and returned it with a rattle to the saucer. Trent hated coffee. Too bad for Trent.

She shuttered at the questions plaguing her soul. Was she mad?

Madness. Could it really be all that bad? It seemed to Kim perhaps a welcome escape. A mad person could care less about dismal finances, about potential pregnancy. A mad person wouldn't notice that her husband was a supreme disappointment, perhaps even a criminal. A mad person could talk to ghosts as easily as she'd talk to her next-door neighbor. Biting her lower lip, she gazed down at the checkered Formica table. A tear dropped and rolled lazily across the red and white squares. *"Oh yeah! Oh yeah!"* howled Robert Plant from above.

Kim began gently pounding her fists upon the wobbly table, causing her spoon to clatter off of the saucer.

"Oh yeah! Oh yeah!"

Clink! Clatter!

Bleep! Blurp!

Kim screamed, "Stop! Stop all of this commotion. You're driving me insane!"

"Oh yeah! Oh yeah!"

Clink! Clatter!

Bleep! Blurp!

"Stop!"

Silence.

"You look like you could use a cigarette."

"Um, no… Thank you," she said to the outstretched hand holding a pack of Virginia Slims. "I don't smoke."

"Sure you do," came an elderly, reassuring voice. "I can spot a smoker a mile away. You are one. And by the looks of you, it's been too long since your last."

He was right. She was a smoker, or at least had been – until she'd met Trent. Then that nasty little habit had taken a long hard leap. Somehow she hadn't felt that her righteous pastor would date a girl with a two pack-a-day habit – no matter how many Bible studies she attended. Trent knew nothing of smokes, or joints, or little red pills. If he had, she would have been tainted, unworthy of his love. Oh, he would never have admitted to this, never would have addressed the subject, but the wall would have been erected. It was simply the way he was wired. At least it was then. Now, Kim had no idea what drove the man.

The spotted, wrinkled hand with the brown tweed arm shook the open pack causing two white cylinders to inch out of the foil opening. "Go on. I'm not going to tell anyone," prodded the gentle and vaguely familiar voice. "It'll do you some good, ease the tension."

Tentatively, with quivering hand, Kim clutched a butt between her thumb and index finger, sliding one cigarette from the package. She did not put it to her lips, but rolled it slowly, examining it. Virginia Slims, her old brand, she'd forgotten how light they were, how smooth. She remembered the soothing effect of nicotine on the system. Would it be so bad if she had one cigarette?

"Allow me." The hand returned, gently plucking the cigarette from Kim's trembling fingers. She heard the flick of a lighter, the soft drawing in of breath, and then the hand was before her, wrinkles and tweed, the glowing head of temptation aimed upward above the snow-white body. "Go ahead. No one need know."

The soft elderly voice tickled her. Where had she heard it before? Her head was cloudy, she couldn't think. Kim saw her hand reach out and take the smoldering object. She held it upright between thumb and index finger, hypnotized by the orange glow. It called to her. "*Take me, Kimmie. I'm here just for you. We're old friends, you and I.*" Oh, how she needed this, needed something to get her through. But what if Trent smelled it on her breath? Just because he was no longer a pastor didn't mean that his sensibilities had changed.

"Trent need never know," whispered the voice in her ear. "Have some breath mints." A box of Tic-Tacs appeared before her. "One won't hurt. You need this."

Kim nodded and slowly brought the glimmering faggot to her lips. At first she did not inhale, but merely puffed at it, testing it. She was mildly surprised at the sight of blue/gray smoke exiting her body.

"Now, I know you can do better than that," came the man's voice. This time it was close. So close, it could have been in her head. She inhaled deeply, drawing the warm substance all the way down, expanding her lungs. A wave of dizziness came over her. She began to wretch. The voice chuckled, saying, "That's alright, Kimmie. It's been a while. Go a little easier on the next one." She obeyed, felt dizzy, but was able, just barely, to keep her stomach from turning inside out. She took another drag, and another, and then it was as if she'd never quit smoking.

"Better?" asked the voice.

"Yes. Much. Thank you," said Kim, a slight smile on her face as she glanced down at the diminishing butt. A strange thought occurred to her. Why would a man have Virginia Slims, a woman's cigarette? Finally, she turned in the direction of the voice, meaning to ask this question.

But no one was there.

Stunned, she looked left and then right. The cooks were in the kitchen, barely visible above the counter. Teens were still in the alcove playing noisy video games. Two waitresses sat gabbing and laughing at a table near the ancient cash register. But there was no old man – anywhere.

Pale, she gazed at the checkered table before her. There sat an open pack of Virginia Slims, one cigarette missing, beside it, a box of Tic-Tacs. Still, there was no man, only the heavy, sweet smell of pipe tobacco.

"*Oh yeah! Oh yeah!*" screamed Robert Plant.

CHAPTER 12

From the journal of Baqash, angel of the order of Cherubim

I am in deep sorrowful contemplation. Distress pervades my being. O, the path that I travel is precarious indeed. How does one reconcile agonies of the heart? I have never before confronted issues such as these. I cry, I cry. And yet, I must commit this account to writing, for I have no other way of relieving this burden.

My dear friend Michael and I had volunteered to survey the great landmass to the south of Pergamos. We were directed to explore, observe the topography and wildlife, and to make a proposal as to how best divide the area into five sectors, each to be governed by a principality of Helel's choosing, and attended by several legion of hosts.

Helel, it must be noted, has assumed a great role upon the earth, involving himself in nearly all ministries, directing others. His skill is equaled only by Michael.

We completed our survey without incident, identifying not five, but six natural divisions upon the landmass. Drawing a map indicating these regions, we wrote a draft explaining the rationale behind the change from Helel's original plan. We had no reason to believe that this would in any way cause ill will.

Upon our return we encountered a huge golden image, a likeness of Helel, adorned in splendor with ruby, sapphire and diamond. As we stared up into the grinning, golden face, Michael drew near to me saying, "Nothing such as this embellishes the glorious realm. There are no images even of the Ancient of Days himself. Why then was this produced?"

Two angels blocked the entrance to the main chamber: my dear friend Pereh and Asmodeus, a quite and tawny Seraph with whom I have had few dealings. We were instructed to wait while they summoned Helel. Several moments passed as we stood stupidly outside the great door, staring at jeweled walls and awaiting permission to enter. Michael gazed up and about the area, his gleaming eyes shining, his lips curled in bemused concentration, taking in the elaborate, but somehow dark interior.

When finally we were admitted, Helel stood beaming benevolently, his magnificent face gleaming in the multi-hued light, his very presence enthralling. There was no question as to how he commanded such loyalty. "Greetings, archangel. Greetings, Cherubim. I trust your sojourn went well." His voice tinkled like the fine crystal chimes hanging above. "Now, what did you find?"

Michael stepped forward, handing Helel the map we had drawn.

Helel unrolled it, holding it open with his delicate hands, and gazing at it as Michael spoke. It was a striking representation of the land, detailing mountains, valleys, forests, deserts, lakes, rivers, all in precise proportion. We had outlined in blue five distinct regions, then, in red had divided two large regions into three smaller vicinities more closely approximating the size of the other three.

Michael explained that the six regions were both more consistent in size one to another, and fit more naturally within the lay of the land.

Helel glanced toward me. "Do you concur with these conclusions, Cherubim?"

"Quite," said I. "The six region structure will allow each principality to govern roughly equivalent territories within the natural confines of the topography. These physical confines, though insignificant to us, will cause the human population to cluster into each of the six regions."

"It will?" asked Helel. "And how do you know this? Have you had the opportunity to observe large groups of humans together?"

"Of course, no," said I. "That opportunity has not been afforded us. Though we did extensive study of animal life indigenous to the area."

"I am not concerned with zebras," replied Helel.

"Excuse me, friend Helel," Michael interjected. "But we studied the animal life in order to gain a better understanding of fleshly creatures. For the humans are of flesh and will require such essentials as water and nourishment. Likewise, they will be hindered in travel by mountains and seas."

Helel gazed long into Michael's eyes. I believe now that he was attempting to determine if the archangel was challenging him as an opponent, or was merely an irritating peer. Finally, he shook his head saying, "Return to this land. Redraw your map with five regions."

"Helel, we have indicated five regions in the blue. We choose to give you the option of the five, even as we proposed the six," said Michael.

"Oh?" he said as if in surprise. "Does the archangel presume to pull rank?"

"Certainly, friend Helel, that is not my intent." Michael smiled, but the corners of his mouth edged involuntarily downward. "I offer only options that you may best fulfill your task."

"I do not believe I requested options," smiled Helel. "Now, I understand your independence, but on earth obedience is a necessity. This is not the realm, you understand."

"Such is obvious," said Michael.

Helel smiled. "Good. Then I am sure you will understand why this map will not do." He ripped the piece in half and handed it to me before dismissing us.

Why did my soul cry against this? These were foreign feelings to I who had spent eternity in the glorious realm. Was this simply an unforeseen aspect of life on earth, or was it something more? I turned to ask Helel when he required the revised map, but upon my turning, I found Helel seated upon the throne. And at his feet knelt Pereh and Asmodeus in apparent worship.

Since that day, I have felt divisions in my soul, an apprehension in my inner emotions. Since that day, I have questioned my own thoughts, my own invisible motivations. Since that day, I've wondered just who I might truly be at the core of my being.

*****

Trent Troxel stared fixedly at the torn map at his feet. It lay in two jagged pieces and was of the same strange substance as the other angelic documents. It bore a detailed likeness of Africa. Mountains, valleys, forests,

51

deserts, lakes, rivers were all detailed in precise proportion. Outlined in blue were five distinct regions, in red, three regions spanning the territory of the two largest blue designations.

Helel, he thought, chiding himself for not making the connection earlier. Helel was Hebrew for light-bearer or morning star. But most people were more familiar with the Latin translation – Lucifer.

CHAPTER 13

Eldon Troxel led the forty-something year-old father and the pre-adolescent son to the front door, handed the freckled boy a carefully wrapped package, bid them farewell, and closed the door behind them, twisting the lock absently. Making his way past the far counter, he flicked off the overhead light, ambled into the back room closing the door behind him, and glanced at his rather battered Elgin watch. 10:45 p.m. It was time to call it an evening.

Almost involuntarily, Eldon's gaze locked on the cool gray safe lodged between an old white refrigerator and the semi-functional washroom. The thing in the safe was running his life now, dictating his days, filling his nights with strange dreams. He hadn't minded – not that much at least – until a couple of days prior. Then Trent had entered the dreams, and then, reentered his life. If the events – the dream and the visit – had been in the reverse order it wouldn't have bothered him so much. Still, either way, it was Trent he was dealing with again. And that couldn't be all that rosy.

Trent: his brother, Maggie's old flame, how would he take it when he found out they'd divorced? The brothers hadn't had a bad relationship really, not until Maggie at least. Eldon wasn't athletic, but had been the consummate sports fanatic. Trent could care less about stats, but had enough natural athletic ability to field an NFL team single handedly – he'd been scouted by Green Bay. Eldon was an academic with a street-level vocabulary. Trent was an athlete that yammered like a dictionary. The one thing they had in common had been Maggie, and in that area they'd been all too similar. Trent had lost her to his preoccupation with football, Eldon because he'd spent his life traipsing around archeological digs on the other side of the planet. The divorce had been amiable, they even still dated occasionally, but it had been a divorce.

Eldon had been perplexed at Trent's entry into the ministry. Trent had never been overly religious, but for some reason had suddenly decided, during his senior year in college, on a pastoral career. Eldon was even more surprised to learn of his younger brother's fall from grace. Trent could be hardnosed, sometimes overly self-righteous, but Eldon had never known him to be unethical. He might break a guy's arm for stealing his girl, but he wouldn't cop a spare pen from the same guy without first asking. The whole thing hadn't made sense.

Eldon punched the combination to the safe, turned the handle, and pulled the thick metal door. There was only a single item within: a worn leather pouch. Tenderly, he withdrew it, placing it on his desk. Why had he dreamed of this thing again? And why had Trent been there this time?

Eldon needed to loosen up, to get a grip. The dream about Trent and his subsequent return was nothing more than a coincidence. Trent had moved back to Chicago, it was natural for him to seek Eldon out. Likewise it was natural for Eldon to think of Trent, perhaps inserting the guy into his nighttime fantasies.

But a dream, a voice in the night, had led Eldon to the specimen before him, directed him in what to do, how to hide it, when to flee.

Eldon paused. It seemed almost as if the air had thinned, as if he'd suddenly jumped several thousand feet in altitude. The pressure seemed different somehow. Eldon shook his head. Probably a storm front coming in, barometric pressure shifting. Still, strange though. The suddenness of it.

What was that?

Had there been a sound in the front of the shop? He remained still, listening, eyes wide though sight was not the sense on which he focused. For several seconds he remained thus.

Nothing.

Sighing, Eldon moistened his lips and returned to his specimen.

Again, what was that?

Eldon slowly grasped his prize – the single piece which had driven him from traditional archaeology and into this semi-secluded life – and quietly moved back toward the safe, listening, yet hearing nothing. The air was still. Goosebumps rose on his arms. Quietly he replaced the pouch and closed the safe.

Clink!

This time there was a sound. In his mind Eldon replayed the scene of the father and son leaving the shop. He had shown them to the door, handed the package to the boy, ushered them out, closed the door, and yes, locked it. He was certain of that.

He remembered twisting the lock. But he'd done it quickly, absently. Had the lock fully engaged?

Clink!

Another sound. Someone was out there. It was past eleven o'clock and the lights were out in the store. Who could be in there?

The answer was both obvious and unsettling. It was a burglar, or perhaps a vandal. No one with legitimate motives would break into a business and sneak around in the dark. And the room was dark. Eldon could see the crack below the door jam. No light peered from beneath.

But Eldon's light would show from the other side. He swallowed, though his mouth was dry. His brown eyes shifted from side to side. Would the intruder realize he was back there? A smart thief, if there truly was such a thing, would at least investigate the back room. Eldon contemplated putting something, perhaps his jacket, at the foot of the door, blocking the light, but then decided against it. If the intruder had already seen the light from under the door, its sudden absence would alert him to Eldon's presence.

Eldon pulled his Blackberry from his pocket, intending to call 911. But the thing failed to respond. He had plenty of bars, had never had reception problems from the store, but still he got only silence – cold, unforgiving silence. He tried again, and yet again, this time turning the phone off and then on again. Nothing. He thought of the store phone, but it was on the counter just beyond the door. Could he get to it unnoticed?

Impossible. He would need to exit the room just to reach around the door and fetch it. Silently, he cursed.

Clink!

What was happening out there?

Eldon glanced toward the back wall, at the stacks of boxes and containers. The back exit was completely obscured, a fire marshal's worst nightmare.

As he saw it, he had two options: stay put and hope he was not discovered, thus allowing the intruder to have his way with the shop, or investigate and possibly spook the thief – or thieves – into fleeing. The glaring downside here was that he could wind up dead or wounded.

Still, could he let someone just walk away with, or worse, destroy all of the relics? The insurance would cover the loss, but his merchandise wasn't easily replaced. It took months, even years to accumulate such a vast variety of artifacts.

Breath held, Eldon rose, and, cautiously eyeing the door, stepped quietly, very quietly, in that direction, placing his ear to the thin wooden door.

Nothing.

He pressed closer.

Still nothing.

He remained silent, motionless, breath held, but the only sound he heard was that of his own pulse throbbing rapidly within his head. There was no movement.

After several minutes – hours to Eldon – he determined that he had either imagined the sounds, or that the intruder had already found what he'd sought and fled. Eldon took his ear from the door and released his breath in a long hiss. Slowly, his callused fingers slid downward across the coarse wooden door, and then, finding the cold metal handle, grasped. The loose knob jiggled slightly with a light click. Eldon caught his breath, held motionless, and listened.

Silence.

Wait. Was that something?

No. There was no sound, not one inconsequential little sound. Not even the annoying sound of the air conditioning kicking out dry cool air.

Hand upon the doorknob, he twisted, slowly, so slowly, till he felt the catch slip. He paused, listened, still nothing. But there had been a sound before. He was sure of that. And thus he had to proceed cautiously no matter how paranoid he felt. Eldon pushed the door, opening it only enough to peek through with one eye. His view was not spectacular. The right third of the back counter was visible along with a portion of the east wall and counter. Over three quarters of the shop was obscured.

Another gentle nudge. Now he could see nearly the full eastern wall.

The room was gray with darkness. Fueled by a streetlight, shadows fell across the floor creating a bleak landscape of the window display. Eldon's jersey-clad suit of armor, "Butkus", he called the thing, was situated in the southeastern-most corner, a silent sentinel in the apparently empty room. Eldon inched forward without opening the door further. He would attempt to peer around to his left, sheltering himself with the door. It occurred to him that he should have armed himself, perhaps using a hammer as a weapon.

"Why hello, Mr. Troxel."

The voice sounded like the rustling of a thousand leaves. It had come from directly behind him.

Heart in throat, Eldon slowly turned to face the intruder.

The man was tall, perhaps six foot eight. His long dark hair glinted strangely golden even in the dim shadowy light. His face was sharp, fierce, youthful, yet hardened with the trials of life experience. His long black leather jacket reached down to mid-shin just above the highly polished snakeskin boots. The stranger held an ancient Byzantine sword pointed directly at Eldon Troxel's chest.

CHAPTER 14

It wasn't that Kim had lost control or anything. It was simply that she couldn't remember the day. The school had let out at two thirty, she'd met briefly with Principal Diane Grady, come home to learn that Trent had lost his job, and then... And then it was nearly eleven o'clock at night. She'd never had blackouts before, well not real blackouts, just the blurred-cacophony-of-beer kind back in college. But those days were long over. Hell, she'd practically forgotten they'd ever existed.

Man, she needed a smoke.

Her brow furrowed. Where had that come from?

Kim swung her two decade-old Tempo into the driveway and then with-drew the keys from the ignition. Everything had the slow motion surrealism she might expect if she'd been under water in an entirely alien environment. Nothing seemed as it should. Shaking her head, Kim climbed out, locked the door, and shoved her keys into her right jacket pocket.

What was that?

Something was in there, a box of some kind. Kim withdrew a half-empty pack of Virginia Slims. Where had this come from?

As with many ex-smokers, Kim had come to detest cigarettes, to practi-cally wretch at the smell. She sincerely wished that all public buildings would be "smoke free" zones, that all billboards advertising the things would burn, and that most cigarette company executives would die long agonizing deaths brought about by their own products. But now... But now, the cravings were back. She longed for a cigarette, needed to feel the gray fumes caress her lungs, to feel the light buzz. She...

No!

What was she thinking? Cigarettes were nothing but suicide for those who wanted to take their time about it. She'd lost an uncle to emphysema and back in her own puffing days could barely walk two blocks without wheez-ing. Cigarettes were the last thing she needed reintroduced into her life.

Give it a break, Kimmie. It's just a cigarette. No big deal.

But it was a big deal. How would Trent react?

Trent doesn't matter.

She was ticked at him yes, disappointed to be sure.

Infuriated! The man deserves nothing but contempt.

But she might still love the guy. And what about Ashley? What kind of an example would that be for her? And the potential pregnancy. It would be stupid, even dangerous for her to start now. Still...

Still, it was her life to live, and a Slim was her only immediate hope of happiness.

Quickly, before she could change her mind, Kim marched to the trash can, lifted the lid, tossed in her old friends, concealing them beneath some TV dinner tins. She then backed away as if something might jump out and grab her.

To her surprise, the trashcan remained perfectly still.

Kim swore under her breath. She had to get her mind together. Had to center her thoughts, determine what she was going to say to Trent about arriving home so late.

It doesn't matter what Trent thinks. Trent is nothing.

With luck, he'd already be in deep sleep, or maybe in the basement with his precious crates. In either case, she'd try to slip in unnoticed. There was no need for Trent to know what time she'd arrived home or where she'd been – as if she knew.

Holding her breath, she placed a trembling hand on the brass-colored doorknob and turned. The door swung open, Kim peeked in. There he was, on the couch – awake, his upright bass lounging lazily across his lengthy frame. Her creamy white complexion flushed to red. What was this? Did he think he was her father, staying up late just to make sure she'd arrived home on time? Shouldn't he be sleeping, getting a good night's rest so that he'd be fresh for the job hunt? Before she could contemplate her own actions she screamed, "Why aren't you sleeping, you lazy pig? Can't you even get a job?"

Trent set the instrument off to his left. "Honey, where have you been?" He was off the sofa now, approaching her, nonplused by her outburst. He appeared genuinely concerned. Why? Didn't he hate her? Wasn't he evil or something?

"Stay away from me! You're not my father. I'm not some kid on a curfew." But even as she said it, she realized that she'd been prepared to sneak into the house just like a kid avoiding her parents.

Her husband smiled, raising his hands as if in surrender. "Sorry, Goober. Sorry. I was concerned. Your mother said you blew out of here like a tornado on a trailer park. And, well," he shrugged. "It's late."

"Somebody needs to make a living around here," she said. His expression was of someone completely perplexed. "I was looking for a second job," she added, realizing how ridiculous this sounded even as she spoke the words. People didn't job hunt at eleven p.m.

Trent gazed at her, hell, scrutinized her. She pictured her own wavy blond hair, disheveled and wind-blown, and her eyes, they were probably bloodshot (though she didn't know why she supposed this), maybe her makeup was even smeared, her clothing wrinkled. Anyone would know that she hadn't been job hunting. "Kimmie," he said. "It's okay. I don't need to know."

"Don't call me that. He calls…"

She stopped, bewildered. She had almost said, "He calls me that." But he who? Trent was the only one who ever called her Kimmie. Fear, anger, confusion, all rushed over her in a flash of spiraling emotions. Why was she pushing her husband away? He was concerned. He loved her. Or, had loved her. Did he still?

Weeping, she collapsed into his arms, squeezing him tight enough to make him wince. He had to know that she'd just lied to him. But he wasn't chastising her. Wasn't pushing. He simply held her, caressed her, nuzzled her against his chest as he kissed the top of her head.

Why did she feel such revulsion? Such love. Why did she have the urge to gouge his eyes, to rip off his clothes, seduce him, take him right here in the living room? Why did she long to give him a swift knee to the family jewels, to twist his neck? To kiss him, adore him, feel him inside of her? To kill him, slowly painfully with the utmost of pleasure?

And why did she smell like pipe tobacco?

CHAPTER 15

Trent dropped the document translation on the old green chair, trudged up the creaky stairs, withdrew a key hidden in his wallet, undid the padlock, opened the door, and applied the same lock to a latch on the kitchen side of the door. He welcomed the sizzle of a frying pan, and the smell of sautéed peppers and onions. Reggie was at it again, motoring around the kitchen, juggling three separate pans, while never missing a pitch on his televised ball game.

Ashley sat at the cluttered table gabbing away on the telephone, her head bobbing back and forth. "Daddy!" she screamed, probably shattering an eardrum of the poor soul on the other end of the line. "I'm talking to my Unca Eldon. Did you know I have an Unca Eldon?"

Eldon, huh? Interesting. "Yes, honey, I'm familiar with your Uncle Eldon. He's my brother."

"He's not your brother. Unca Reggie's your brother – silly!"

Trent chuckled. "Uncle Eldon's my brother too. He just doesn't live with us. May I speak with him, please?"

"Unca Eldon, are you my Daddy's brother?" The girl listened intently, furrowed her eyebrows, and then laughed aloud. "You're silly Unca Eldon."

"Ashley – the phone."

"Daddy's getting really perturbed. I gotta give him you."

Trent retrieved the phone, gave his daughter a squeeze and a peck, and sent her off to destroy something valuable while Daddy was on the phone. "You calling to offer assistance?" he asked in lieu of a greeting.

"Well, hello to you too. I'm doing fine. Thanks for askin'."

Trent rolled his eyes. "My apologies, El. But, I doubt you called to trade small talk and recipes."

"Not exactly." The voice was tentative, maybe even frightened. "Listen, Trent. You're into something. And whatever it is, you're way over your head."

Trent had to laugh. If Eldon only knew how far over his head, he'd send scuba divers down to salvage him. "Readily admitted, El. So, come to my rescue."

"Can't do it, Trent. Trading in black market artifacts would make my rep smell like puke. No legitimate source would touch me again."

"I'm doing nothing illegal," said Trent. "And even though I don't trust the source of these relics, I've got a pretty good sense that he came by them honestly."

"You're talkin' outta both sides, Brother." Eldon paused. "Listen, I got a visit. A very frightening visit. The guy was weird, threatened me with a sword from my shop. He claimed to represent someone looking for a document of wifehood – like the one you showed me. He got really ticked when I wouldn't help him connect with one. Heck, I thought the guy was gonna stab me." Eldon sighed. "Anyway, he's probably gonna track you down. Stay clear. Call the cops. Come clean."

"Curious," said Trent. "Someone desires that piece?"

"Yes."

Trent began pacing. "Someone seeking that item just after we'd met. I wonder who else knows that I possess these relics." Trent paused. "Did you say he offered compensation for the document?"

"Trent, don't even consider it. You've got a family. You can't afford jail time."

"Yes, Eldon, I have a family. They need to eat."

"That's what paychecks are for."

Trent reached down and twirled the salt shaker, watching tiny granules scatter across the table. "I was fired, El. I'm unemployed."

There was a pause, a sigh, and muttered words before Eldon replied. "Well, my advice is that you find another job. But whatever you do, stay away from this guy. Drop those relics off with the cops, tell 'em what you know, and don't look back."

"It's not that easy, Eldon."

"Who said anything about easy?"

*****

Kim gazed in through the rain-streaked storm door. Inside, Trent sat on the couch reading a Dr. Seuss book to Ashley. It looked like "The Cat in the Hat," but it could have been "The Cat in the Hat Comes Back." The covers were similar. Ashley looked happy in her fathers lap wearing one of his old T-shirts for a nightgown. Trent looked tired, concerned, his eyes red, his hair disheveled.

The Slims had been there again, a quarter pack. But this time there'd been some pills too, little red ones. She couldn't remember the name of them, but she and her high school pal Suzie had called them "little-red-hots".

She felt queasy, and almost fell over, but managed to right herself with the slippery railing.

What time was it?

Dark. It was dark. School let out at 2:30. It shouldn't be dark yet. Kim fumbled with the cellophane bag in her pocket, pinching the pills between her fingers.

Little-red-hots.

When was the last time? High school? No, freshman year of college.

Little-red-hots.

Then Suzie had dropped out. Kim had become responsible.

Little-red-hots.

Responsible. Nothing stronger than Jack Daniels and joints.

Little-red-hots!

Responsible!

Little-red-hots!

Kim turned from the window and seated herself in a puddle on the top step, pulled the plastic bag from her pocket, and shook her head in disgust. "What am I doing?"

She opened the bag, and withdrew two little-red-hots.

*****

Ashley was almost asleep in Trent's lap when the phone rang. She stirred, shifted her head, hugged her stuffed bear, but didn't sit up or request another book. Trent was very thankful for this. The girl was trying to stay up to see Mommy. But Mommy wasn't home – again. As with the night before, Kim was not answering her cell phone. Trent had no clue when she'd show, or what state of mind she'd be in.

"House of Troxel, may I take your order?" whispered Trent, still holding Ashley on his lap.

"Mister Troxel?"

"Yes." Trent didn't recognize the voice.

"I am glad to have found you Mister Troxel. It is my understanding that you're in possession of an authentic Egyptian document of wifehood. I am willing to pay quite a substantial sum for such a piece."

CHAPTER 16

From the journal of Baqash, angel of the order of Cherubim

"Friend, Pereh," I cried. "Bring me to Helel. I must speak with him."

Pereh studied my face. "You are distressed, friend. The eyes tell that tale already. But it is not so easy to see the prince. He is busy attending his duties."

The prince. Helel had somehow acquired the title, "Prince of earth."

"Friend Pereh, we are brothers you and I. Do this thing for me. Grant my audience with Helel before my soul rents asunder."

Pereh smiled, shaking his head. "You have always had a flare for the dramatic, Baqash. I believe that I understand the source of your tribulation. Many have come forward with similar concerns." He stopped, pondered, and then with a laugh, said, "You shall see the prince. And when you do, he will dispose of your misgivings."

We found Helel standing in the great room, his robe of precious stones flowing behind him, sending varying hues across the floor and walls. His charismatic smile and triumphant eyes captured me at once. Again I was impressed as to the unsurpassed beauty of this creature.

"Greetings, Cherubim. What has brought you before me this day?"

I hesitated, unsure of how to formulate my thoughts into a cohesive sentence.

"Is it that you take issue with my methods here on earth?" offered Helel. My mind went to Pereh. What had he told Helel to cause such an abrupt beginning?

"Not exactly," I answered.

"Not exactly," he repeated. "Then exactly what is it?" He stood casually, smiling at me from before the throne.

"The title, 'prince of earth,'" I asked. "Is that one which the Ancient has given or was it derived independently?"

Helel laughed, high pitched, yet strangely restrained. It was almost a weary sound. Surly others had posed similar questions. "I understand perfectly," he said. "The next question will address this holy chair. Do I have permission to sit upon it?" He patted the throne playfully. "Let me assure you, Cherubim, your fears have no basis."

He stepped down, pacing the room as he spoke, his cloak waving behind in a glittering dance. "I ask you, do I will to ascend to heaven, to raise my throne above the stars of God? Do I desire to make myself like the Most High? Cherubim, you know the answers to these questions. The petty title 'prince of earth' is no affront to the king of the universe." Helel stepped forward, his demeanor stern. "Earth is a rock. The Ancient rules all of creation. Now tell me, where is the conflict?"

I admit, I was taken aback by his statements. They made my fears, my contemplations, seem unreasonable, petty. What possible dissonance could arise from Helel, the most beautiful and wise of all creation?

"You plead your case well," said I. "Still, there is another matter."

"Yes?" he said, drawing out the "s".

"When last I stood in this room, it appeared that you accepted worship from Pereh and one other."

Helel finally drew close. "First, do not assume that I am in any way required to respond to your allegations. I respond of my own free will." I acknowledged this, and thanked him for his consideration. "I will, from time to time, accept praise, this is true. Though, I do not require it of my subjects. This praise is freely given from those who work closely with me and understand my wisdom and beauty."

"But is this not misdirecting praise from the Ancient?"

"Was it not the Ancient who created me as I am?" countered Helel. "Was it not the Ancient who clothed me in splendor? Was it not the Ancient who granted me an intellect above all other created beings? Is it not the Ancient you worship when you bow before me?"

I stood mute, unable to respond. The logic of his statements seemed clear. How foolish I must seem to one such as he. How misguided. Smiling, Helel approached me, draping his arm over my shoulder. "Ah, my curious seeker, you are an intelligent being. You ask probing questions. Certainly, you see that I am no threat. The Ancient has placed us here for his own purposes. I will need those such as you, Cherubim, to do the work set before us. I need those of fiery spirit and free of thought, those willing to understand that things are not always to be as they always have been. The earth, the universe, these are new creations. Is it not your desire to embrace this newness, to put aside the old ways and seek the new and better? Do you not wish to come beside me in this great adventure, friend Baqash?"

I was overwhelmed by the confidence of this superior being. How glorious was the path he proposed, how incredible the adventure before us. Yes, I would serve Helel, prince of this world, in his holy mission upon the earth. There was no need to question further. All was as it should be.

CHAPTER 17

From the journal of Michael, archangel

It is with unfathomable regret that I commit to written form the events of this day. I do so primarily that there be accurate record of all that has transpired.

There is something terribly wrong on earth this day. Devotion to an able captain is progressing toward true worship. And this we must not accept. How could Helel, I, any of us accept worship due the Ancient of Days? Yet, accept it Helel does. And I submit that he not only accepts, but indeed encourages and expects this adulterous homage from his fellow hosts. Allow me to site as example the following:

Baqash and Pereh approached Helel concerning a mutual project. Pereh immediately bowed before the self-proclaimed prince of earth, prostrating himself on the marble floor and singing praise to the smug Helel. Baqash bowed slightly, greeting Helel with praise to our creator, while uncomfortably shifting his eyes toward his companion, anxiety visible in his gaze.

By all that is holy, Helel should have rebuked Pereh harshly that very instant. Instructing him that never, never should this behavior be repeated, that the Ancient of Days alone is to be worshiped, that all else is blasphemy. But amazingly, it was not Pereh who was to be rebuked. Rather, it was Baqash.

Baqash!

Baqash who had approached with praise to our creator upon his lips, Baqash who loves the Ancient above all, Baqash who trusted Helel implicitly, Baqash whose inquisitive mind left him open to such as Helel.

Oh, how my innermost being groaned. "No!" I screamed as Helel instructed Baqash to humble himself and pay respect to "the prince of earth." And I wept as I rushed forward. I wept as Baqash, my dear friend, knelt before this false god and slowly, haltingly, against all that he was, whispered a prayer in the name of Helel.

I approached the throne indignant and offended. "Oh, that he was not so dazzled by your brilliance, Helel. For clearly then he would recognize the blasphemer which you have become." I turned to my friend. "Arise, Baqash. Leave this place."

Baqash rose, saying, "Michael, you misinterpret what you have seen. Do not challenge what you don't understand." The quiver in his voice belied his uncertainty.

"Yes," cooed Helel. "You have misinterpreted." He leaned back in his golden throne smiling. The vast chamber seemed to close in on us, the numerous tapestries to darken, to stare at us from the walls, the chimes to hush as if listening from afar.

"I plead with you, Helel. Cease this apostasy before it destroys you and all who would draw near."

"Apostasy? Really, archangel, is that not a bit much?"

His manner was superior, condescending. He spoke to me as to one of little consequence. In truth, I had instinct to strike him. Yet, I tempered my emotions, remained civil – for the moment. "We have both served faithfully through time eternal." I said. "Respect our relationship. Remember why you are here and who you are – a servant to the creator. If this elevated position causes you to stumble, retreat." I took a step forward, softening my tone. "There is no dishonor among the hosts. Do not allow pride to swell within your bosom and blind you to the gravest of errors."

Pereh, who had remained silent to this point glared at me with corruptive emotion. "Leave the prince be, archangel. This is not of your concern."

"I will handle my own confrontations, seraph," stated Helel, his tone cool, his manner superior. "The archangel can cause me no harm." He rose from his faux throne, and floated off of the vast platform and to the floor. Pereh stepped back, behind me, and out of view. "You do understand, Michael. You can cause me no harm."

Dancing colors, the result of jewels and crystal about the chamber, played across his face, making it seem not more beautiful, but malevolent, distorted. "My intent is not to harm, Helel. How could you imagine that it would be? But you make a mockery of our calling, and I demand that you cease this charade."

The slap came quick and sharp. Never before had I been struck such. Still, I did not move nor flinch. "None! None, archangel, make demands of me. Accept that fact, or leave me now, never to return."

"No, Helel, I will not leave. This kingdom is not of your design. You simply seek to steal it from the true creator."

"That is untrue!" shouted Baqash. "Friend Michael, we have served with Helel. We are aware of his qualities. There is a reason that he has ascended to leadership upon the earth." He gazed at me, earnest eyes pleading. "Michael, please. Do not pursue this in your misunderstanding."

I turned to my friend, sorrow welling within me. "Baqash, you are my dearest companion, but you are deceived. I do not dispute the glorious attributes bestowed upon Helel. But, dear friend, he has perverted these gifts in order to glorify himself."

"And so it would seem, archangel," said Helel, "that we are at odds. You serving the old, Baqash the new."

"There is nothing new, Helel, that was not created by the Ancient himself."

"Oh, please. Do not bore me with this."

I moved forward as if to strike the blasphemer, and truly, I might have done so, but found firm hands upon my arms. The hosts Asmodeus and Semyaza had taken hold of me, Pereh, having summoned them without my knowledge. I offered no resistance. What was I to do, fight them off? Surly I was capable. But what end would be served?

Helel smiled, as if in victory. "Do not challenge me, archangel. You do not have the fortitude. Where you trust in another for your strength, I rely only on my own superior ability. Do not forget the tournaments of our past. We were equals then, but I have grown while you have become complacent." Then, with the wave of his hand, he showed me away. "Be gone, archangel. This meeting is adjourned."

I chose not to respond to this heresy. Helel was beyond redemption. But Baqash, perhaps I could still reach Baqash. "Will you be party to this?" I asked. "Even after what you have seen, what you have heard, will you follow this blasphemer?"

Baqash did not answer, but only lowered his head, his courage failing him, his devotion ruined. "Baqash is loyal," said Helel. "He knows that all need not be as it has always been. There is a new day, Michael. Join it, or be crushed by it."

I did not dignify this with a response, but merely looked once more at Baqash. "Dear friend, you know this to be wrong. I see it in your very being. Do not become party to blasphemy." Baqash turned away as I was led out of the vast chamber by the two brutes. I wonder if I shall ever again share the company of this most beloved friend.

CHAPTER 18

The man at the door was large, round, his royal blue blazer tight around the shoulders and separated by a full foot at the belly. His red checked tie, yellow polyester pants, and white loafers left Trent with images of every used car salesmen cliché ever imagined. "Norman Spellman," said the man, extending his pudgy right hand.

"*Honest Norm,*" thought Trent. "*Have I got a deal for you.*"

"I hope you don't mind," continued Norman as he pumped Trent's hand three times. "But I'm a few minutes early. If you're right on time, you're probably late on somebody's watch." He smiled, one golden tooth glinting in tandem with his seemingly-polished bare head as he marched past Trent and into the small living room. "Quaint, very quaint," he said, gazing about the room. "Well, I'm sure you'll find more suitable lodgings once we transact business, eh, Mr. Trookel?"

"Troxel," said Trent as he closed the door and strode into the hallway. There was something not-right about this man: something in his manner, his expressions. "We'll do this in the kitchen," said Trent as he led the way.

"Who is it that you represent?" asked Trent as he settled into the chair opposite the man at the Formica table. Spellman placed his brown vinyl briefcase on the table and opened it. What was it about this guy? He seemed... unnatural, somehow almost synthetic, an approximation of a cliché.

"My client, Mr. Trookel, may I call you Trent? My client, Trent, chooses to remain anonymous – for obvious reasons."

Trent gazed at the yellowed, overly-long fingernails, at the hooded eyes, brown on a pale beige canvas. He inspected the jowly face, poorly shaven and flushed. "Obvious to you perhaps," he said. "Not to me. Why don't you explain."

"Well..." The man faltered. It seemed almost that he was struggling with something internally, a fight for control or influence. He flinched, blinked, inclined his head at a peculiar angle and stared almost sightlessly at Trent.

"This is a legal transaction." Trent continued. "The parties should be known to one another."

The large man leaned forward on his elbows, the blazer straining at the seams, the smell of English Leather assaulting Trent's senses. "You're doing business with me, Trent. I will then transact business with another. Now, may I see the merchandise?" He grinned, attempting to appear casual, but his bald scalp sparkled with sweat. Trent doubted the man regularly dealt in six-digit transactions. Perhaps this was why the man seemed so ill-at-ease, to struggle internally. This was a big deal to him. Heck, maybe the guy really was a used car salesman, somehow moonlighting in ancient artifacts. Maybe he was a month and a half behind on his mortgage just like Trent, with gas and electric bills two months past due and credit card debt scratching at seven thousand – just like Trent.

Or maybe he was something else entirely. But, what? Trent had difficulty pulling his misgivings into something more concrete.

"It's here," said Trent as he reached beneath the table and clasped the leather pouch. Did he really want to do this? Could he do it? He'd acquired this thing from a demon – a demon! What events might be set in motion by the selling of this relic? "How did your client learn about this piece – that I possess it?" asked Trent, still leaving the thing on the cool vinyl floor.

"My client moves in certain circles," said Spellman with a lulling roll of the head. "He has contacts. He hears things."

"That's wonderful, Mr. Spellman, but I told no one of this piece."

"No one? You took this item to your brother for appraisal. Couldn't he have told someone?"

Eldon? Eldon was against this whole thing? Could he have told someone about it, unintentionally sending a buzz out in "certain circles?" Eldon was an archeologist. He had connections in that field. Perhaps he'd done some inquiring, attempting to learn where Trent had acquired his relics. It was possible at least. And Trent really didn't see how the demon could profit from the sale of the piece.

Trent glanced at the refrigerator, at Ashley's multiple drawings hanging about the thing, at the school photograph of his precious daughter, at the hand-drawn birthday card proclaiming, "I love you, Daddy." He lifted the soft leather pouch, placing it before him on the table. His family needed to eat, to have beds to sleep in, to have electricity, water, security. He'd have to worry about his immortal soul later. "You have the check, I presume."

"Of course," smiled Spellman, withdrawing a white business-sized envelope. "Two hundred and fifty thousand dollars, as agreed."

CHAPTER 19

From the journal of Michael, Archangel

Only when we are unhindered in rebellion are we truly free in dedication. Only if we are unshackled can we stand immobile and true. For it is our ability to choose against which grants sweet aroma to our stalwart choice for. Yet with this liberty, some will surly choose the destructive course, the way of darkness, of death.

Such a great assembly but once have I seen: every Cherubim, all Seraphim, the Chief Princes, the Principalities, all of every order, those stationed in the golden realm, those stationed on earth. All gathered for one purpose – judgment.

Such a foreign concept. Never before has there been a cause for judgment. Truly it is an alien notion to any host. Great contemplation, even trepidation, befell the masses. Though thousands came forward, scarcely a word was spoken. Host squeezed tightly against host. Each desired proximity to the event, yet silence carved cavernous gulfs between them.

Gabriel, Raphael, Uriel, and I flanked the great throne, thus affording us a view of the masses. Both land and sky were invisible behind the sheer numbers of hosts. And I saw fear in the eyes of angels. None gazed directly at another, heads were lowered, eyes darting from host to host, wings lowered and limp, lips curled strangely downward on golden faces.

Helel, at the center of the first row, stood haughtily, his cloak shimmering with precious stones. Of all present, he appeared the only one at ease. His head cocked, arms crossed, legs spread, he seemed to believe himself in control of the situation. But even the bravado of Helel lasted but moments. For as the last hosts arrived, a voice boomed, "Helel, in the pride of your heart you say, 'I am a god; I sit on the throne of a god. But you are not a god though you believe you are as wise as a god.'"

An audible gasp cascaded through the hosts. All knew the charge. Yet, to hear it spoken by the Ancient of Days made the steadiest host tremble. Helel took a moment to respond, appearing almost to retreat, to bow before the might of his former Lord. Yet when he did speak, it was in arrogance. "Am I to assume that you take displeasure in my accomplishments?" he asked, his voice melodic and firm. "Have I not tended the fields? Have I not embraced the land which you created? Have I not beautified it beyond the original state? Where then do you find fault in the perfections of my deeds?"

"Get you behind me, Satan!" thundered the Ancient, the word Satan meaning adversary. "Your pomp shall bring you to the grave."

Helel sneered, his countenance becoming dark, his eyes wild, uncontrolled. "You may call me Satan if you so desire. But, know this – I act not alone." Turning to the multitude, Helel cried, "Come forth those who would testify on my behalf. Stand beside your prince as he is unjustly accused."

All was still, every angel silent. Helel gazed across the masses, his smoldering eyes condemning those unwilling to comply. "Do I not have one faithful soul, one faithful witness to my perfection?"

Blasphemy!

Silence.

But then, surprisingly, movement.

From among the hosts hovering above, the angel Pereh floated down to stand aside his prince. "I shall stand with you, friend Helel. You are all that you have claimed."

My arms became stiff, my being still. One of the multitude had chosen Helel, the Satan. Worse even, Pereh was a companion of Baqash. Could my dear friend be influenced by a companion's folly? I searched the crowd for Baqash, but could not discern him amongst the clamoring masses…

*****

From the journal of Baqash

…"Is that all?" cried Helel, as Pereh soared down to stand beside him. "One? Merely one of the thousands to labor beside me?" Helel stepped toward the multitude; his six wings arched high in agitation. "Should not one as perfect as I be permitted to lay claim to an inconsequential kingdom of my own? Have I not proved my perfection?"

O, how my soul rent, the division so profound as to immobilize me. Yes, I intended to support Helel, but my Lord, my dear, dear Lord was the opponent. How could I come against the creator of all, the one who brought me into being? I gazed down upon Helel, upon Pereh by his side. These were not blasphemers. Dissidents perhaps, those of a different mind, but not blasphemers. Surly the Ancient could not truly mean to pass judgment on such as these.

I gazed again at my dear friend Pereh. We had determined to go forward together, to stand unified beside the prince of earth. But Pereh's resolve had proved the greater, mine faltering at the last. Still, the time had not yet passed. Terrified, I prepared to move forward, to make my stand. But before I could move, a burly host named Baal stepped forward and took his place alongside Helel and Pereh. "This, I will do," he said, his voice low, rumbling, arrogant.

With that, another host came forward, then another, and another. Soon multitudes were aligning themselves with Helel, yet still I remained immobile. Did I lack the fortitude to do as I desired, or was there something more, something deeper holding me still?

*****

From the journal of Michael, archangel

...About half of those who had been stationed on earth, and several thousand who had been but visitors to that sphere had now come forward. And then I glimpsed a sight that will forever rent my soul. For my dear, dear friend Baqash became visible to me, and it appeared that he might move forward to join the ranks of the accuser. I started toward him, but the Ancient held me immobile, indicating that the decision must be made by Baqash alone. My friend Baqash gazed at Pereh, then at me, his eyes tear-filled and confused, apology on his lips. But he refused to look onto the Ancient as he moved forward. No! Please, no! I wept bitterly for my lost companion, dear, dear, Baqash!

The Ancient of Days indicated that any who wished to return to him were still free to do so, but once sentence was passed on Helel and his minions, they would forfeit this liberty. Several hundred did slowly migrate from the condemned crowd, but even still, nearly a third of the total number of hosts remained aligned with Helel. Baqash, downcast and trembling was among that number, though why, I cannot fathom. What had Helel done that could cause such folly in one who had been so completely dedicated to the Ancient? What could have transpired for Baqash to forfeit his eternal destiny?

Finally, when all had settled, when all had aligned themselves with a chosen master, the Ancient spoke. "You were the model of perfection, full of wisdom and perfect in beauty. I placed you in Eden, the garden of God; every precious stone adorned you: ruby, topaz and emerald, chrysolite, onyx and jasper, sapphire, turquoise, and beryl. Your settings and mountings were made of gold; on the day you were created they were prepared.

"So, I drive you in disgrace from the mount of God, I expel you, O guardian Cherub, from among the fiery stones. Your heart has become proud on account of your beauty, and you corrupted your wisdom because of your splendor. So I throw you to the earth."

At this, Helel barged forward, his true disposition displayed to any who still could have wondered. "You may cast me down, but I will ascend to heaven. I will raise my throne above the stars of God. I will sit enthroned on the mount of assembly, on the utmost heights of the sacred mountain. I will ascend above the tops of the clouds; I will make myself like the most high!" His voice had climbed into hysteria. What his followers thought of Helel in this moment, I cannot know, but that they knew fear was evident.

The Ancient of Days responded calmly, rationally, to the outburst. "You are brought down to the grave, to the depths of the pit. By your sin, you have desecrated your sanctuaries. I throw you to the earth."

And with that, a great wail erupted from Helel as he bellowed for his followers to charge the golden throne.

Confusion, chaos, as the condemned fluttered about not yet sure how to respond. But there was one, this Baal who had so boldly aligned himself with Helel; he held no hesitation as he forcefully grabbed the nearest host by a wing, and hurled the startled angel aside as he bound toward the throne.

Gabriel swooped down colliding with the charging Baal. The condemned host was nearly toppled, stumbling back several steps, before regaining his footing. Gabriel had the momentum, but Baal was large and broad, sturdy as an earthly oak. Baal's large arms reached around the smaller Gabriel, prying the loyal host from his breast and slamming him to the golden street.

I raced forward, shouting commands, organizing the loyal army as Helel's minions swarmed forward. They charged, they feinted, they attacked, but their purpose, their commitment seemed hollow, unsure.

These dissidents were to be thrown to the earth, so, as I charged into Baal with anger and determination, I soared upward pulling the huge host with me, clutching him under his upper left wing, and across his broad neck. He fought furiously, reaching, grabbing, clawing at my face, biting my wrist. Several times I nearly faltered, nearly released him. But, finally reaching the rim of our heavenly realm, I spun and spun about, thrusting Baal from me, sending the traitor tumbling into the cold black void.

Others followed my example, piling upon the dissidents, wrestling them to the ground, then lifting them, by their wings, their legs, sometimes even by their hair, and hurling them into the blackness. Our numbers were roughly double theirs. The outcome predetermined, yet they clawed, spit, cursed, their very natures seeming to change from angelic to demonic as they committed to their hopeless cause.

Some fled, hiding in dwellings, scurrying behind fountains, even attempting to mingle with the faithful. But as the number of condemned decreased steadily, the number of faithful remained consistent. Where we had begun with an advantage of two to one, soon it was three, then four, and then twenty to one.

Cries and screams filled the hallowed lanes as one by one the condemned were hustled away. Tears were shed for the fallen beloved. Some pleaded with their former companions, begging them to return to their senses, but by this point fates had been sealed, judgment cast. As I wrestled with a stout, troublesome foe, a familiar voice caught my attention. I swirled to my right. Baqash was being lifted to his destruction by two loyal hosts, one clutching his long golden hair, the other his left calf. His pleading eyes met mine one final time, and I could do naught but turn away.

O Baqash, why? Why did you falter? How could you have come to this? Dear, dear friend, I shall miss you. Today I weep for the purest of hearts now turned black. Why, Baqash? Why?

*****

From the journal of Baqash

...As I was cast forever from the glorious realm, I felt the Ancient's presence wrenched from my being, sensed a rush as his spirit fled, evaporating as mist before my clutching fingers. I heard the agonizing shrieks of the lost, then realized that it was my own voice which filled my ears. I gazed down upon the weeping eyes of my dear friend Michael perhaps for the last time.

We rose, higher, higher, the glorious realm, in all of its tumult, diminishing below. Yet, still I struggled against my assailants, clawing at their eyes, kicking and squirming, wrapping my wings around the neck of one, and spitting in the face of the other.

I was thrust roughly into dark cold space, to float aimlessly for days, perhaps weeks. It seemed no star pierced the eternal night, no sun warmed my extremities, and no sound reached my ears. Even my own wretched and endless squeals simply slipped silent into the dark, condemning, void.

And I am cold, so terribly, terribly cold.

CHAPTER 20

"Hello, Kimmie." The voice was old yet smooth, familiar yet forgotten. The heavy, sweet smell of pipe tobacco tickled Kim's nostrils as she buried her eyes into the red and white checked Formica tabletop. Kim knew, but did not know, that the package of Virginia Slims and lighter had appeared before her. Somehow they reminded her of something beloved, like a childhood pet, they seemed to purr, to call, to nuzzle. Of course she wanted one. Didn't she always have a Slim after little-red-hots? Mechanically she withdrew the slender cylinder from the foil encasement, sniffing the air, anticipating the aroma, and, with jittering fingers, lifted it to her lips.

Not looking up, Kim took a long drag and exhaled the blue/gray smoke in billows causing it to roll across the table like a London fog. She didn't know why, but felt it best not to acknowledge the man beside her. Another puff, another long drag, another, another. Suddenly shuddering, she realized that there was no ashtray at the table. What was she to do with her ashes? They were becoming long and bent, ready to fall. It would make a mess. They might soil her clothes!

Her eyes flitted forward, then to the left, then forward again, but never to the right. That was where the other sat. The one in tweed, the one who spoke to her. "An ashtray," she whimpered. "I need an ashtray." And one was before her. With a squeaky sigh, she tapped the paper to plastic resolving her dilemma.

"Is that better?" came the hypnotic voice. Kim nodded, brushing a blond lock from before her face. Then, taking another long drag, she placed the cigarette in the ashtray, pulled her knees upward so that her heels were resting on her chair, slipped Trent's over-sized sweater over the knees to seemingly swallow her whole, and cradled her long legs with her arms.

"I understand that your husband made a rather sizable profit recently. Would you care to tell me about it?"

Kim reached down and pulled the cigarette to her pouting lips, inhaling deeply, remaining silent.

"Kimmie, I understand that he sold an ancient document. Where did he get it?"

Pressing the cigarette butt into the ashtray, Kim withdrew another from the package, fumbled, and retrieved it. Reverently, she drew it to her lips.

"Kimmie, you mustn't ignore me. You do hear me, don't you?"

"I... hear." Her voice was choked, weak.

"And you do know the answer to my question."

"No. I..." She took a long drag. "I don't know."

"Kimmie, are you telling me that you don't know that your husband just sold an ancient document for a quarter of a million dollars?"

Kim gazed across the room. It was hazy, indistinct, like her mind. She couldn't make out details. It was all distant shadows, almost as if the room wasn't really there. Or maybe... she wasn't there?

"No," she said. "Trent told me that he sold the piece, that I could stop working. But... I can't stop working. You... still want me to work, to leave the house, to come here." She bit her lower lip and settled her chin between her upturned knees.

"Yes, Kimmie. That's very important. For another has made it difficult for me to enter your dwelling undetected. Now, where did Trent get that document?" The voice was becoming agitated, less soothing. Kim fumbled with her cigarette, dropping it onto her left leg. She squealed, frantically batting it away like she would an attacking bumblebee. No, no, no! A hole! A hole in Trent's brown wool sweater. "He'll know! He'll know!" she screamed.

The other placed a firm hand on her shoulder and whispered in her ear. "No. He will not know, because you are going to buy a new wardrobe with some of that new money. And if Trent doesn't like it, you're going to tell him it's your right as his wife. You can even tell him to back off."

"I can say that?"

"Most definitely."

A wry smile grew across Kim's lips. "I think I like that."

Kim saw a hand reach out, remove a cigarette from the package, and pick up the lighter. It disappeared to her right, and then reappeared before her, cigarette smoldering and beckoning. "Now, where did he get the document?"

"I don't know."

"Was it in any way associated with the name Baqash?"

Kim started. The name, Baqash, she knew it. The same way a preschool playmate's name is remembered, distant, concrete, yet indistinct, without recent point of reference. She knew the name, somehow, but not in connection with the document that Trent had sold.

"No," she said. "I don't remember Trent using that name."

"Are you certain?" The voice was harsh, agitated. "You seem familiar with the name."

Kim drew her arms more tightly about her legs. "That name… I don't know. It's familiar. But I don't think Trent has ever mentioned it."

"Your husband holds such important information from you. Surly, you must wonder what else he's hiding. Perhaps some slut on the side."

Kim took another long drag and nodded, thinking of the baby, the biggie she was hiding from Trent. She hated it when he kept things from her.

"Are there other documents, Kimmie? Other artifacts?"

"There are boxes, crates. There's a challis."

"How many boxes?"

"I don't know. A lot, I think."

"And you don't know where they came from?"

"They were delivered. Trent keeps them locked in the basement."

"Who else knows about them?"

"Reggie and…" She hesitated. For some reason she couldn't bring herself to speak her daughter's name to this one. "Reggie knows. But I don't think he knows where they came from either."

"Who else?"

"No one."

"Who else, Kimmie?"

"No one."

And she was alone.

CHAPTER 21

Eldon climbed the seven steps, glanced through the three small rectangle windows on the wooden door, and rang the bell. His thoughts were of Trent, Reggie, and his wacky dreams. He knew it was time to dance with the fire, but wanted nothing more than to disappear into the cool Chicago night. After thirty seconds, he rang a second time, and was gratefully turning to leave when Reggie opened the door.

"Reggie, hi. Uh, listen, sorry I haven't been too good about returning your emails. I've been…"

"Eldon! Did you see the Cubs game? Four/three in the ninth and they blew it – fumbled an easy pop up." Reggie paused, eyeing Eldon curiously. "Does Trent know you're here? He doesn't like you, you know. He thinks you stole Maggie from him, but he has Kim now. She's a nice lady. Do you want some chicken? It's good."

Eldon smiled, his brown eyes crinkling and ruddy cheeks stretching with his wide grin. He'd not realized how much he'd missed Reggie, who not only shared his brown eyes, round face, and dark hair, but also his love for Chicago sports. Stepping through the screen door, he gave his brother a firm hug. "I've missed you, Reg. Don't you let me go that long without seeing you again."

"Okay, Eldon. I didn't mean to. Do you want some chicken?"

Eldon patted him on the back. "Nah. I guess I need to see our brother."

Reggie nodded and retreated from the tiny living room with a familiar waddle.

There was nothing wrong with the place. The home was small, but definitely Trent's. A bookcase littered with dusty tomes stood against one wall, an old CD player churned out jazz classics at a moderate volume, their dad's old roll top desk sat in a corner, and Trent's upright bass, blond and battered, angled lazily across an old plaid couch beside a pillow and ruffled blanket. A typical middleclass setting. So, why did Eldon's legs jitter? Why did the sweat on his brow seem to freeze in place though the room was uncomfortably warm? Why did Eldon want not only to flee this room, this home, but maybe even the city itself?

Trent emerged as if from nowhere, worn and dusty. Waving halfheartedly at Eldon, he managed a controlled drop onto the couch. A quirky grin slipped across his broad lips as he heard Reggie motoring around the kitchen, clinking and clattering. "Get your bib on, El. Chef Reggie's in the house."

Eldon smiled. "Some things never change." He gazed at his exhausted brother. "You okay?"

Trent nodded unconvincingly. "Fine as a peacock in a quill factory." He massaged his temples with his palms. "I suppose you're here because I sold that wedding document."

"Well, yeah," Eldon shrugged. "Someone leaked the sale to the paper. It seemed like a pretty ignorant thing to do."

Trent chuckled softly. "That seems to be the consensus. My wife has accused me of everything short of assassinating Lincoln." Trent reached to his right and drew his bass across to his chest and began plucking softly.

"What are you into, Trent? You've gotta give me enough info that I can... I dunno, give some advice, help you out of the mess – something."

"Really? You're offering help?"

"Yeah, really."

Trent's lips curled into a broad grin. "What an entertaining little deviation. You Kick me out of your shop, threaten to call the authorities, and then show up offering help." He glanced sideways at Eldon, winking. "Are you wired, El? Are you undercover, going for the big sting operation? Are you going to nail me for possession of old stuff?""

Eldon leveled his eyes at Trent. "Listen, I know that you sold that piece, my guess is that it went to the same bozo that broke into my shop. So, what's this all about? Who's supplying you with artifacts, and where are they getting them?"

Trent thumped harder on his bass, the deep tones resonating about the tiny room. "Sorry, El. I sincerely wish I could tell you everything, but I can't."

Before Eldon could respond, a little blond girl wearing a long white V-necked T-shirt entered the room carrying a plate of sizzling fried chicken. Eldon went cold. It was the nameless child from his horrific dream. The girl that the monster had carried to the fire. The one the dream Trent had tried to save – unsuccessfully.

"Hey, sweetie," said Trent. "I thought you were in bed."

"I got her up, Trent," hollered Reggie from the kitchen. "She needs to meet Eldon. Eldon needs to meet her. Introduce Ashley to Eldon, Trent. They need to meet."

Trent smiled, shook his head and shouted in the direction of the kitchen. "Thanks, Reg!" Then, to the girl he said. "Ashley, this is your Uncle Eldon. You talked to him on the phone the other day."

Eldon hesitated, just staring at the girl. How could this be? How could the girl from his dream be real? He'd never seen her before.

"Hello, Unca Eldon," said Ashley. "Unca Reggie made you some chicken." She placed the plate on the coffee table before Eldon.

"Um, hi, Ashley. Glad to meet you."

"Unca Reggie said that Daddy and you got in a biiiig fight." The girl stretched her arms as wide as they would go. "He said that Daddy and you are both smart, and someday you will figure out that you're still brothers."

"Ouch!" chuckled Eldon. "From the mouths of babes, I tell ya. Come here and give your uncle a big ol' hug." Eldon trembled as he embraced the child.

After a couple minutes of good-natured banter with the kid, Trent shooed Ashley off to bed and the estranged siblings fell into stilted conversation. How did Trent like being back in Chicago, was he going to visit their ailing mother anytime soon, when was his wife due home? Trent remained closed to any discussion of the relic's origins, though Eldon pushed to the point of being obnoxious. Why not? It wasn't as if he was in danger of damaging the relationship.

Shortly after 10:30, they heard a sound at the front door, someone jockeying with a key. Eventually, the door swung open allowing an attractive woman of about thirty-five to enter. With slightly disheveled golden blond hair, bewildered blue eyes, and carrying two large Sears bags in each arm, she looked lost and hopeless. She gazed about as if examining a new and unfamiliar place, and then dropped the bags where she stood, allowing the contents to spill across the gold and brown carpet as she strolled unsteadily toward the kitchen leaving the door ajar. Eldon noted a strange buzzing, nearly undetectable. The sound of multiple bees or wasps. Nothing was visible, though. He saw only the vacant-eyed woman. But there was more. Somehow he felt – in his gut – there was more.

"Kimmie." Trent set his bass aside and rose from the couch, catching his wife's attention.

"Trent?" She squinted her bloodshot eyes. "I didn't see you."

"Where have you been, Goober?"

Kim turned and stared at Trent, her pupils wide, unchanging. "Shopping," she said.

Trent furrowed his brow, scrutinized her. "That I had surmised." He hesitated, then pointed at Eldon. "Hey, uh, Kim, this is my brother Eldon."

She turned and glared at Eldon, the eerie quality in her blue orbs causing him to avert his gaze. "Eldon?" she said. "You married Trent's old flame. I certainly hope you didn't bring her with?"

"Uh, no. We're divorced." Eldon glanced toward Trent, noting the slight tightening of his jaw. Eldon hadn't yet shared that little piece of information with his brother.

"Oh!" She seemed to contemplate this revelation for a moment. "I suppose that's best, isn't it?"

"Kim!"

"It's okay, Trent," said Eldon, rising from his seat. "It's an awkward situation." Then to Kim he said, "Pleased to meet you, Kim. I'm sure your big lug knows he's right where he belongs, married to you."

"I suppose," she said, and turned absently toward her packages. "I went shopping," she restated. Then, with a mischievous grin added, "Back off."

"Back off?" said Trent.

Kim responded in a girlish sing-song tone. "I can tell you to back off, you know. Do you like my outfit?"

The brothers stood in awkward silence as Kim cocked her head and wandered about the room inspecting the walls, tapping on books, contemplating the roll-top desk. She blew dust from the top of the television, then turned and kicked one of the shopping bags across the room. Eldon felt fear, real honest to goodness fear, as Kim stared at Trent with the gaze of a serial killer contemplating an unsuspecting victim. "You've been keeping something from me, Trent."

Trent offered a less-than-brilliant expression. "Kim, what are you talking about?"

"Trent," she purred his name, her tone becoming sultry as she moved to press herself against him. "I'm talking about your precious crates."

"Sorry, Goober. I can't tell you about those." To his credit, Trent actually sounded quite gentle.

"Hmmm," cooed Kim with a curl of her lips. "Do you really find those old crates more appealing than your own wife?" Her hands rose slowly, purposefully to her flowery blouse, and she began seductively unfastening the buttons.

"Kimmie!" roared Trent, forcefully pulling her hands from the fabric before the woman could reveal her breasts.

"Don't call me that! Ever!" Her voice was high, shrill. She broke free of his grip, whirling about, wooing and hooting like some drunken jungle beast. Twirling and twirling, her new cotton skirt billowing out like a carnival ride, hair bobbing with the random flips of her head, she danced toward the couch, nearly tripping over the long low coffee table situated before it. Then, finding her way to the front windows, she called out, "Hello, hello, where are you, Mister Tweed? I know you're out there!" Her ghostly reflection gazed back through the glass at the bewildered brothers, wild, untamed, yet somehow frightened.

Suddenly, with a violent screech, she darted across the small room to the opposite wall, randomly grabbing books from walnut veneer shelves, and hurling them over her shoulders. They flapped through the air like drunken sparrows, cascading down upon Trent and Eldon, bindings separating from pages, knocking family photographs from the walls, and shattering the bulb of a small yellow lamp. Trent's bass, already scared and nicked from twenty-plus years of use, took several hits, each time responding with a low rumbling tone.

Trent was struck repeatedly as he shielded his face with his long, taut arms. Eldon scrambled behind a vinyl reclining chair and few of the projectiles found him.

"Kim! Stop!" shouted Trent in near panic. "Could we just talk?" Crime and Punishment whizzed past Trent's ear.

Ashley and Reggie appeared in the hallway. Great! Just what the kid needed to see – her mother doing the Bride of Frankenstein shuffle! "Daddy, what's Mommy doing?"

"Ashley!" Trent fended off Webster's Unabridged Dictionary. "Reggie, take Ashley to her room and stay there with her!" Kim whooped and let East of Eden fly.

"But, Daddy, what's a matter with Mommy?"

"Move! Now!"

Reggie swept the girl up with his right arm and rushed her into her nearby bedroom, slamming the door behind him.

Trent ducked and plowed through the onslaught of hardbacks, nearly catching his wife around the waste before she pivoted from his grasp and sprinted down the hallway. Trent turned, slipped on Les Miserables, righted himself, and pursued Kim.

Eldon contemplated the front door, so close, so inviting, so safe. But no. He was here. He was involved. Dance with the fire and all that. Cautiously, slowly, he made his way toward the kitchen, stepping over random books and displaced knickknacks. He found Kim scratching furiously at a locked door to the far left. Trent stood, ineffectively attempting to calm her.

"Open the door!" she screamed repeatedly. "Open the damn door! I need to see what's down there. I need to know what you're hiding." She clawed again as Eldon took a tentative step closer. This was astounding. Her nails were actually indenting the wood, and by the looks of it, a quarter of an inch or deeper. Trent placed a hand gingerly on her shoulder. "Kimmie, what's going…"

"I told you not to call me that!" Kim whirled, fingers crooked like talons, she raked her nails across Trent's cheek with a spat of red. Startled, Trent pulled away, his left hand pressed against his damaged face as he nearly stumbled over the kitchen table.

"Kim! What are you doing?" he screamed.

Eldon moved forward slowly, respectful of the crazed woman. Grasping a folding chair from beside the table, and holding it before him as a shield, he approached his brother. "Trent, you okay?"

Trent glanced quickly at Eldon. "Superficial damage. I'll live."

"What's goin' on here, brother?"

"No clue, El." Trent stepped back, allowing Kim her space. She couldn't get through the door, and both men knew that reasoning with her was not an option. They watched nervously, silently, as for several minutes Kim clawed and punched, howling and cursing at the obstruction. Eventually, she collapsed in whimpers to the floor, her bloody fingers resting on cold tile. Cautiously, Trent knelt beside his trembling wife, patting her gently, whispering softly. "It's okay, Goober. It's okay. I'm here, Sweetie."

She shook her head like a frustrated toddler, and squealing, began crawling about the floor. "Where are my cigarettes? Where are the little-red-hots? I lost them all. I lost them. Where's Sam? Sam Melter always has cigarettes. I need a Valium. Does anyone have a Valium? No! Something to pick me up. Little-red-hots for my baby. Little-red-hots for my baby."

Trent gazed up at Eldon, clearly pained. "I'm at a loss, El. She's never been like this before. And this cigarette thing – she doesn't smoke. And the pills..." Trent trailed off. Given a few more minutes of this, he'd be as bonkers as Kim.

"What's this about a baby?" asked Eldon as he knelt beside his brother. "Is Kim pregnant?"

"No. I mean, we were trying, but... I don't know."

Eldon sighed. Yep, dance with the fire. He was up to his elbows in it now. "Trent, you'd better tell me everything."

Trent nodded.

CHAPTER 22

Four faces march beside me, and perhaps one inside.
Six wings embrace my lover, Trent rides his final ride.
My baby punts and hollers, through many eyes he'll see.
Four faces smirk and drool, four faces discern no glee.

Trent had difficulty reading the poem. Not just because of the multiple cross-outs, sprawling handwriting, and strange doodles all about the page, but because of the words themselves, the bizarre tainted words, the reference to Trent's final ride and to a baby. Could Kim really be pregnant? Why hadn't she told him? And what about the drugs and cigarettes he'd found in her purse along with the poem? He knew things had been tense since they'd left the church, and especially since Baqash entered their world. But Kim was a strong woman. He hadn't anticipated this, hadn't expected her to turn to drugs as an escape.

"That's a pretty freaky piece of writing," said Eldon as he gazed at Trent from across the round and wobbly card table. They were in the basement, cold and gray, a strangely appropriate setting for their moods. "Any idea what it means?"

"Yep." Trent had spent the previous three hours at Kim's bedside, nursing her to sleep, stroking her hair, holding her hand, and contemplating her words. "The reference to my demise is obvious, as is the indication that she's pregnant."

"And the four faces and six wings bit?"

"That, to me, sounds like the description of a cherub, or perhaps, of a demon who had once been a cherub."

"A cherub? Aren't those the cute little buggers with wings and bows?"

Trent leaned forward, his duel-colored eyes intense. "The biblical description is a bit more extreme. They're described as having four faces, each face pointing in a different direction, and either four or six wings. Apparently, there's some variety within the species."

"Lovely, so why is the baby seeing through many eyes? Does your wife think she's giving birth to a cherub?"

Trent picked up a pencil from the table and began twirling it between his fingers. "That's a conundrum."

"And how does all this tie together? The artifacts, Kim, you losing your job?"

Trent leaned back in his chair, examining his brother and touching the gauze on his left cheek. Only a handful of people on the planet would take the story at face value – and Eldon wasn't one of them. Still, Trent would need Eldon's expertise in validating the documents. Only the truth would persuade Eldon to comply. Trent allowed himself a grim smile. "Hold on to your lexicon, El. You're not going to believe this."

He didn't.

"Aw, fer cryin' out loud, Trent. Maybe you could pull this crap with your superstitious congregation, but I've got a PHD fer bleedin' Sunday."

"As expected," said Trent. "The consummate intellectual. You'll never believe anything unless you massage it with your grubby little fingers."

"Listen, I'm not the one dealing in stolen archeological treasures."

"Nor am I, Eldon. Trust me."

"Oh, sure – the honorable Pastor Trent and his pet demon."

Trent lowered his head. He'd been a fool. Eldon would never take him seriously. Why had he even tried? "You know, Eldon, I was thinking that blood is thicker than water, but I'd forgotten it's still not as thick as crap." He tossed his pencil onto the table. "I think, perhaps you should leave."

"I think that sounds just about right."

"I think somebody needs some hot cocoa," came a voice from the top of the stairs. Both men gazed up to see Reggie's stocky form descending the creaky stairs, a tray with three cups of steaming liquid in his hands. "Have some cocoa. It's good."

Trent rolled his eyes in exasperation. "Reggie, thank you. But now is not a good time."

Placing the tray on the rickety card table, Reggie met Trent's gaze. "I know you don't think it is, Trent. But when you guys are by yourselves, all you do is fight. But when I'm with you, you laugh. You've always been like that. It sounded like you might need to laugh."

Eldon glanced at Trent and then smiled in Reggie's direction. "Reg," he said. "It's been great seeing you. And I will be better about keeping in touch. But I've gotta go. There's stuff between Trent and me, well, hot chocolate just ain't gonna cure it." Rising, and moving to Reggie, he gave his younger brother a warm hug. "I love ya, kid. Be good." Then he made his way toward the wooden stairs.

Trent watched Eldon retreat. In many ways, he'd prefer the man leave – but not now, not with his entire life spinning out of control. "Listen," he said, rising from his seat. Eldon paused, but did not look back. "You don't believe in demons. I can accept that. I certainly wouldn't have believed this, not even during my pastoral days. But my family's in danger here, and frankly, I need your help."

Eldon turned slowly. He wasn't convinced, but he wasn't walking either. "I need the truth, brother."

Trent sighed, nodded, and stepped forward holding his right palm out before him, displaying the hand-shaped scar. "What's this?" asked Eldon.

"This," said Trent, "is what happens when a demon grabs your hand."

The brown eyes squinted, examining the hand. "No. That's what happens when some schmuck spills hot grease on his hand while working at his father-in-law's restaurant. Try again, Trent."

The hand dropped to Trent's side. "No, Eldon, I'm not going to try again. Believe me or don't. Play the grand enlightened agnostic if that's what keeps your cozy little universe spinning, but help me. If not for me, for Kimmie, for Ashley, for Reggie."

Eldon emitted a long pronounced sigh and appeared in some way pained by Trent's words. Ashley's name seemed to strike him somehow. Trent could see the change at that moment, the tightening of his face, the narrowing of the eyes. "What is it you're trying to accomplish with these relics?"

Trent ran a hand across his ruffled hair. "Eldon, these things are ruining my life. The demon has threatened my family. He wants me to glean something from these documents, I need to determine what."

"I don't believe in your demon." Eldon's words were harsh, final.

Trent looked down on his brother. "But, I do believe, Eldon. I honestly do. And while you may not know if the demon is real, you can know that I am. Believe in me, Eldon. Believe that I honestly need to do this, and that I honestly need you with me."

Eldon broke the gaze, sidestepped Trent, and selected a cup of cocoa from the tray. He glanced at Reggie, smiled, took a sip, then asked, "So, this leaves us where?"

Trent hesitated. "Okay. Fair question. Baqash has given me translations to each document. Obviously he intends that I read them."

"Have you?"

"Quite a few. Taken at face-value, it's pretty spectacular reading."

"And what are you supposed to get out of all this?"

"I'm unsure. I think he wants me to discover something in the writings. Something to help him somehow defeat Satan."

"Ambitious bugger."

"Perhaps." Trent began to pace the dark gray room. "But, I'm not all that concerned with his motives. I'm seeking something that I can use to get him away from my family – permanently."

Eldon stepped forward, facing Trent directly. "Okay, let's take a step back here. What kind of documents are we talking? More marriage certificates, maybe a divorce or two? I don't see those overthrowing any devils."

Trent hesitated. No way was Eldon ready to see the angelic documents. Even if Eldon had been open to the supernatural, it was a safe assumption that he wouldn't be capable of translating the language of angels. Thus far, everything that he'd read had been of angelic origin, but Trent had scanned through other transcripts and many were written by humans, many were very, very old. "We're looking at quite ancient writings, literally the earliest writings known to man. We need to authenticate the relics and translate the documents. I need to know that these transcripts are accurate, and if they're not, what things have been changed."

Eldon nodded. "So, you think all of these pieces are authentic?"

"There's no indication otherwise. The wedding document I sold has been validated, and despite your skepticism, Baqash has proven to be all too real. So yes, I believe that tests will prove them true. But the translations. That's the real issue. Are the translations accurate?"

Eldon regarded Trent. "Depending on the writings, that could be a pretty hairy assignment. I'll have to ship at least some of the pieces off for testing, carbon 14 dating and whatnot. And as for translation, I'm good, but there's a lot better out there. If we stray beyond Egyptian, Greek, Aramaic, or Hebrew, I'll be pretty much useless."

Trent beamed at Eldon, feeling the butterflies of hope dancing around his belly. "Sounds like you're signing on."

Eldon shrugged. "We'll see how things go. I never claimed to be bright – just educated. There's a difference, ya know."

"You're smart, Eldon. Don't pretend," chimed Reggie, obviously pleased that his siblings were conversing at sub-nuclear levels.

"That reminds me," said Trent, realizing that his younger brother had been present for the entire discussion. "Reggie, you can't tell anyone about this – not even Kim. That's very important. Do you understand?"

Reggie grinned and drew his hand across his lips as if zipping his mouth shut.

"And why should all of this be kept from me?" It was Kim's voice, from atop the stairs. "Is this a little boy's club down here?"

CHAPTER 23

Trent and Kim had early-morning coffee at their favorite hangout: the Swedish Covenant Hospital cafeteria. It had become their date of choice simply because it was a short five block walk from home and nothing else was as convenient when they were out for a stroll. The coffee wasn't great, the food less so, the place was too bright and had that hospital antiseptic smell to it, but it was their place, and Kim was comfortable there.

Trent had insisted they talk, and Kim had no desire to do so in the presence of Trent's creepy brother Eldon. Thus the stroll and the cafeteria. Kim sipped her too-dark coffee and stared across the table at Trent who sat spinning a peppershaker like a top. "Drugs, Trent? You're accusing me of drug usage?" She shook her head. "What are *you* on?"

Trent cocked his head, gave the shaker another twirl. "An aspirin regime to thin the blood, a couple of vitamin supplements, and too much caffeine for any sane man. But the question is you, Kimmie, what are you on?"

Kim felt a sharp mental twinge at the name "Kimmie". "Nothing, Trent. Nothing."

Trent leaned forward, elbows on the table. His dual-colored eyes, strange yet beautiful, were intense, his jaw set, the white gauze on his left cheek adding a creepy element to his normally innocent look. "Kimmie, I don't know that any space shuttle has ever been as high as you were last night. Do you remember any of it?"

No, she didn't. None of it. Not one recollection of that day since two-thirty the previous afternoon. "Of course I remember it. Is this another one of your fantasies, Trent – like your demon?" Trent narrowed his eyes at her. "Yes, I heard what you boys were talking about this morning." Demon? Where had that come from? In truth, she didn't remember.

Trent pointed to his bandaged cheek. "Do you remember how my face became injured?"

"It's your face, Trent. Keep track of it yourself."

He slapped the table, causing a group of chatting nurses to turn at the commotion. Then, with a grunt, he dug into his pocket, retrieving a cellophane bag containing little red pills. "Do you want to tell me what these are, or should I go ask those nurses? These pills were in your purse."

Little-red-hots!

"I... don't know," she said.

Little-red-hots, oh she could use one right now.

"Kimmie..."

"Don't call me that."

"Goober, Honey, tell me where you got the drugs, how long you've been using."

Little-red-hots, where had they come from? She wanted them, needed them, but... It had been years, over a decade, why would she want them now?

"Please, Kim. Tell me what's going on. I'm concerned for you, for Ashley. Do you realize that she saw you last night? You were trashing our living room like some orangutan on speed and our daughter saw you. What explanation can I possibly give her?"

Ashley. She would like little-red-hots. No. That was silly. Ashley wouldn't be ready for at least another couple of years.

Trent now reached into his shirt pocket, withdrawing a folded piece of green paper. Kim recognized the kind as having come from her poetry notebook. Trent unfolded the page and slid it toward her. "Can you explain this?"

Kim stared down at the wrinkled page. She didn't recognize the words, though it was clearly her handwriting.

Four faces march beside me, and perhaps one inside.
Six wings embrace my lover, Trent rides his final ride.
My baby punts and hollers, through many eyes he'll see.
Four faces smirk and drool, four faces discern no glee.

"It's a poem," she said. "So what?"

Trent reached for her hand, touching it tenderly with his. "Kimmie, are you pregnant?"

*****

Trent thought of other times, of Kimmie's impish grin, the light of her sparkling blue eyes, the way her blond locks would tumble before her eyes, of the unconsciously seductive way she'd cock her head or twirl her hair. The way she'd whisper his name as she suggested some intimate "alone time." But that was not the woman before him now. Not entirely at least.

Kim averted Trent's gaze and produced a tight smirk. She seemed to him to be moving off somewhere, becoming less in tune with their conversation. Thirty minutes ago she'd been almost her normal self, but now, no, she wasn't much like Kim at all.

"Pregnant, Trent? Cute. Interesting. I'll need to give the matter some thought."

"Goober, please."

"Please, what? Please and thank you? We teach children to say please and thank you. Are you a child, Trent?"

"Kimmie…"

"No!"

"Kim, Goober, just tell me, are you pregnant?"

Kim stretched out across the table, her tiny chin on the hard green surface, arms spread out, her hands fiddling with utensils. "What if I am? That is my prerogative."

"Yes, it is. And we've been trying to have another baby. I'd just like to know."

With a quick swipe, Kim snatched the bag of pills and sprang from her seat. "Mine! I got 'em! Mine!" She spun around like a gleeful child, toppling her chair in the process.

"Kimmie!"

She was losing it completely. In a public place – a hospital no less.

99

Kim stopped, suddenly, a cold glare in her ice blue eyes, a strange near-ly-alien expression creasing her features. "I'll tell them what you've done. I'll tell them all what you've done. Baby maker!" she screamed. "You're just a baby maker!"

"Kimmie!"

"Miss, is there a problem?" It was a nurse, alerted by Kim's outburst.

Kim jerked her head in the woman's direction. "You're not going to lock me up. Oh, no. I know your type. I've seen your type before." Then suddenly she went sweet, the madness melting into a mist. "This man was trying to sell me drugs," she said, displaying the bag of little red pills. "Whom should I notify?"

*****

Eldon left Trent's home around six p.m., having spent over twenty hours poring over relics. The pieces were incredible. Not once did he find any hint of tampering, and most of the pieces looked to date far back – very far back.

Never before had he seen such an intriguing collection. There were enough obscure pieces in that basement to keep a full team of highly skilled archeologists occupied for several years. Many of the writings appeared to be religious in nature. As such, this collection could prove as significant as the Dead Sea Scrolls.

But, where had they come from? Eldon's natural skepticism denounced Trent's ridiculous story of demonic origins – though he was becoming increasingly convinced that Trent actually believed the claim. There was a true mystery here. Why was Trent given these and by whom? In his gut – Eldon trusted his gut like some people trust a medical specialist – he still believed the pieces to be stolen, and that Trent had somehow stumbled into some bizarre fencing operation.

Just as Eldon ambled around to the driver's side of his red Ford Bronco, he felt a strange chill creep over his body. It seemed a large strangely shimmering shadow traversed Trent's lawn. Eldon gazed skyward. Nothing. Not a cloud, no plane overhead, no sparrows or robins. Eldon shook his head with a wry chuckle. Trent's fantasies were playing on his mind. What a load of horse hockey.

CHAPTER 24

From the journal of Baqash, the fallen

Confused and disoriented, I rose unsteadily to my feet, brushing insects from my ravaged form and gazing about in utter mortification. Dark gray clouds hung low in the colorless sky. Strange sounds assaulted my ears: the rustlings of pursuit, the clamor of battle, shrieks of pain, and gasps of death. The sky erupted in shards of radiant light as if nature itself was savaging revenge on the forest. Trees and foliage burst into flames as one after another they were struck by sizzling darts from above. Luminous orange particles clung fiercely to plants igniting all they fell upon.

Feeling strangely vulnerable, I began hiking, perhaps hoping to find that elsewhere all was as it should be. I wasn't of here – wherever "here" was. I knew this more from intuition than from my few shards of fragmented recollection. I was of another place, a magnificent place, with streets of glimmering gold and structures of radiant gems reaching into the clear and perfect sky.

But how had I come to be here, in this terrible land?

I squinted, attempting to wrestle memories from cloudy oblivion. There had been a trauma, a horrid chill, a fatal defeat. And fear. Oh, a fear so ferocious that I'd been willing to do anything to escape its bone-like fingers.

Lightening flashed, pulling me from my contemplations. This place was not right. Perhaps another would be better. I continued my trek: no particular direction, no intended destination. Simply walking. I had hiked for perhaps a day's span when I spotted the loathsome one floating above the lightening-spattered horizon. Catching sight of me, the thing paused, and then altered course to intercept. Hovering before me, he gazed down, a scowl upon his long hard face. Dull. His aspect seemed dull. The eyes were dim, tedious. The wings did not move in harmony, but independently, like writhing serpents. A sane being would fear such a thing. And yet I knew no fear.

"Where do you go?" asked the loathsome one.

I had no compulsion for dialogue and ignored the question.

Obviously perturbed, the creature dropped down before me, repeating the question. "I said, where do you go?"

I strode silently past him.

Snorting, the thing followed. "Do you not venture to Pergamos?"

Pergamos? The palace of Helel. Beautiful, shimmering Helel. Interesting. It had not occurred to me that I would be expected. "No, I do not venture to Pergamos."

The repulsive creature flew before me, hovering slightly above ground level. "Have your senses left you? Where else is there for such as us?"

I continued walking.

"If you do not desire to serve Helel, why then did you choose this fate?"

"Did I choose this? It seems a strange choice."

The creature snorted in disgust. "Look at yourself and then tell me what you chose."

I did as instructed, gazing over my form. Where I had expected to see a magnificent golden body, I found a withering, boiled mass, nearly as loathsome as the one before me. With this realization came the first true stirrings of memory: the battle, the fall, the damnation. "Yes," I said. "I suppose I did choose Helel. Though, in truth, I cannot recall the rationale."

The dull-faced creature snorted in frustration. "Fool. How does one choose such a fate with but trivial commitment?" And then, with a harsh flutter of uncoordinated wings, he was gone.

I continued onward, ignoring the retreating form, my eyes staring blankly ahead. Then, perhaps fifty paces on, I paused, gazed onto the horizon, turned, and strolled slowly, steadily in the direction to which the fallen host had disappeared.

*****

Once-fine tapestries hung about the walls, dingy and stained. The marble floor was dark and crumbling. Throngs of desolate hosts crammed the immense chamber. These things were a motley lot, their forms naked and misshapen, their manners coarse, brutish; their darting eyes lacked reason. They scrapped and spat, cursing at one another as they flitted about the space with torn and ill-formed wings. Their odor was off-putting, their gaping grins and lulling tongues far worse.

The burning carcasses of numerous beasts lay upon a large circular platform: lions, elephants, apes, huge reptiles, all sizzling and popping. A lanky form sat upon a throne situated at the far eastern wall. "Who will challenge Melkart the victor?" said Helel, as he rose, his long golden hair fluttering behind him, his beautifully sculptured face betraying no motive. "You," he said, pointing to a skeletal host just ahead and to the right of me. "Have your skills been tested?"

The gaunt face tightened, his eyes averted the gaze. "No, my lord. I anxiously await your call."

"Then consider yourself called," said Helel, his hushed melodic voice dancing about the chamber.

Then, ever so casually, the demon prince's gaze fell upon me. The dark eyes glinted as his thin lips curled into a foreboding smirk. I had been seen. Whatever was to befall the one now called, would befall me as well, of this I was certain.

The chosen one moved forward, awkwardly pushing his way through the jeering crowd to step upon the great circular platform.

"You know what must be done," said Helel. "Proceed."

I stared up at the poor lost host. A great creature was just beyond him – a mastodon, enormous, lumbering.

The brooding host stepped tentatively toward the waiting beast, his eyes focused in concentration, his frail form taut. Then, to my astonishment, he stepped through the beast's flesh and to within the creature. The shaggy form lurched, then twirled and shook – an incredible sight due to the creature's sheer mass. Then, with a thunderous boom, it flung its colossal form to the floor causing the very chamber to tremble. Just as it appeared the flaying form would thrust itself into the flames, it halted, rigid and still. Then, relaxing, the beast rose clumsily to its feet. To my astonishment, superimposed about the physical form of the mastodon was a spiritual entity – the host. And it was this tiny, quivering spirit which now controlled the massive form.

Could this be possible? Were we capable of inhabiting the flesh? I gazed in amazement as the beast/host took three tentative steps, the new master of the form learning to manipulate the limbs. After several awkward struts and pirouettes, the thing turned to face Helel who was now seated sideways on the dull golden throne, one leg dangling over the armrest. A low, rumbling voice emerged from the strained throat of the mastodon. "I-am-ready-my-lord."

Helel glared. "It should not have taken so long to subdue a stupid beast." Then, with a dismissive wave of the hand, he said, "Proceed."

The thing turned, and for the first time I noticed another form, a lion, circumventing the platform. And about the feline's form, the same spiritual glow as was upon the mastodon.

The lion roared, "Identify yourself."

"Loki," grunted the mastodon. "The seraphim Loki."

"Melkart," replied the lion-thing, as it crouched and leapt, attaching itself to the hirsute neck of its unprepared foe. The mastodon howled, throwing its massive head from side to side in an attempt to disengage the assailant. Forelimbs wrapped around the impossibly wide neck, claws imbedded in the leathery flesh, the lion head thrust downward again and again with intensifying fury. The mastodon shrieked and spun about, frantic now as the lion plunged deeper.

Then, suddenly, the mammoth wrapped its thickly muscled trunk about the giant cat, and with a desperate heave, ripped the feline free, hurling the beast toward the flaming pyre. The lion screeched, flipping about in the flames, and then rolled out onto the platform, its mane ablaze.

Melkart flopped about the floor in a maddened frenzy until the mastodon wrapped its powerful trunk about the lion's torso, lifting, and then slamming the creature against the hard marble floor, again, again. To all appearances, the lion was lifeless. Certainly Loki believed this as he lifted the now-bloodied figure above his shoulders, trumpeting a victory call.

Whipping its head about in a movement unbelievably swift for a creature so tortured, the lion lunged at the exposed area of the Mastodon's neck, causing the triumphant trumpet to reel into a screech of incomprehensible agony. Shaking frantically, the mastodon pulled at the lion as Melkart held firm with knife-like fangs sinking deeper into the soft under-tissue. The snake-like trunk loosened and dropped, as the mastodon tumbled headlong into the blaze with a great splay of flittering sparks. Releasing its grip, the feline landed with a sickening thud upon the floor.

I stood hushed, mesmerized, as the lion slowly, painfully shifted. Broken limbs clattered together as Melkart willed the shattered form to rise upon broken hindquarters. Standing upright as would a host, he roared, "Melkart is victorious!"

It was then that Loki staggered free of the flames, eyes wide and unfocused. He lurched, stumbling about the platform. "Dark. I am... Cold. Dead. Dark. Why... so cold?" He was insane – insane!

Sensing a presence beside me, I turned to see Helel. "Cherub," cooed the demon lord as he stepped closer. "Perhaps you would like to test your might against that of Melkart?"

I inclined my head. "I'm curious. What is the purpose of the contest?"

Helel smiled a still-beautiful smile. "Of course, you are a late comer." Now his gaze was one of venom, his grin of seething disappointment. "I would have thought you more loyal." Another pause. "These are meant to determine rank and order amongst us. Those found worthy may one day become gods."

Gods? How could this be so? It seemed folly at best. Was it even possible for there to be another god than the Ancient One?

I contemplated the cold, dark eyes of Helel, knowing that to debate the issue would do naught but infuriate him. "And how am I to possess a beast?"

Helel grinned. "The beasts are dull of spirit. Their minds are tiny and unimaginative. Merely take hold and subdue the meager intellect." Helel turned. "Ah, it seems a suitable host has been selected."

I followed Helel's gaze to see a great ape, large, black, and brutish, such as I had tormented with fruits a lifetime ago. Behind this was a lion, a replacement for Melkart's battered beast.

*****

The possession process was strangely invigorating. As I imposed myself about this creature, its mind seemed to lash out, to force me away, to nearly scream in hopeless protest. I could not tell how long I wrestled for control, nor whether the ape bucked about as had the mastodon. But eventually my superior will prevailed.

And suddenly. Suddenly I was gazing through fleshly eyes. How dull the colors. How indistinct the image, how uneven the hearing and foul the odors. What strange sensations these alien muscles and bones. How disturbing, the bodily fluids racing through veins and arteries.

I rose to meet the gaze of Melkart. Already, the lion crouched in preparation. I feigned right, and then rolled left avoiding the first lunge. I did not yet manipulate the limbs well. Still, I moved with forethought and strategy which the ape could never possess. The lion whirled and leapt, colliding with me, digging deeply into my back. The pain. The unimaginable pain.

But, not madness.

I had seen the seraphim, Loki, had witnessed the effect of fleshly death upon him. I could not lose this battle, could not allow a defeat that would bring about lunacy.

Somehow, I broke free, falling out of the lion's reach. Before the feline could reorient, I bound forward, slamming into a surprised Melkart, and hurling both creatures into the nearby blaze. Flames lapped at my face and hands, but I could not accept defeat, not if it meant madness. If Melkart was not destroyed then my mind would be destroyed. And in a place already teaming with insanity, I dared not risk losing what reason I retained.

I forced the lion's head into the heart of the blaze. But with a panicked swipe, Melkart broke free, scrambling from beneath me, and rolling from the inferno. As the lion-thing beat at its blazing head, I grasped a long bone from the fire, one with a broken and jagged end, and lunged upon the lion, thrusting the weapon deep within its chest. The crowd erupted in cheer as the lion tumbled forward onto the floor. I gazed down at the immobile beast, the brown eyes staring blankly into nothing, the chest so still, the limbs so stiff. Where once there had been a living creature, now lay decaying meat.

Unexpected emotion flooded my mind. Such power. Such unimaginable potential. I had never truly contemplated the taking of life. But, here, this. Was this not god-like? Was this not a power beyond compare? Turning toward Helel, I screamed, "Another opponent!"

And Helel did bring another, and another, and yet more. And each time I was victorious, becoming increasingly adept at manipulating the ape. Soon I was without fear, and this was my advantage; for I was willing to enter the flame, to feel the searing heat, to come to the brink of death – but only to the brink. Only once did I falter, and this but momentarily. I faced Pereh, my friend of old. Yet once I realized that he held no sustaining loyalty, well, then neither did I.

Pereh is now a mad thing.

Soon, after yet another brutal victory, Helel moved to beside me. "You are prideful," he smiled. "In my experience, pride could be a downfall."

I appraised the demon prince. "I've done only as you have asked."

"Yes, indeed. You have done just as I had hoped you would do." Helel turned. "Baal, let us determine if Baqash's confidence is well founded."

A familiar form, a host of immense strength, stepped forward. His great sloping forehead rolled into tiny eyes, sitting above an ill-formed nose. Two flap-like ears protruded behind boiled cheeks. His shoulders were broad and well defined. This was Baal, the second only after Pereh to align himself with Helel that fateful day.

And then the crowd erupted in riotous laughter as a creature was brought forward by a tittering host who drooled and chortled, nodding at the absurdity of it all. On his palm sat Baal's fleshly host. Not some great ape, nor a lion, or a mammoth. No, this was a tiny thing – a toad, green with black spots. Though my inclination was to laugh at the absurdity, I could only frown. This was to be my opponent! How audacious was Helel to even call it a contest?

Baal, for his part, simply stepped forward, dissolving into the tiny creature, easily overpowering the simple mind, and quickly taking control of the form.

"Baal," I barked hoarsely through the mouth of the ape. "Come-to-me. I-will-end-this-quickly."

The toad croaked, unable to form even rudimentary syllables, and quickly hopped forward. I swatted at the thing. But Baal anticipated the move, evading at the last. The toad hopped about, coming up behind me. I twirled, slapped, missed. The motley throng hooted and howled at my expense.

Grunting in frustration I cursed and screamed, "Baal! This-is-useless. Let-us-be-done."

I bounded after the toad, dove, missed again. By this time the crowd was in hysterics. I caught a glimpse of Helel angled comfortably across the throne, his expression one of amused curiosity. The outcome of the contest was a certainty, but this ridiculous toad might hop about for hours before finally I smashed it to pulp.

Cursing, I bound forward, swatting and stomping. But the tiny creature simply hopped this way and that evading the furious attacks. Bone and flesh now rained down on me, hurled by the riotous spectators. I picked up the pale white skull of a wolf and hurled it at the Baal-toad. It flew wide, skittering and bouncing on the platform.

Once again, I bound forward, but my right knuckle came down on a moist piece of flesh, causing me to topple sideways. Before I could right myself, the toad hopped onto my belly and into my mouth, immediately scrambling over the tongue and into the throat.

Even as I gnashed my teeth, the Baal-toad squirmed deeper and deeper into the ape's narrow throat. As a spirit being, I had no need of oxygen, but I currently inhabited a fleshly form, and fleshly forms require air. I rolled about the platform, attempting to cough the tiny creature out, grasping at the slimy thing with the ape's clumsy fingers. My vision began to darken, a crimson grayness closed in upon me. I felt the gorilla's mind slip away, diminishing to a fading wisp.

Somehow I stumbled out of the now-dead ape. Nothing seemed as it should be. There were shadows and sounds, everything a distortion. And fear. Fear of everything: of the jeering crowd, of Helel, even of the now dead ape. I tried to focus, to gather my thoughts, but they were as a phantom, inconsequential and unformed. I stumbled, weeping, babbling. It seemed something flitted before me. I snatched at it, but found only air. There was a noise to the left, a buzzing. I whirled to see it but it was gone. I began screaming, barking curses at the laughing throng, waving my arms from side to side.

I knew my wits were awry, but no longer had a basis in reality on which to compare. I could feel all sense distorting, dissolving. And then I was spent. Oh, I still existed, but the last remnants of my former self were as golden leaves beneath a coat of virgin snow: dead, decaying, gone.

CHAPTER 25

Trent heard the creak of stairs and the subtle padding of bare feet as he read the document translation. He looked up, smiled, dropped the pages to the concrete floor and rose from his seat. Kim had been missing for over twenty-four hours, had not shown up for work that day, nor answered her cell phone. Trent had called every known friend, relative, and institution imaginable. The last time he'd seen her she'd been virtually incoherent, storming down the brightly lit hospital corridor spouting fantasies about a drug-dealing Trent. He'd since spent several hours seeking advice from mental health professionals.

Now he stepped toward her, probably a bit too quickly. "I called the school, your parents, the police. I even checked the hospitals. Where have you been?"

Kim angled her head, frowned, and said, "Oh. Trent. There you are." She smiled. "If it's all the same with you, I'd just as soon you left my life."

Trent felt as if a grenade had exploded in his belly. Hadn't they been healing? Hadn't they been putting past failings behind them? "Kimmie, Goober. I realize you've had some issues lately but…"

"Me?" she nearly smiled. "Excuse me, but I'm not the one having conversations with demons here."

Trent glanced at Eldon, who sat a few feet away examining an original document. Scratching his nose, Trent stepped slowly, and yes, a bit cautiously toward Kim. His face was still bandaged and swollen from Kim's raking nails. He had no desire for a repeat performance. But he needed Kim to understand. He needed her to believe, if not in Baqash, at least in him. "Kim," he said. "The demon is real. He could be right here, right now, in this room, and no one will believe me."

"Trent, you're talking crazy."

"Because I believe in the demon?"

"Because you believe more in your demon than you do in me."

Trent looked down on his wife, at her cool blue eyes, her confused blond hair. This was his wife, the woman he loved until his very soul ached, and he didn't have a competent thing to say to her. "Kimmie," he ventured, reaching out for her hand but she stepped back. "We spent the majority of our marriage dealing in spiritual issues. You believe, Goober. Why is this so hard for you?"

Kim's lips tightened, she drew her arms tightly across her chest. "You, Trent. You were the believer. I just went along because it was expected. You couldn't exactly have a heathen for a pastor's wife now could you?"

Trent stared dumbly at her. She was lying. She had to be lying. Kim was simply pushing his buttons, trying to manipulate him. He paced, then paused, then paced again, wiping his sweaty palms against his corduroy pants. "So you're telling me that our whole marriage has been a lie? That's what you're saying – right? You simply played a role to get the man you wanted?" Trent slammed his palm on the unstable card table, causing Eldon to start. "And why would you even want me if it took playing some charade? Was I some kind of prize, some toy to be won? Look, I've got my very own pastor, woohoo!" He squeezed his forehead between his palms. "So, what is it now? Have things gotten too real for you, or is this just some insane excuse, another grand illusion?"

Kim stared at him for several moments before turning and moving up the stairs. She paused, turned. When she spoke her voice was low, her tone even. "Do you know what, Trent? I actually started to fall for it, to believe in your supernatural nonsense. But then you turned out to be a fake. Just another phony playing on the trust of the gullible. You're not the man I thought I'd married. How can you expect me to be the woman you married?"

*****

The guy was beat. Eldon had never seen him defeated before. Trent was the one who would play just as hard when his team was down thirty-three/zip as he would when they were neck-and-neck or flying high. Even years before, when Maggie had dumped him for Eldon, Trent hadn't resigned himself to it. Instead, he'd turned around and broken Eldon's arm. No, that hadn't gotten him his girl back – quite the contrary, she'd rushed to Eldon's rescue – but it was a far cry from sitting around like a drenched puppy in a thunderstorm.

Eldon sat down beside his brother on the steps of the front porch and shooed a mosquito from Trent's arm. "You alright?"

Trent didn't respond.

They sat in silence for several moments. Eldon knew Trent was bound up, probably couldn't express a tenth of his turmoil. But hey, they were brothers, or at least they were trying to be brothers again. He'd hang close. If nothing else, Trent would know that he wasn't alone.

When finally Trent spoke, he asked, "Is my life a lie?"

Sure brother, everything you've done is a lie. Your wife makes the wicked witch of the west seem like a Girl Scout, you were disgraced as a pastor, got fired by your father-in-law, and talk to demons that aren't there. You're a real loser, bro.

"No, Trent. Your life is not a lie."

"I think it is, El."

"Listen, something's going on with your wife. She had drugs. You still don't know where she got them, how long she's been using."

Trent shook his head. "It's me I'm talking about, not Kimmie. She was right." Trent hiked his flannel sleeves above his elbows. "I'm hollow. El, you didn't know me when my faith was strong. We'd already had our rift and you wouldn't reconcile. But it was real. It was dynamic. I know you don't believe, but it was true."

"So, what happened?"

"There's the conundrum. I suppose I just let it slip away, started relying on my own skills. I don't know. At some point I just realized that God was no longer a part of my life. And... And, Eldon, somehow that just didn't bother me the way it should have."

Eldon sighed and leaned back on the cool concrete steps. "Tell me about your fall. How did the church folks figure out you were pulling something screwy?"

"They didn't."

"'Scuse me?"

"They didn't find out. I stepped down voluntarily."

"You stepped down?"

Trent nodded.

"That took some guts. What exactly did you do anyway?"

Trent dropped his head. "I suppose you could say I was unfaithful."

"As in, you slept around, had an affair?"

"No! I... Listen, El." He paused, searching for words. "I want to be truthful with you, but... I don't have the fortitude, the integrity to confide in you. Even Kim doesn't know the whole story. If I try to tell you everything now, I'll probably skirt the real issues, try to make myself look better than I am. I'd rather tell you nothing than tell you a half truth. That may sound weak, but it's where I am right now."

Eldon sighed, dropping his head and contemplating a beetle as it made its way slowly across the concrete step below. "It sounds like you haven't forgiven yourself. Whatever it was that you did, it's in the past. Move on, brother."

Trent shook his head. "Eldon, I was in a position of trust, of spiritual leadership. Do you realize how many people have had their faiths damaged by my actions?"

Eldon stared at him for several moments. For the first time he saw Trent not as the jerk who'd broken his arm, but as a complicated and honorable person. "If you're right – about the demon thing. If demons opposed to this Baqash are aware of what he's up to, or at least suspicious, we could be knee deep in some serious sludge, right?"

Trent chuckled. "Nice try, El. But you've made it quite clear that you believe none of this."

"Yeah. And that hasn't changed. But, I'm listening now. Take it while you can."

"It doesn't matter anymore."

"Like I'm gonna believe that from you."

Trent shook his head. "El, please. I'm really not in the mood."

Eldon turned slightly in order to make better eye contact. Or, more truthfully, to get in Trent's face. "Trent, you sit here asking me if your life is a lie. Well, here's your chance to prove it ain't. I'm willing to hear you out. Yeah, maybe I'm just doin' it to help you lose the dumps, but take your shot."

Trent grunted. "You're a real pain, you know that?"

"Yeah well, I learned from a master."

"Would it be inappropriate for me to slug you?"

"And ruin our sterling relationship? Shame on you."

They both chuckled, and then fell into an awkward silence, Trent contemplating his shoes, Eldon staring at low-hanging clouds. "So," said Eldon finally. "Are you gonna tell me how we defend ourselves against the unseen? I mean – supposing that the world is just insane enough for you to be right – how do we know demons aren't sitting next to us right now listening to every word we say?"

"You sure you want to ride this road?"

"Yeah. Yeah, I am. What are the odds that we're being watched?"

"By Baqash, certainly – at least some of the time. But I don't believe he's here continuously. Demons, including Satan, are temporal. They exist in a specific place, at a specific time, just like us. They have bodies; it's just that we can't see them unless they want us to. As for us being observed by other demons," Trent shrugged. "If we haven't been watched yet, we will be as soon as Baqash implements his scheme."

"What about angels?"

"What about them?"

"Wouldn't they be protecting us?"

Trent closed his eyes as if in deep thought. Then, opening them, stared directly at Eldon. "I don't know, El. They might. But I don't even know if they would consider me to be on their side anymore."

"So we can't count on a cavalry of angels coming to the rescue?"

Trent shook his head. "I honestly don't know."

"But you still believe this stuff."

A pause. "I do."

Eldon stared at Trent, who sat with a downward gaze, elbows on his knees, chin on his knuckles. Trent was a complicated man who was seriously complicating Eldon's life. "Can demons read our thoughts?" asked Eldon.

"You really don't need to humor me, El."

"Just answer the question."

Trent shook his head with a drawn-out sigh. "No, I don't believe they can read our thoughts. There's nothing in the scriptures to indicate…"

Trent didn't have the opportunity to finish his sentence for the screen door clattered open behind him. It was Kim. She had Ashley cradled in her right arm, head resting on Kim's shoulder, and a bulging gym bag slung across her left side. Trent and Kim locked eyes, his gaze then falling to the over-stuffed bag.

"Hi, Daddy," murmured Ashley, barely opening her sleepy eyes. "We're going to sleep at Grandma and Grandpa's house."

Trent opened his mouth to speak, but Kim beat him to it. "Don't, Trent. Don't try to stop me. I'm taking Ashley for a night or two. I just need some time to think."

"Kim…"

"Don't make a scene in front of Ashley. We'll talk later."

Trent acquiesced with a weak nod. The man's face had gone ashen. Trent really did love this woman.

Kim then turned to Eldon. "Are you going to let me pass, or should I call the police?"

"I'm movin', lady." Eldon rose and stepped to his left.

Kim marched past the two men and down the steps. Little Ashley smiled as they reached the bottom. "Unca Eldon. I'm going to Grandma's house."

Eldon forced a smile. "You have fun, sweetie." And then he added, a bit louder, "You're wrong about him, Kim. He still is the man you married."

But Kim didn't answer. She was already in the driveway and opening the car door. Eldon wasn't sure, but just for an instant, just as she placed her drowsy daughter in the back seat and closed the door, he could have sworn he saw something flickering about her frame, wings perhaps, tattered, serpentine. Kim angled her head toward Eldon in a peculiar twist. She was smiling, a broad toothy smile. The knowing smile of the insane, or perhaps of the damned. And then all was as it had been. Eldon blinked, refocused. Nothing. It had probably just been the way the light had reflected off the windshield.

CHAPTER 26

A correspondence from Pereh, the fallen, to Helel the Satan

Pereh, faithful servant and watchful eye, to Helel, great prince of this world, lord of the flies, conqueror of all that is seen:

My luminous king, the events, the ones of which I now write concerning, are none of my doing, nor of my fault. No fault is mine. I am witness only. All had been well – well indeed. Your plan, a brilliant plan, has produced many fine offspring. Quite fine. These men are tall of stature, thick of muscle, fierce and intelligent, with flowing red hair and deep piercing eyes, the likes of which I have never before witnessed within the flesh. No, never. The humans consider them warriors of great renown and have dubbed them Nephilim. Surely, should your enlightened scheme continue for but a few generations, these Nephilim would rule this dusty rock of earth. Surely, and without question.

I have laughed at those who disparage your decision that we, your angels, should lie with human females in order to produce a superior race. Laughed, yes. Such fools: Chemosh, Melkart, Asmodious. Ha! All fools. Each procrastinating. Each mumbling curses. "Human filth!" they say. "I lie not with vermin." "Let me consort with lizard," says Chemosh. "They smell not as foul." O' the blasphemes my loyal ears endure.

Let it be noted that it is true: I have not yet lain with a fleshly female. But this is no lapse. No lapse indeed. My commitment true. Simply, I have yet to find a human specimen worthy of this undertaking. For truly, should I spawn offspring, I should desire to bring forth only those worthy to serve you, great Helel. Only those worthy.

Baqash, my sullen companion, ridicules me this. "You are fearful," he cries. "You have not the capacity for the undertaking." Yet he lays wallowing among the pigs, covered in muck and feces, frightening mere livestock for amusement and chiding me as though he thinks me mad. Who is truly mad? I think the friend of pigs, no?

But enough. This message is urgent in nature, disturbing in scope. Yes, urgent and disturbing. For the hosts of the golden realm have appeared as a whirlwind, a great cloud of raging fire accompanying them, their chime-like voices reverberating within my skull, driving me to near lunacy.

Foul. Such foul creatures.

Led by the loathsome Michael. Yes, the archangel, traitor to your sweet friendship, and bane to all who bow to you, O' great one. And their purpose? Oh, their purpose, dear Helel, this I must convey. For they seek to rid the earth of any who would lie with the fleshly ones, to curtail the conception of your glorious race of Nephilim.

They come into the very bedchambers themselves, ripping your faithful free of their weeping brides, throwing your angels to the dust, binding them with shimmering ropes of gold, and then dragging them off to Tartarus, a place known to be lower than Hades itself. The shrieks of your faithful pound about my skull. Their eyes, wide in horror, mouths cursing and vomiting.

I watched from a vantage of safety, beyond the cackling Baqash and his precious swine, as dozens of your faithful were dragged spitting and flailing from their chambers of pleasure by these despicable hosts. I tell you true. Yes, true. Our number fought well, scratching, clawing, biting. Not one went peaceably. Not one. Many took to the skies, others hid within the livestock, possessing horses, sheep, mules. But the hosts outnumber us greatly. Their force was overwhelming.

Two, three, even four hosts would descend upon each so-called demon like vultures on an eyeball, overpowering your loyal servants. Many of our number scampered about in desperate hopes of escape. All cursed the archangel and his mindless cronies. Oh, yes. We all cursed him.

I witnessed Michael as he pulled one of your legion into the dusty streets. It was Muwtsaq, a thick, hard creature, with four tattered wings and a cavernous nose. At the sight of the archangel, Baqash bolted upright from amongst the swine, a cry of grief exploding from his lips. Michael must have recognized the timbre of his old friend's voice for he turned toward the sound, his entire form moving with his head. Muwtsaq took opportunity at this diversion, raking Michael across his glimmering face, pulling free.

Yes, free!

Before the archangel could respond, Muwtsaq had overcome a human female, her belly swelled with child, her eyes wide with incomprehension as your servant wrestled with her soul, subduing her, taking command of her form.

So beautiful, so beautiful.

The female rose, yes. But it was Muwtsaq who controlled her as her arm darted to the left, snatching a scythe, a simple farming tool, but also a potential weapon, deadly to the human form. Michael moved forward as if to recapture his prey, but Muwtsaq pulled the blade of the scythe to the woman's belly. "I can destroy the unborn child with but a slash. I have no qualms," said Muwtsaq through the woman's twittering lips.

Michael paused, his presence radiating out like mists of flaming amber. "Muwtsaq, release the female. Your fate is set. The fire awaits."

But Muwtsaq did not desire the company of fire. The woman's arm pressed the tool to her belly causing a trickle of blood to slip from the supple flesh. "Would you murder a human, archangel? Would you destroy the life within?" The scythe dug deeper yet, the flow of blood increased. Magnificent.

By this time, several murmuring humans had gathered to watch the spectacle. They could not see the archangel, nor could they see Muwtsaq. Their puny fleshly eyes could only perceive the woman holding a blade to her swelled belly. They prattled, yes. Some gasped even, as if horrified at this sight. Still, none sought to intervene. These humans, we have taught them well, no?

"The murder would be yours alone, and serve no purpose," said Michael to Muwtsaq. "All who have been ordered held captive will be taken. There are no options for you."

"I disagree," said Muwtsaq as he began to back away, glancing about, seeking an avenue of escape.

"You will not flee," commanded the archangel, his voice so self-righteous, his face haughty and unforgiving.

Fool!

Suddenly, Michael bolted forward. Muwtsaq pulled the scythe across the woman's belly, deep and forceful, causing blood to gush forth onto the dusty street. Then he fled the body with a curse. The woman shrieked as she collapsed to the dirt. "My baby! My baby!" she cried as her trembling hands found the gash in her belly. The archangel hesitated, clearly desiring to pursue his quarry, but feeling irrational obligation to the fallen female. Just as Michael reached to within the hysterical woman's womb, trying to tend to the wounded infant, Baqash bolted from the pig sty, jabbering and skittering. Something had slipped from within Michael's robes. His journal. Baqash scooped it from the bloodstained ground and fluttered off beyond the crude human structures, prize in hand, an expression of loathing and love on his twisted visage as he giggled and hummed.

Michael, oblivious to this intrusion, continued to work on the infant, trying to restart the tiny and ravaged heart, to undo what could not be undone. All the while, the woman screamed and the crowd stood silent and mesmerized. Only one human moved, a male, most likely the woman's husband. He raced forward, dropped to his knees beside her, and pulled her upward into a sitting position as he screamed and bellowed, asking "Why?" and cursing whichever of us he considered the responsible "god." I believe the name Chemosh received the most attention.

When finally Michael rose, his bronze face was solemn and fierce. The child had perished. A sweet thing to be sure on such a day of pain.

Two heavenly hosts appeared above, both grappling with the cursing and struggling Muwtsaq. So sad, I suppose.

Three more hosts raced before me in pursuit of another of our number. Then two more captured another to my right. Those targeted by the hosts seemed destined for capture. The time and manner of their confinement, the only question.

Certainly, I considered joining the fray, adding my strength to the masses, assisting your loyal legions in their time of need. But our numbers were already depleted beyond all hopes of victory. Beyond all hopes. And truly, am I not your eyes? Do you not require my report? My intelligence? Surely, I am of greater use free than bound. My place is to see, to report. And continue to report, I will. This I vow.

CHAPTER 27

Black smoke caressed Trent's eyes, even as he daubed them with a damp towel. The heat became more intense and the smoke glowed an orange beacon as he moved further down the groaning stairs. He'd fallen asleep on the couch, translated pages still in his hands. How long he'd slept, he didn't know. Not long, he thought. The fire couldn't have raged too long before the stifling smoke sparked him to action.

He could not yet see the flames for the smoke, but heard the pops and crackles, tasted the musty fragrance reminiscent of so many childhood campouts. The intense heat molested his arms and face. His left foot was just settling on the concrete floor when he heard thuds and thumps.

Trent was struck from behind, just above the knees, causing his lower body to lurch forward as his head was thrown back. The damp towel he'd worn like a hood flipped over his face with a splat causing his already hindered vision to go entirely blank as the base of his skull connected with the sharp edge of one of the lower stairs.

Rolling off of the staircase, he clutched the back of his throbbing head with his left hand while fumbling for the towel with his right. The towel seemed to play with him, not becoming looser, but tighter as he rolled about. He was choking, the mingled tastes of terrycloth and smoke forming a musty clot in his throat. Was Baqash or some other imp trying to kill him? Had a demon pushed him down the stairs and pulled this wet towel tightly over his face? Trent reached across with his left arm, clawing at the terrycloth fabric, but something was there – a hand! Someone, some *thing* was trying to kill him.

His right elbow shot backward, connecting with something firm but giving. There was a loud "ooof", and the hand on the towel fell away.

Got the sucker.

He was in the process of turning for a frontal assault when he heard a cry above the crackling flames. "Trent! No!"

He hesitated, muscles taut, fist held at ear level, poised to strike. "Reg?"

"Yeah, Trent. Don't hit me."

There was a sharp tug at the back of his head, and the towel came free, revealing a hazy Reggie with a towel pulled across his mouth and nose. Trent fell to his hands and knees, gagging and gasping, involuntarily gulping in the thick smoke-filled air and retching with each inhale. "What were you trying to do – strangle me?"

Reggie shook his head. "I was trying to get the towel off of your head."

Trent nodded and retched like a cat hacking up a hairball, amazed how quickly the smoke had affected him. His stomach tightened into a fist-like knot, and he actually wished he had something more than air to vomit.

"I dropped the fire extinguisher," said Reggie.

"What?"

"The fire extinguisher. I dropped it when I tripped on the stairs. I'm sorry, Trent, I dropped it."

The fire extinguisher. Well, Trent felt like an idiot. All he'd brought was a couple of damp towels, Reggie'd had the foresight to bring the heavy artillery. "Did you see where it landed?" Trent's eyes stung, and his lungs strained in the smoke.

"No, Trent. I can't see very good down here. I think maybe that way." Reggie pointed toward the heart of the crackling.

"Great."

Both men coughed and hacked. Neither could see much. Trent retrieved his towel, daubed his eyes, and then held it loosely before his mouth and nose. "Okay – *hack* – listen, Reg. We're not going to – *hack* – last very long down here. I'm going to try to find the extinguisher."

*****

The "little-red-hots" caused Kim's hands to tremble in a kind of tingly dance of energy as she drove. It was a pleasant sensation. Darting between cars, in awe of the swishing colors of neon signs, of the ocean-like roar of the traffic, and amused by the slower vehicles. "Four doors and a hat!" she laughed as she skirted around an elderly driver. She heard the sleeping

Ashley shuffle in the back seat. "Oops!" she giggled. "Mommy better be *Quiet*!" The girl shifted again. Kim continued to giggle.

"Perhaps you should be quiet, Kimmie. It may even behoove you to slow down a bit."

Kim inhaled the sweet and familiar fragrance of pipe and giggled once again. "Are you giving me driving lessons, you old fart?" She laughed uncontrollably at what she felt had to be the funniest joke since Seinfeld.

"You are still of use to me, Kimmie. Please slow down."

Laughing, Kim bolted through a red light. Roosevelt Road was still busy at this hour, but not that busy. It was a weekday, and after ten p.m. They made it through unscathed, though a couple of drivers honked, and one communicated non-verbally with his left hand.

"Kimmie, slow down. You are nearing your turn."

The voice was firm, authoritative. Kim pulled her foot entirely off of the accelerator, allowing the car to slow quickly. Her eyes darting back and forth like a cat cornered by a pit bull terrier, she stopped giggling and simply said, "Yes, we're close." She was in Oakbrook, almost to Daddy's house. Daddy would be glad to see her. Mother too.

"Now, Kimmie. Once again, explain to me exactly what Trent was hiding."

Kim slammed the breaks at a yellow light, causing the car behind to screech and fishtail to a halt. "Old stuff," said Kim.

"Yes, ancient artifacts, documents. But your husband could not read the documents, could he? They were in other tongues – old tongues."

"Oh! This is my turn." The light was still red. Kim was in the middle lane, but maneuvered in front of the car adjacent her, and onto the cross street. "Trent... could read them," she said, trying to focus. "He had translations." Kim took a sharp left onto a residential street. "I need a cigarette, Sammy boy."

"Did Trent reveal the contents of the documents to you?"

Kim shook her head, trying to focus. "It was about demons, angels – stupid supernatural stuff."

"Tell me, what did you do with this 'stupid supernatural stuff?" '

Kim took a hard right near a large two-story brick residence. She was now on her parent's street. "I need little-red-hots."

"What did you do to the artifacts, Kimmie?"

The Tempo slipped quickly around a casually-paced Lexus. "I burned them. You wanted me to burn them."

"Mommy?" Ashley's voice was soft, weak, she was still mostly asleep.

"Yes, Kimmie. I told you to destroy anything your husband received from Baqash."

"I really need a cigarette."

"Mommy, who are you talking to?"

"Specifically, Kimmie, think hard, what specifically did Trent tell you about Baqash, about his purpose, about the contents of the documents?"

"Oh! There's Daddy's house." Kim accelerated.

"Think, Kimmie."

"Mommy, you're scaring me."

"I don't know. This demon guy wants to… to kill Satan or something so he can get in good with God. Where's my cigarette?"

"The imbecile! And you're certain you destroyed them?"

"Mommy!"

Kim pulled a sharp right onto the driveway, and into the back of her father's Infinity.

*****

The fire extinguisher was about ten feet to Trent's left, wedged between two crates. "It's over there, Reg." Trent pointed toward the partially obscured object. "Between those crates."

"It's too hot, Trent. We can't get to it. It's too hot." Reggie coughed and gasped. "I'll call the fire department."

"No!"

"There's a fire, Trent. The fire department is good at putting out fires."

Good ol' Reggie and his infallible logic. "I'm aware of that, Reg. *Hack*! But no one can know about these relics. They're worth – *hack*! – millions and I have no believable explanation as to how I acquired them." Trent took three tentative steps toward the extinguisher. As if anticipating his move, flames leapt out, causing him to hop back. He tried again, the flames persisted. It seemed almost they had an intelligence of their own.

The smoke was heavy, vision almost nonexistent. The thick air burned his lungs. Twirling ash singed the hair on head and arms. Trent felt weak. His eyes burned. It felt like sandpaper, dry and coarse, scraping against his iris every time he blinked. Nausea overtook him. He dropped to his knees. He could hear Reggie's voice, but couldn't make out the words. It seemed that didn't matter any longer.

Then suddenly he was cold. Chilled to the marrow cold. And there was a voice. Not Reggie's, but familiar, so very familiar. Trent found himself on the concrete floor, curled in a fetal position as flames lapped about his head. And yet, still he shivered.

And still came the voice.

Louder now.

Deeper into his being.

And then Trent knew nothing at all.

CHAPTER 28

Eldon leaned back in the old wooden chair, wiped his nose with his plaid handkerchief and gazed at the baffling object before him. Why had the thing so consumed him? This one find, this simple fabric, had prompted his abrupt exit from archaeology proper, had restructured his life, and, if ever discovered by his former colleagues – not to mention the Turkish government – could get him arrested.

He'd been digging in eastern Turkey. The day had been hot, dry, long – a typical summer day near ancient Pergamos, now known as Bergema. The archeological students and volunteers had all returned to camp, and his team had undoubtedly landed in the canteen to eat, drink, commiserate, and, most importantly, to flirt. Eldon's associate, Avraham Mazar, a tall gangly man in his mid-thirties, had obviously taken a fall for the cute little staff artist, Deborah Clayton. Deborah, for her part, had remained detached, uninterested. Eldon figured that she was simply being coy, leading poor Avraham around like a stray dog. Eldon wondered what ever had happened to them – to them all: Avraham, Deborah, Stu, Willie, Saede. Certainly, he'd never work with any of them again. Not after the stunt he'd pulled.

As was his custom, Eldon had been the last to leave the dig for the day. He'd liked to walk about, to watch the sun vanish behind the western hills, sending golden light and lengthening shadows across the sand. It was a time for Eldon to gather his thoughts, to plan the coming day. The season had been almost over, the students, volunteers, and local workers would all depart in less than two weeks, leaving only the staff behind. Nothing of significance had yet been uncovered, and Eldon had wondered whether his antsy investors would spring for another year or redirect their dollars to other more dramatic digs. Over the years Eldon had learned that investment-types had attention spans roughly equivalent to those of toddlers on a sugar high.

Eldon had turned, intending to join the others, maybe even to coax fellow sports nut Willie McBride into a wager on the pre-season Bears/Dolphins game. But a sudden weariness assailed him. It wasn't that he was going to pass out, he didn't fall to the ground or stagger drunkenly; he was just very tired, very drowsy, the tempting fingers of pending oblivion dancing about his brain. He'd seated himself against one of the many ancient columns still standing about the area, and leaning back, was almost immediately in a deep slumber.

The dream had come almost at once, a strange dream, Eldon ducking into a small opening between large rocks. The dream Eldon had rocked a large stone until it fell aside, and then picked up a lantern and stepped into the opening. Surprisingly, this had taken him not into a tiny gap between stones, but onto a downward path, a passage which spiraled deeper, deeper, perhaps a full fifty feet below the surface before finally opening into a large cavernous space.

But this area was no cave, no natural cavern. It was a palace, or a temple. The walls were high, reaching what seemed to be well above the fifty or so feet he'd just traversed. The floors were of marble, with mother of pearl and gold inlays. Great tapestries hung about the immense walls, tattered and stained. There'd been a large circular platform in the center of the area littered with chard bones, both human and animal. And at the far end of the chamber, upon yet another rise, had been a golden throne. Eldon had approached this, though even in the dream, the seat had unnerved him. It was a large thing, entirely made of gold, with no crushed velvet seat cushion or padding of any kind. Etched into the fine metal were representations of strange creatures baring multiple faces and wings. It seemed the metallic eyes of these beasts followed him as he stepped onto the platform and stared down at the thing.

There was an object on the throne, a pouch, leather, he believed. A voice had then spoken, a deep melodic voice seemingly coming from nowhere, yet everywhere. "Take this object, hide it, read it," the voice had said.

And then Eldon was awake, fully refreshed, no hint of lethargy. He'd shaken his head, glanced about him. The sun was still hanging low over the western sky just as it had before his snooze.

Strange.

He'd risen, turned to head toward base camp, and then froze before the small opening from his dream. "Naw," he'd said as he scratched his head and kicked at the dirt. He wasn't a man who believed in dreams, premonitions, or fate, but his curiosity had been too great to ignore.

Eldon had hesitated before entering. This was just a little creepy after all. Somehow he'd found the nerve to roll the stone aside. The opening was dark, but still he could see the start of a downward path. He'd taken a lantern, held it in through the narrow opening, and glanced about before entering. It was cold inside, much colder than he would have expected, and that smell, even now Eldon could remember that awful stench of death and decay.

Still, he'd continued down the spiraling path as if led by some outside force. The passage itself seemed of a weird consistency. Though it looked like stone, the surface seemed to give with each step, as if Eldon had been treading on some sort of rubberized material. And Eldon had felt strange too. The further he went, the more his body seemed to tingle, almost as if he'd been receiving tiny electrical jolts. His mouth had dried to a near parch, and once, when Eldon had scratched an itch, he'd noticed that his skin seemed to have taken on an almost powdery quality. He'd considered turning around, fleeing the crazy place, but felt unable to do so, almost as if he'd been continuously nudged forward by some outside force.

Everything had been there, the great chamber, the marble floors, the chard bones. Shivering, Eldon had ignored it all and moved directly to the golden throne.

The object was there, seated on the royal seat, as he'd known it would be. He'd swallowed, set the lantern to the right of the chair, and lifted the leather pouch. "How in freakin' bloody Sunday could this be?" he'd muttered. Surly there was a rational explanation, but none came to mind.

He'd gently opened the pouch, withdrawn the contents, and carefully laid the thing on the marble floor. What he'd found within had been like nothing he'd seen before or since. The material was similar to supple leather, but thin, very thin, almost like tissue. It was cold, much colder than the already chilly room temperature, and was smooth to the touch, even in places where characters had been etched. There was a small swatch missing from the upper right hand corner, as if someone had sliced a sample from the fabric. Eldon had carefully lifted the piece, set it atop the pouch and rolled it open, noting that no marks had come through the fabric despite the thin material. And the characters on the page, they were... unusual, resembling no known linguistic family.

Take this object, hide it, read it.

Somehow Eldon had known that he could not share this find with his colleagues. It was irrational, illegal even, but he'd known he had to hide the thing, keep it, study it. Even now Eldon couldn't fathom his rationale of that evening. But he had taken the thing, hidden it, and, to the bewilderment of all, left the dig the following day, never to return.

In the ensuing three years, Eldon had run every conceivable test on this remarkable find, compared the writing to every known language group, and was no closer to determining its origin than when he'd begun. He'd found no means of translating it, of identifying the strange substance, nor of determining how it had come to be in that chamber. But still he pondered the thing, retesting it, attempting to duplicate the strange writing, and sometimes simply caressing it.

A sharp knock on the door brought Eldon back to the present. "Time to play Joe Retail," he said as he rose from his chair, picked up a gray tarp from the floor, and covered his prize before moving into the front room and closing the door behind him.

The abrupt rap repeated, louder this time. "I'm comin', I'm comin' already." Eldon glanced forward as he made his way up the dimly lit aisle, stepping over and around random artifacts, nearly tripping on a set of pygmy spears dating back a thousand or so years. It was Trent and Reggie at the door. Eldon twisted the lock, and pulled on the door. "What's up, guys?"

Trent barged past him and then pivoted. "Eldon, I'm very sorry. This is going to be a tremendous burden, but I know no other way."

Eldon stared at his brothers. They were both red, burnt, with eyebrows singed to extinction. And Reggie, there was something about Reggie. Not an injury, nothing physical. But Eldon had the strangest compulsion to go to him, to wrap him in his arms and squeeze as he'd never done before. It was almost as if he felt this would be his last chance ever to do so. That something, somehow… "Trent, what happened?"

"Kim set the crates on fire – some of them at least. Reggie and I attempted to douse the blaze. I succumbed to the smoke. The lousy demon came to my rescue, or at least to the rescue of his precious collection." Trent stepped forward. "El, I'm losing my wife and possibly my child. Kim has become unstable, even dangerous. My house is damaged, and a demon is nettling me. I can't tend to all of this at once. My family must come first, but I can't ignore Baqash and his demands."

"Trent, I… don't know what to say."

"Say that you'll take this burden from me." He scratched his reddened nose. "See that truck?" Trent pointed at a yellow Ryder truck parked a couple of spaces down. "It's all there: the relics, the documents, the translations. I'm sorry, El, but I've got too much to lose. I need you to study the translations while I tend to Kim." He stepped forward and placed his palms on Eldon's shoulders. "Eldon, I apologize, but I'm asking you to be my brother again."

CHAPTER 29

The demon had driven Trent's family apart, caused Kim to nearly burn down the house, and endangered everyone he loved. Trent felt bad, awful really, about dumping the relics, the whole Baqash thing, on Eldon. And truly, he still didn't know how the demon would respond to this act of rebellion. But first and foremost he needed to protect Kim, Ashley, the unborn baby, somehow keep them from the demon – get them back.

He trudged across the small living room, fell heavily on the sagging couch, laid his head on the pillow, and stared at the plaster ceiling. The bed linens, the sofa, the carpet, the whole place still smelled of smoke. Kim had started the fire: sweet, precious, deranged Kim. She could have killed him.

Despite his frenzy of concern, he must have fallen asleep because the sharp sounds from the basement first seemed a dream, something indistinct, distant, unreal. But then the clatters and thumps came closer, closer, till his fuzzy brain finally realized that these were actual sounds. Battling the fog of sleep, subduing the image in his mind, the strange six-winged creature flitting around his evaporating trance, Trent rose groggily from the makeshift bed. Scratching his disheveled red hair, he called out, "Reg?"

No reply.

There was a buzz near his ear. A wasp flew by. Unusually large, black, juicy.

Somewhere deep in the pit of his stomach he had a profound concern for his younger brother.

Trent inhaled deeply, attempted to calm himself. Surely, Reggie was

fine. Trent was just experiencing the aftereffects of a lingering night-mare.

Crash!

"Reg?"

Thud!

Trent hefted his lanky frame from the sagging sofa and shuffled toward the back of the house. The place seemed all a chill. Why hadn't Reggie answered his calls?

Another wasp, another and another. Where were these things coming from?

As Trent marched across the kitchen Linoleum and toward the basement door he heard a horrendous roar, the sound of metal against metal and rushing waters commingled into one. Trent's stomach suddenly did that roller coaster thing. Baqash! Reggie! He bound forward screaming his brother's name.

Trent hesitated at the top of the stairs, almost fearful to descend. The fire had been bad enough, but having a furious Baqash come to his rescue had been a near-nauseating experience. The demon had moved around the room, almost as a phantom, strangely grotesque, visible, but not visible, suffocating the flames with his own translucent form. Trent only half remembered it as he'd been in and out of consciousness. Reggie had seen nothing through the smoke, and Trent wondered if Baqash had somehow blinded him to his presence.

"Reg, You down there?" Trent hollered from the doorway. The thumps and crashes were sporadic, but quite loud. "Reg! I'm getting concerned here. A 'Hey, Trent, I'm fine' would really help clarify things about now." He knew Reggie was nowhere else in the house, the doors to each room had been open as he'd made his way down the short hallway, and there was no place else for him to be but the basement. "Reg, a little assistance."

Once again, the metal-on-metal, rushing waters wail assaulted his ears. "You!" it roared.

Hundreds, perhaps thousands of wasps, swept up the stairs in a cloud of buzzing fury. Huge wasps, deeply black, with bulging eyes of green and red. Swirling, darting, screeching as no earthly wasp had ever done. Even before Trent could comprehend the madness of it, he was thrown back against the exterior door, his head connecting with the window pane causing shards of glass to cascade over his head as he dropped to the floor.

"Where are they?" cried the voice.

Trent shook his head causing tiny pieces of glass to drop from his hair. No one was visible, though the cloud of wasps obscured all but the tiniest of views. "Baqash, are you insane?"

"Not insane! Not insane! Baqash insane!"

And then Trent saw him, his brother – Reggie, ascending the stairs, a pained grimace stretching his lips into unnatural proportions. His gate was uneven, his stance awkward as if his back was suddenly misaligned. One shoulder sat perhaps four inched lower than its twin. His nostrils flared and a thick bile dribbled from his lips. He was covered in welts of red. Wasp stings, assumed Trent. There was a curious red substance on the fingers of his right hand – blood and matter.

And he was missing his left eye.

Clotting blood surrounded the torn and empty socket as the right eye darted left, right, left, right as if in search of its life-long companion. A wasp darted into the socket, settling within.

"Reg, no." Trent could not grasp, could not accept the sight of his beloved brother before him. "Baqash, please. No. He has nothing to do with any of this."

"Baqash? Baqash. Always Baqash," croaked the Reggie thing.

"I won't help you. I'll fight you. You'll get nothing from me unless you release my brother." Trent was stammering, his thoughts barely coherent.

"You will learn," said the demon housed in Reggie's skin. "A lesson."

There was a flickering about Reggie, the half image of serpentine wings coiling about the smaller man's arms, drawing them up toward his neck. Wasps flitted this about his head as if anticipating the final act.

The one eye gazed at Trent, seemingly pleading. If there was anything of Reggie in there, it was projected through that one miserable eye. Though Trent was a mere five feet from his brother, he could not move fast enough to prevent the tragedy.

Reggie's own hands locked about his head.

There was a sudden twist, the sound of a cracking whip.

Reggie's one eye rolled up as his now-limp form tumbled backward down the wooden staircase in a series of muffled clunks and thuds, causing the unholy swarm to scatter and dart.

"No!" screamed Trent as he leapt forward, but even as he took the first stride, the basement door slammed shut, barring him from Reggie's corpse. The kitchen cupboards flew open. Plates, bowls, and saucers shot out, smashing in explosions of glass and ceramic against the opposite wall and windows. Trent buried his head under his arms, protecting his face from the flying fragments, and tried unsuccessfully to scoot out of the line of fire.

The window behind the kitchen table shattered splaying needle-like glass about the room as the decade-old microwave oven rocketed toward the back yard. The table then shot upward, colliding with the ceiling, then dropping to the floor with a crash and a crack. One leg broke off, and the table tumbled sideways, scattering the buzzing swarm. Trent crouched in the alcove near the basement door. There was something sticky wet on his face. He was bleeding.

"Baqash! Baqash! Baqash!" roared the disembodied voice of a train wreck. "Baqash a fool!" Trent couldn't argue with the assessment. "Where are they? Where are the writings? Were they destroyed?" The refrigerator lifted to about three feet off the floor, causing Ashley's multi-colored drawings to slip from the decorative magnets, and to float softly downward. Pill bottles, a green vase, an old Betty Crocker cookbook, all perched atop the appliance scattered as the dingy white rectangle soared across the room and crashed against the doorframe to the master bedroom adding splintered wood to the glass-covered Linoleum.

"They're safe! They're safe!" cried Trent, wondering if he could somehow slip out the back door before the demon decided to hurl a major appliance in his direction. The back of his head was matted with blood and he had no idea how badly he was bleeding. "Your precious collection is fine. You saved it yourself."

Suddenly, Trent was off of the ground, hovering as the refrigerator had. Strong invisible hands clamped about his triceps, but he saw nothing. There was an odor, a familiar smell. Something he'd noticed recently about the house, smooth and sweet, yet musty. He couldn't place it, but it was distinct. "Where, offspring? Where are they?"

"Safe," replied Trent, trying to focus even as his eyes rejected the input. He may have dumped the things on Eldon, but he wasn't about to lead the demon to his doorstep, not if it didn't already have that information. "You killed Reggie!" he screamed. "You can take your writings right back to hell – but not until I have Kim and Ashley returned and unharmed!"

Trent was slammed against the ceiling, the ugly green and white floor spinning beneath him. The demon spewed profanities, demanding to be led to the "writings". Trent felt nauseous, nearly vomiting in the demon's face. "Not without my family," choked Trent as he struggled to expel a wasp from his palate.

"Fool!" cried the demon as Trent was thrown across the room and through the shattered window. The sensation of flying was surreal, vaguely euphoric, and utterly terrifying. Trent saw the room receding, twisting. He felt the harsh coldness of the broken window, glimpsed the light-colored brick of his home. He landed abruptly, with a splat, in the muddy backyard between the red Weber grill and the rusty yellow swing set, his head inches from the crumpled microwave.

An alarming thought struck him as he lay still and moaning on the ground, nothing broken, but nearly everything aching – that wasn't Baqash.

CHAPTER 30

To a parent, there's nothing like watching your child sleep. They're so peaceful, so precious, so still. When sleeping, they don't say "no", or color on the walls. They don't spill cereal or cut their own hair into uneven tufts. They just breathe. That, and cling tightly to a favorite stuffed toy, no matter how old or tattered. They float through dreams of kitty cats and puppies, of friendly dragons and candy cane castles. Kim stroked Ashley's soft blond hair. So precious.

"You didn't destroy the writings, Kimmie."

Kim hugged her daughter, gave her a peck on the cheek. So much potential. Could this be a future Olympic gymnast, a congressperson? Could she be the one to cure cancer or AIDS? Maybe she'd simply lead a joy-filled life as a wife, as a mother. Who would be her Prince Charming? When and where would she meet him?

"Kimmie. The writings, the relics, they were not destroyed. Where are they?"

"I… I don't know. I… need my little-red-hots."

"Your mate hid the crates. Where would he have put them?"

Kim wished that she could see Ashley's eyes. She had such beautiful blue eyes.

"Kim, where would your husband hide the writings?"

"I burned them."

"You didn't burn them all, Kimmie. Trent has taken them away. Where would he take them? Is there someone he could trust? Anyone who would hold those for him?"

"Trent doesn't have any friends here."

"He has a brother."

"Yes – Reggie."

"The other one."

"Eldon."

"Yes. Would he have given them to Eldon?"

Kim frowned. Trent hated Eldon. But… No. Had she ever met him? She wasn't sure. She thought she had, but, no. She couldn't have met Eldon. Trent hadn't seen him for years.

"No," she said. "Trent hates Eldon."

"Where does Eldon live?"

"I don't know. In the city, I think. I don't know."

"And there's no one else, no other friends?"

Kim shook her head. "Can I have some little-red-hots now?"

A cellophane bag containing little red pills dropped into her lap. Eagerly, she pulled it open, spilled a half dozen pills onto the girls bed, fumbled with the slippery little treats, and swallowed three of the things dry. She closed her eyes waiting for the waves of giddiness to overtake her. Why had she given these things up for so many years?

"Kimmie."

Kim smiled. Sam was trying to say something to her.

"Kimmie, I need to take the girl."

Sam was being silly. What girl?

"Kimmie, Ashley is coming with me."

No. Ashley couldn't go with Sam. Sam was dead – wasn't he? Maybe she should ask Sam sometime. She looked down at her sleeping daughter. No, Ashley couldn't go with him. Ashley had to stay here with her mommy.

"Kimmie, it's my turn to see Ashley. She's my daughter too."

Kim looked up into Trent's downcast face. He seemed so lonely, so sad. He missed his daughter; maybe he even missed Kim too.

"Kimmie, it's my turn to take Ashley. I'll bring her back tomorrow."

Sam was funny. He looked just like Trent. Sam would make a good dad. Trent was a good dad. He should see his little girl too. Kim watched nervously, not knowing, yet fully knowing, what was wrong as Trent lifted her daughter, still sleeping, from the bed, and quietly left the room. The girl's under-stuffed Teddy bear dropped from her arms, landing near the doorframe. Kim swallowed another little-red-hot.

She would never see Ashley again.

CHAPTER 31

From the journal of Baqash, the fallen, AD 70

Such rubbish!

What foolishness Helel demands. "Welcome to the revolution," he cries as if blissfully unaware that the war was lost centuries past. We have been banished, all love, compassion, anything worthy within our souls, long since evaporated. Can Helel not be content to let us roam this miserable rock in wretchedness and despair? Must he call to Pergamos an assembly of the lost, to gather us as soldiers to fight his pointless battles?

Apparently he must.

But I tarry. There is a tale to be told, and I best be about the telling. Pergamos, now a city of humans, has changed in many aspects since the first days, becoming one of three leading cities of this vast region. The mortals have constructed great buildings and monuments. Egotistic sculptures of fallen hosts, thought by humans to be gods, litter the streets. Dionysus, a rather scrawny creature in reality, seems to be the favored spirit, but Zeus, Trajan, and Asclepieum, all appear as stone figures. O that the fleshly beings could know who it is they worship. If only they could see the tattered wings of Trajan, so broken and useless. If only they could witness Zeus rolling about in the dung heap, an idiot's grin upon his lips. If only they could see Baal laugh and mock as infant humans are sacrificed in his name, or how Chemosh, the "god" of the Moabites, fosters illness and bloodshed amongst his devotees merely for an evening's entertainment.

Of significance to my tale is a vast library containing thousands upon thousands of human writings. Truly, the humans believe this a treasure of knowledge and wisdom beyond any other. And though much of the works within are fanciful, often inspired by fallen beings, wisdom as well can be found, and in some instances, even truth. It is this truth which frightens Helel.

The assembly in many ways resembled the one held centuries earlier. Foul-tempered and repugnant hosts skittered about, pushing, pulling, jockeying for position, seeking a clearer view of the dull and dirtied throne. Aside from a few scraps, the once-fine tapestries have fallen from the great walls. Pillars have crumbled, causing the immense ceiling to droop, and even for rays of sunlight to sneak in through the resulting fissures.

Pereh, the fool, and I made use of the cleft ceiling, slipping in through a gap, and gazing directly down upon the dreary seat of Helel. Others followed, pushing us down and to the left, causing us to scrap for position. Still, we were afforded an acceptable view, and I was content to wait quietly for Helel to begin. Not so, my chattering companion.

"Melkart! Is that not Melkart?" he cried.

Yes, it was Melkart, the one I had first defeated while inhabiting the ape. He drooled and twitched in a most annoying fashion, appearing quite dull of intellect. Still, though defeated in this arena, he had risen under the tutelage of Baal to be worshiped as a god within the human city of Tyre.

"And beside him, Baal!" hooted Pereh. "Baal! His strength is rumored to rival Helel's. Shall we go? Shall we join the gods?"

"No! Quit your jabbering. I am content."

"You are never content."

"Go if you will. I shall remain."

"Ah! I see," cried the buffoon. "Baal defeated Baqash in the arena. Baqash still fears Baal. Do you not wish to learn the ways of a god like Melkart or Berith? Do you not wish a city to wear your name as Baalbek wears that of Baal?"

"I care not for cities."

"True. Baqash much prefers the company of pigs."

It was then that the crowd erupted in a frenzy of barks and howls, scraping and climbing, twirling and yapping. Helel had stepped onto the crumbling platform, his demeanor confident and purposeful. Still, even as I howled in anticipation, it was obvious to me that he carried many of the same infirmities as his followers. Yes, he was still beautiful to behold, his skin glistened, his amazing grin curled just so, disarming even the most strident foe. But his radiance belied the subtle deterioration of this once impeccable being. The movements, though smooth, were unnatural – forced. Almost as if he pretended to be what he had once truly been. Even the voice, though melodic and strong, projected a disturbing cadence. Still, this was Helel. And though I often loathed him for all he had cost me, the sight of such dignity, of such confidence brought vigor to my soul.

"Welcome to the revolution!" he bellowed. "Welcome... to the revolution."

"Wooooo!" cried the rabble. "The great Helel!"

Helel nodded and grinned for several moments before finally displaying his palms, quieting the throng as a human governor might settle his supporters. "We have seen some strange times, you and I. Some difficult times. Discouraging times. We were cast out." He gazed solemnly about the assembly. "But we have prevailed. We were left to rot by those we called friends, brothers, lord! But we have prevailed. We have turned much of humanity toward our cause." Helel pivoted to the left, and his voice rose to nearly a fevered wail. "Many of you in this very chamber are worshiped as gods. My goal is that all become gods. That all receive the worship which is your due."

Helel paused as the crowd bayed and wailed. Truly, it seemed an amazing moment, and despite myself, I became engrossed in the master's words. "But we have an enemy," he continued, "an opponent who wishes to stifle our effort. The one we once called lord." The throng hissed and spit, jostling about, causing a glorious clamor. Helel scanned the crowd, making eye contact with every being, making his message personal, intimate. "Now as the human populace strives toward intellectualism, as they seek literacy and science, our opponent seeks to enlist the humans to his cause through knowledge of truth."

Helel walked to the front of the platform, gazing at the multitudes before him. Admittedly, the gaze was infectious, not one could doubt his sincerity. Yes, myself included. My misgivings would not surface until later.

"Truly I tell you, this we cannot allow," he said. "Thousands have already turned from our idols. Thousands more will follow." Helel narrowed his gaze, his modulating eyes becoming as hypnotic slits below his brows. "But as our adversary adapts and even as human culture adapts, so must we. This move toward intellectualism, we can use to our benefit. Those who worship knowledge consider themselves above belief in the unseen. So be it. We shall guide them further toward that end. No. They may no longer believe in you. They may no longer call your name or sacrifice their children on your alter. But neither will they call upon our adversary or his golden hoard. And in this, we shall cripple him." Helel paused, scanning the sea of brutes. "Certainly, some will continue in their current beliefs. These enlight-ened ones; we will treat as always, guiding them from trust in the ancient one and toward our own ends. But the intellectuals, well, they shall become great and haughty in their own eyes. Self-sufficient, or so they will believe. In truth, their denial of the unseen, their reliance on science alone will make them splendid tools for our cause."

Helel turned, pacing from one end of the platform to the other. "We must redirect the scholars and theologians. No truth-inspired document must survive, no copies made. For it is through these writings that the opponent means to rob you of your godhood. Instead, we must inspire new writings. New directions of thought. Destroy and recreate. That, my lovelies, is our mission."

And suddenly I knew, I knew within my being, that this was a futile ef-fort. That the task before us was beyond our capacities. These documents he wished to destroy, they were many and varied. Copies of copies of copies had already been produced and dispatched. If this was to be the plan, if this was Helel's grand scheme, how possibly could he succeed? And as I gazed into the face of our leader, as I observed the quiver of the lip, the darting of the eyes, and furrow of the brow, my being went cold. For it was at that moment that I realized that Helel feared this as well. And it was then that I truly understood what a fool I'd been.

CHAPTER 32

Trent knew he must regain control of his life. Priority one was obvious: get Kimmie and Ashley back. Priority two: somehow dispose of the artifacts, and with them, Baqash and any other demon tag-alongs. Priority three – and this was quite possibly at the core of the crisis – once Baqash was absent, determine just who Trent was as a person. The demon had been with him for so long, through so many life decisions, Trent no longer knew with certainty who he was or what he actually believed.

He turned slowly, his body protesting, his head swimming. "Probably a concussion", he thought. Being a former football player, he was familiar with the symptoms. The demon had trashed his home, nearly leveled it really: hurling appliances, hammering in walls, and ripping out the plumbing and wiring. Somehow, there hadn't been a fire – or an explosion! Certainly the gas pipes had been exposed. Trent had slipped away, apparently unseen, as the demon – or demons – tantrumed. Perhaps he'd been followed by an imp, but he'd seen no evidence of that yet. Probably the thing had simply been too preoccupied with irrational rage to bother with him.

Almost mechanically, he'd called Eldon. Trent had to warn his elder brother of the pending danger. He had to tell him about Reggie.

But Eldon hadn't answered.

Trent was alone.

Alone with the haunting images of his now-deceased sibling.

His fault.

It was all his fault.

Somehow he'd allowed this monster into his life and Reggie, pure, sweet Reggie, the most innocent soul Trent had ever encountered, had died a horrifying death. What were those last minutes like for him? Trapped in his own body, a demon crowding out his very consciousness. The horror he must have known.

Trent needed to connect with Kim. He needed to end this. But he was concerned, unsure of how to proceed. Had Kim been influenced – even possessed – by some grotesque demon? That would explain her behavior. Or, possibly even worse, had she just finally showed Trent who she truly was at the core? Either way, Trent didn't want an encounter such as he'd just had. Not in Ashley's presence. He needed neutral ground.

After driving about aimlessly for nearly two hours, he'd settled on a Motel 6 near Kim's parent's place. He could have afforded a much nicer hotel – he did, after all, have a quarter of a million dollars in the bank – but that would have felt to him like celebration. There was nothing to celebrate. Motel 6 fit his mood. He'd contemplated contacting Kim immediately. But something had held him back, something nettling in the back of his brain. Kim was no longer Kim. Trent would need to proceed carefully if he was to avoid the death of another loved one. Ashley could not be involved.

Trent stared blankly at his own tear-stained lap. What was he going to do? What was he going to do?

*****

"Kimberly." The voice was indistinct, far away. "Kimberly, may I come in?" It was Mother's voice. Why was Mother at her house? "Kimberly, it's nearly seven A.M. I really think it's time you and Ashley get up."

Kim's eyes fluttered open. They were sticky, lids glued together by green crusty matter. "Eye boogers," she giggled as she attempted to focus on the empty cellophane bag atop Ashley's Winnie the Pooh pillow.

"Kimberly?"

"Just… Just a minute, Mom." She rolled onto her back, groaned, and made an unsuccessful attempt to rise. Morning already? That just couldn't be.

"Kimberly, do you girls want breakfast or lunch?"

"Oh, just come in, Mother. That's what you want." Kim really didn't feel up to dealing with her mother just yet. And what was her mother doing here anyway?

Kim heard the door latch turn and felt a warm rush of air from the hallway dance over her face. Kim's room had always been the coldest in the house.

"Honey," Kim heard a hint of nervousness in her mother's voice. "Where's Ashley?"

"Ashley... Oh, yeah," Kim said, still trying to focus. She rolled her head to the side, to the other bed. The blankets were crumpled in a pile at the foot, a few of Ashley's Barbie dolls littered the floor. "I think..." She blinked and cocked her head. There was Ashley's stuffed bear by her mother's foot. "I think... Trent took her."

CHAPTER 33

From the journal of Baqash, the fallen, AD 110

The library was like so many others we had visited. The windows faced east, allowing maximum exposure to the sun. The floor was of green marble, meant to diminish glare and thus reduce strain on fleshly eyes. There were two great reading rooms, one for Greek, one for Latin. About the walls were recesses housing thousands of scrolls. Statuettes and busts of favored authors littered the shelves, and in the center of the hall stood a golden statue of a divine patron; in this case, the fully armed but shapely form of the goddess Athena, whom I knew as the far from feminine Athemetis, a wiry host skilled not in war and crafts as the goddess was here portrayed, but in manipulations and deceptions.

Pereh and I entered in the early evening, after the facility had closed. The attendants, slaves, copyists, and restorers had retired, leaving only a slumbering librarian in the hall. But we tended to him straight away, possessing him jointly and then forcing him to gut himself with a tiny blade found in a drawer.

Pereh, as per usual, flitted about yammering and baying as he flung parchments about, ransacking works by earthly legends such as Homer, Virgil, Plato, and Aristotle. Pereh was fond of shredding any and all papyri and parchment, sending fragments hurling in all directions, sometimes igniting the works, and occasionally burning the libraries to the ground. To me, the process was futile. Human knowledge continued to expand. Significant writings had been copied and circulated for centuries. How could even the legions of Helel hope to collect all of these and inspire credible replacements? A futile folly to destroy all truth and inspire writings that supported Helel's grand scheme.

As I poked about the library, sifting through letters and poetry, genealogies and legislation, I came across a moderately-sized cubby nearly hidden in a corner behind a statue of Aristotle. Within this niche was a rough wooden box large enough to contain perhaps six to ten parchments. I withdrew the box and opened it. The interior of the container was lined with a fine purple silk padding which gently cradled seven rolled documents. I extracted one from the center of the bunch, severed the restraining ribbon with my teeth, and unrolled the thing. "*Paul, called to be an apostle of Christ Jesus.*" This was yet another copy of the dozen or so letters written by that traveling nuisance Paul. How Helel had hated that man. I began destroying the piece, biting and clawing, shredding the thin leather. The thing was almost destroyed, nearly unrecognizable, when I noticed something unusual, something odd at its conclusion. With a curse, I spit fragments from my mouth, and read the scrap.

"*I Paul, write this greeting in my own hand. If anyone does not love the Lord – a curse be on him. Come, O Lord! The grace of the Lord Jesus be with you. My love to all of you in Christ Jesus. Amen.*"

I had seen these words before. Surely, this piece had been copied numerous times. But it was not the words which caught my attention, but rather the large shaky scrawl at the bottom of the page. A signature.

Cocking my head and grunting, I held the thing to my face, eyeing it, sniffing at it. The ink of the signature smelled the same as the ink of the text. Interesting. The words, "*I Paul, write this greeting in my own hand,*" appeared on many such documents, but only as a part of the text. Never had there been an actual signature beneath.

I became curious – a fault of mine, this is true, but one I tend to indulge. Dropping the fragment, I withdrew another parchment, untied it, and rolled to the end. Yes, it was there also, in large ungraceful print, a signature reading, "*Paul, apostle of Christ Jesus.*"

I opened another and another and another. Each bore the signature. But what's more, each smelled of a different time and place. Some offered the sharp scent of salt, as by the sea, others the pungent odor of beasts of burden. Each ink was of a different shade, some midnight black, some nearly brown from exposure to the sun. The qualities of the writing materials varied as well. These were not produced at the same place, or even at the same time, yet each signature matched that of the previous.

Could these be the originals?

It seemed unlikely, but not impossible. Surely the original writings of Paul would be somewhere. I had not heard of their destruction, an event which would have caused quite a stir within the ranks. I recalled the hullaballoo created when, centuries earlier, some of our kind stole the Ark of the Covenant. Surely I would have heard if Paul's writings had been discovered.

But what did this mean to me? I cared not whether I destroyed an original or a copy. Truly, I wanted nothing more than to be done with the horrid things. Enraged at myself for my own foolishness, I shredded another document, tossing shards above me, howling and screeching like Pereh.

I reached for another, a shorter, lighter letter, and hesitated.

These were the original writings of Paul; I was becoming more convinced of it. They did not offer the flowering adornments of later copies. The written characters were not so perfect, the writing materials of a lesser grade. These looked like day-to-day writings, not sacred copies produced to impress or honor. How might I use this find to my advantage? I did not know, but surely it would be fool-hearty to squander such a boon.

Cautiously, doubting my own motivations, I returned the parchment to its case. I had destroyed two of the letters. Five remained. Gazing about the floor at the shards of parchment I devised the beginnings of a plan. No, I did not yet know how to utilize the remaining letters of Paul, but the ones I had destroyed, these I could use immediately. Quickly, I gathered the pieces scattered about my feet, making sure to collect the signatures themselves. Then I closed and locked the box, hefting it under one arm.

"Come, Pereh!" I cried. "We have great news for Helel."

Pereh looped and fluttered, paused in contemplation, then tittering, charged the statue of Athena sending it crashing to the cold marble, shattering in a dozen directions. "I never liked Athemetis," he said, landing clumsily beside me. "What have you done? What do you have?"

I smiled, holding the fragments above my head. "I have destroyed the original writings of the troublesome Paul. Helel shall reward me greatly."

Pereh gazed at me, eyes blinking independently of one another, tongue slapping lazily from cheek to cheek. "And this box you carry? It is empty?"

"Certainly."

"No, not certainly." His disposition was troubling. "Open the box. Let me see." He reached out, as if to snatch the thing from my grasp. I pulled it back, cradling it beneath a wing.

"No." I replied. "What needed to be done has been done."

Pereh nodded and giggled. "Baqash has not destroyed *all* of the writings of Paul. Baqash keeps some for himself." Pereh teeters between the sane and the insane, often playing the fool. Unfortunately, he is not quite so stupid as I would like to believe. Frequently he steps beyond his lunacy to inspect an issue with surprising clarity, even insight, before strolling casually back into his personal oblivion. Often he uses such times to approximate the forms of selected humans, taking on his subject's physical appearance, mannerisms, voice, vocabulary, even odors, in order to manipulate and deceive. At such times none of his inherent dementia is displayed. He appears perfectly sane, perfectly rational, perfectly human. While Pereh had not, at this time, taken human guise, this was clearly one of his lucid moments, and he would not be easily fooled.

"I have no plans for the writings," I said, silently cursing the timing of his lucidity. "But they may benefit us at a later time." I leaned forward, my lips nearly touching one of his twitching ears. "Do not divulge this little breech of protocol to anyone – Helel in particular. No need for him to know what only you and I now know."

Pereh gazed a cold gaze, his many wings raised as if to threaten. "Keep the box if you will, but give me those shards of Parchment," he demanded with sudden ferocity. "Helel will be pleased to know that I, Pereh, have destroyed the writings of Paul."

*****

Eldon Troxel tossed the pages onto his desk, yawned, scratched his two-day stubble, and eyed the transcript. "Naw," he said aloud, rising from his chair and chugging the last of his hours-old coffee. "The original writings of

Paul the apostle – not a chance in hell." He lifted a crowbar and marched to the nearest of the sixteen crates. "Not a chance in hell."

CHAPTER 34

Trent sat up in the squeaky twin bed, threw aside the tangled covers, grabbed the remote, flicking the TV to off, and pivoted, allowing his bare feet to meet the worn tan carpet. Reaching to the nightstand, he grabbed his open can of 7-up and chugged the last of the warm, sweet, and very flat, liquid. His stomach felt like downtown Baghdad on a bad day, and the stuff usually helped it to settle. He tossed the can into the oval wastebasket. It was time to call Kimmie.

He'd wanted to call the night before but had been too rattled after Reggie's death at the hands of the rampaging demon. He just couldn't have dealt with the emotional tension. Instead, he'd settled into this tiny hotel room, ordered a pizza, and spent the night alternating between bad late night TV and fitful non-sleep. Now it was late morning, and he could put it off no further.

Trent tapped the auto-dial on his Nokia. He longed to hear Kimmie's voice, to reconcile, to regain some control in his life, to have some small portion of his existence stop spinning into that ever-widening black hole.

"Hello." It was the stern voice of Curt Baldwin, Kimmie's father.

Trent rolled his eyes. Great. What was he doing with Kim's cell? "I need to speak with Kimmie," was all he said.

"Troxel, is that you?" The tone was smooth, condescending.

"That would be me, Curt. May I speak with my wife?"

"I suppose you have no idea as to the whereabouts of my granddaughter." There was a hint of suppressed joy in the voice.

"Excuse me?"

"My granddaughter. Kim claims you have taken her."

"That's an interesting fiction, Curt. Is there something I need to know here?" Trent gripped the tiny silver-colored phone tightly, fearing, knowing. A man couldn't walk away from a demon and expect no repercussions.

Kim's voice in the background. "Daddy, is that Trent?"

"Curt, let me talk to Kim."

"So, you are unaware of Ashley's whereabouts?"

"Daddy, Give me the phone."

"Certainly," said Baldwin. Then Trent heard a soft rustle as Kim came on the line.

"Kimmie, what's this about Ashley?"

"Don't start with me, Trent. I want my daughter."

"Our daughter. Please, Kimmie, tell me what happened." Trent was up now, pacing about the small room.

"Trent, I know what you did. You drugged me and took Ashley."

"What?"

"I remember you being here, carrying her out of the room. I woke up still drugged, some pills spilled on the bed, but…" She paused. "Trent, I went to the house. It's nearly demolished. What happened there and where is my Ashley?"

Trent paused. "You were there. Did you go to the basement?"

"Yes. It was a disaster like everything else. What happened there?"

"Reggie? Did you see Reg?"

"No one was there, Trent. Are you going to tell me what's going on?"

Trent pivoted and crossed the room in four long strides. The demon had obviously moved Reggie's body. To where and for what reason, he couldn't begin to guess. "The house, that's a tale for later. I don't have Ashley." He paused, scratching his nose. "When did she disappear?"

"I suppose you're going to tell me that your demon trashed our home."

The lady caught on quickly. "A demon, yes. I don't know which one."

Trent pulled the phone from his ear as Kimmie slammed her end against something – probably the kitchen counter. "I'm sick of your delusional demon crap! Where is Ashley?"

"I don't know!" He responded in kind. "I don't know!"

She didn't reply right away, and was probably contemplating the situation. Obviously she didn't know where Ashley was either. How long had she been gone? What demon had stolen her – and why? Had Baqash decided to make good on his threat to kill a family member? *Please! Not that!*

"Okay," said Kim, in a more reasonable tone. "You're not going to tell me where Ashley is, but where are you? I know you're not at home, it's unlivable."

Trent sighed. "I'm at the Motel 6 on Roosevelt, just a few blocks from you."

"I'll be there in five minutes."

"Kimmie, those demons you don't believe in, one of them killed Reggie."

CHAPTER 35

Eldon rubbed his eyes. He'd been up all night for two nights. It was now morning, and he was ready to fall over. But there were the parchments – *those parchments*. An archeologist's dream. Sipping coal-black coffee from his Chicago Blackhawks mug, he gazed through bloodshot eyes at the thing before him: Paul's letter to the Ephesians. Could it really be the original?

He'd found the box in one of the crates, perhaps the sixth he'd opened. It was about the size of carry-on luggage. The wood was unfinished and rough. There was nothing impressive about it. Once opened, he'd found the purple silk lining cradling five parchments; there were empty spaces for two others. The two Baqash destroyed?

No. That was a load of crap.

Obviously, whoever had produced those fictional transcripts had known what artifacts were present and had simply written the tale to fit the collection, perhaps in hopes of greater profit due to the supposed spiritual significance of the pieces.

The parchments themselves had been just as described, each in a different ink, on a different quality parchment, each with the large uneven signature of Paul the apostle at the bottom. He'd spot translated several sections, and then taken digital photographs of each, uploading these into his laptop, and then importing them into his ancient dialects translation program. Quickly, he'd discovered that he had the biblical books of: Ephesians, Galatians, Philippians, I Corinthians, and I Timothy. To his practiced eye, he could tell that, yes, everything was consistent with the stated period: the materials used, the lettering, the ink. But he lacked the equipment for radio-carbon dating. And even if he could accurately date these back to the first century AD, there was no way of verifying the signature as Paul's.

But his gut.

His gut told him these were the real deals – actual original writings of Paul. How in blazes had Trent put his hands on this stuff?

Eldon rose, strolled across the small room, and reached around the open crates to turn up the air-conditioning. May, and it was already blazing. He was just about to grab a java refill when he noticed something at the bottom of one of the crates, a small shred, slightly grayish in color, nearly translucent. "Naw," he said; his heart jumped as he located his crowbar and began prying the front off of the container. The boards responded with a loud squeak and a whiff of sawdust. Gently, Eldon pulled away the loosened barrier, making sure that none of the contents toppled. Fortunately, each item was securely packed, and Eldon was able to maneuver his hand between the boards and the artifacts, steadying the things as he pulled the restraint away.

He knelt and reached for the small gray shred. How had he even seen the thing from his vantage? It was between two containers at the bottom of the crate and should have been invisible in the shadows. He stretched out his hand between the obstacles, forcing his thick forearm into the tight space. The thing was nearly out of reach, but just a little more. Yes! He had it, barely, just with two fingers, but he was able to inch it toward him.

He recognized the texture immediately: cool, perhaps ten or fifteen degrees below room temperature. Smooth, almost silky. Thin, like onion paper, but incredibly durable. As he finally held it before him he realized that it wasn't a scrap at all, but a perfect square, a swatch, as if someone had cut it out and placed it there purposely.

His heart thundered in his chest, pounding against his ribcage, demanding the freedom to flee.

The coincidence was just too strong.

Almost mechanically, Eldon crossed the small room to stand staring down at the emotionless gray safe lodged between the fridge and the john.

Two minutes later the mysterious gray document he'd smuggled from Turkey lay on his desk.

Hands trembling, throat constricted, Eldon placed the cool silky swatch at the upper right-hand corner.

It slid seamlessly into the missing section of the piece.

A perfect match.

CHAPTER 36

"Explain yourself," said Curt Baldwin as he marched into Trent's tiny hotel room, his craggy face taut, his blue eyes intense, nearly luminous. Obviously, he was in one of his "power" moods. Great. The man was impossible when like this. Though the flipside was not an improvement. When in powered-down mode he was nearly lethargic, only responding in the most rudimentary fashion. Trent had often wondered how Baldwin could swing from timid to ferocious so drastically and so frequently, but wrote it off as a bi-polar eccentricity of the nearly wealthy.

Kim trailed behind her father, stepping almost ghost-like into the room, her shoulder-length blond hair tangled in twisted clumps, her angelic cheeks splotched and red, dark hollow rings beneath bloodshot eyes. She pulled a knit sweater tightly about her increasingly skeletal form though the outside temperature was climbing toward an unseasonable ninety. Kim looked like a drug addict, strung out and in need of a fix.

"Oh, Kimmie," said Trent as he rushed to his wife. Kimmie: his little Goober, his wife, his lover, his best friend. He was losing her, really losing her. Surprisingly, Kim didn't reject the hug or the multiple kisses showered about her head. Neither did she return the affection. Rather, she followed her father's movements with her eyes as he paced about the diminutive room like a jungle cat seeking prey.

"A quarter of a million dollars, you've procured, and you stay at a Motel 6?"

Trent turned to face Baldwin while maintaining hold of Kim. "A man with priorities," he said, not hiding his distaste. "I thought you'd be more concerned about your granddaughter than my accommodations."

A dismissive wave. "The girl? You don't have her, and you know nothing more than does your wife. Less, I'm sure." Baldwin smiled, narrowing his eyes at Trent and nodding slightly as if sharing some sick inside joke.

Trent pulled away from Kim and stared into the craggy face. There was something there, something in the man's expression. "You know where she is. You know where my Ashley is."

Baldwin grinned. "No, Pastor. That information I lack. Though, I believe I do know whom she is with."

Kim looked up, her eyes red, her manner confused. "Daddy, what are you talking about?" Her voice quivered in near hysteria. This was a mother fearing for her child.

Trent glared at the man, understanding beginning to slice through the clouds. Had Curt just called him "Pastor?"

Baldwin nodded.

Trent knew.

"Really?" asked Trent as he moved toward Baldwin, bending at the waist in order to stare directly into the smaller man's eyes. No, they didn't swim one color into another; they didn't modulate as if dancing to some silent harmonic. But neither did they dilate and contract. They didn't focus. It was as if they were fixed to a specific setting. This was not Curt Baldwin, or at least, it wasn't Curt Baldwin who controlled this body.

"Really," Baldwin confirmed.

Trent stood upright and paced about the man, encircling him, his stomach tight, his palms sweaty. "How long?" asked Trent. This was incredible, he'd never guessed, never suspected. "It's been a long while, hasn't it? Yes, of course it has. It would have had to have been quite a while."

"What are you two talking about?" asked Kim, irritation rising in her voice.

"Several years," replied Baldwin. "Since you first met Baldwin's daughter. She seemed a useful tool."

"Tool?" Trent nodded. "Interesting. What was this tool meant to accomplish?" Many men might have attacked the creature. Many more may have fled ranting like lunatics. But Trent's natural response to conflict was inquisitive interrogation. Yes, he longed to smack Baldwin's haughty face, to force him to return Ashley, to break his demonic will. But irritating the beast would accomplish nothing more than to endanger Ashley further. Better to engage him now, learn what he could, improvise from there.

"Hello! I asked a question here!" Kim was understandably upset.

"The girl fell for you, my puppet minister," said the Curt Baldwin thing. "Seeing this, I obtained influence through Baldwin, a weak and listless creature. I coached her, helped her to appear devout. I used her to seduce you, to misdirect your faith, your teachings. I had hoped you would rise within the ranks of your denomination, influencing the assembly toward my ends. You might have gained me a true stature within the ranks of Helel's legions."

He stepped forward, staring through Baldwin's intense blue eyes into Trent's face, some strange indefinable emotion abusing his features. "But then something novel occurred to me. You were quite fallible, prone to rash decisions and poor judgments. You were impetuous and overly curious. In short, your temperament was so truly similar to my own at the time of my fall as to be hereditary." Baldwin leaned further forward. "So I determined to facilitate your fall, to encourage you to make the same mistake I had made. It would help you to understand my perspective, my predicament. And then perhaps we could seek redemption together."

What complete lunacy. "Interesting tale, demon. Unfortunately it makes no sense. Why would you need a human?"

Baqash cocked Baldwin's head and grinned. "I have long sought to dis-associate myself with Helel and to regain the lost kingdom. Helel is such a poor excuse for a god. He really is quite deficient. But the Ancient One no longer hears my cries, and what host would plead the case of a demon? But a human! Ah, the Ancient loves his humans. If I could convince a human to petition on my account..." Baldwin shrugged.

Trent laced his fingers behind his head as he paced "Double talk," he said. "Let's address the real issue: where is my Ashley?"

Baldwin inclined his head toward Kim, who stood quivering as if standing naked in a mid-winter night. "It seems your wife has been influenced by the imbecile Pereh. Apparently she considered him an appropriate guardian for your offspring."

Bile rose in Trent's throat as he turned to face his wife. "Kimmie, is this true?" he asked, trying to maintain control of his voice, trying not to scream at the already fragile woman. How could she have done this? How could she have given precious Ashley over to a demon – to anyone? No, this was another trick, another hoax from Baqash. Kimmie might be in a weird place right now, might even be abusing drugs, but voluntarily give up her daughter?

But Kim didn't answer. She just stood there staring, shivering. Trent's stomach tightened further yet. "Kimmie, did you give Ashley to someone?" Kim looked from Trent to her father and back again. Obviously she understood none of this.

"The dear lady is confused," smiled the Baldwin thing. "Allow me to make matters clear."

*****

Kim was numb, nearly disconnected. This whole scene seemed to be happening to someone else, someone far away. Kim had grown accustomed to the far-off feeling, the cloudy random thoughts. But the little-red-hots had never caused her to hallucinate. Yet surly that was what had just occurred. One moment her father was standing smug and confident, tormenting Trent with his arrogance, the next, a man, tall, statuesque, with familiar features and long nearly golden hair seemingly stepped out of him as if through a doorway. Her father tensed. His eyes grew wide, clear, and surprisingly lucid, and then he slumped to the floor like a marionette with its strings sliced.

Kim's heart raced, her mind suddenly becoming clear. This was real. Real! She didn't know how, couldn't begin to comprehend it, but it was really happening. "Daddy!" she screamed as she fell to her knees. "Daddy, can you hear me?" He was so still, so lifeless. "Daddy!" No. She was hallucinating. She had to be.

Kim found her father's wrist, felt for a pulse. Nothing. She went to his neck, tried to find the jugular. You'd think the vein would be obvious. Where was it? Here! Yes, she thought so. She pressed her fingers to his neck. Nothing. She leaned forward, put her ear to his lips as her tangled mane tumbled across his inert face. Was he breathing? She couldn't tell. Wouldn't she be able to tell if he was breathing? Oh, just for one little-red-hot, right now.

"Kimmie, is he...?"

"Shut up, Trent!"

"Curt Baldwin is not dead," proclaimed a strange familiar voice. "Merely unconscious. Check the pulse again, this time gently. Pay attention, girl."

She did as instructed. But where? She couldn't feel anything. No... There! A faint beat? Yes. Yes, that was it, soft, but regular. Now, she could feel it better, she'd found the right place to feel the pulse.

"Is he okay, Kimmie? Did you find the pulse?" Trent was kneeling beside her. How long had he been there? Most likely through the entire episode. Still, she ignored him and cradled her father, allowing her head to rise and fall with his slow, even breaths.

*****

"Back to the matter at hand," said Baqash. "You must aid me. We must curtail Helel's plans that I might be redeemed."

For a being who had lived for eons, Baqash was oblivious. "You think you can prove your worthiness by trouncing Satan? That's absurd."

"Trouncing, hardly," said the demon. "I seek only to expose him to the world. Helel will find it most difficult to manipulate a populace that truly acknowledges his existence."

"And you think this will redeem you in the eyes of God?"

Curt Baldwin coughed, gurgled. His eyes fluttered, but didn't quite open. He seemed to be coming around. "Daddy, Daddy. It's me, Kimberly. Daddy, are you alright?"

"I was cast from the golden realm because I foolishly chose to follow another leader," continued Baqash. "I hope to demonstrate that it is no longer Helel that I serve."

161

"And these artifacts, these documents, will prove this how?"

Kim's father coughed again, this time moaning and opening his eyes partially. Kim stroked his face, leaning close. "It's okay, Daddy. I'm here."

"Pastor, are you blind or merely ignorant?" Baqash's voice seemed to rankle. Multiple wings shimmered at his back and then disappeared. "I have assembled documentation of the supernatural, of the existence of Satan. Within this collection are angelic documents, written on a fabric of the realm, a fabric not of this earth. There are original writings of Paul, a challis of King David. Once your brother verifies the authenticity of these items and publishes his finds, who could remain doubtful?"

"And so this is some sort of twisted repentance?"

"I have repented!" hissed the demon, his face flickering like an old silent film.

"Did you really? Then, why the games? Why tempt me? Why engineer my disgrace?"

"I deceived you, dear pastor, because I needed you to fall, to know what it was like to experience that emptiness in your spirit. Because only in experiencing that yourself, would you understand my condition; only then would you be willing to intercede for one such as I."

"And you fired me from my job..."

"For the same reason that I arranged the sale of the marriage contract. I needed you to be dependent upon me financially, emotionally. We have followed the same road, you and I. Both devoted to the same master before unwittingly following another. You and I, Pastor, are the same."

The words pierced Trent's being like a razor-sharp icicle, chilling him to the core, causing him to pause, close his eyes. The same? The same. Impossible! Yes, Trent had walked away. Yes, he'd stumbled. But he'd never knowingly aligned himself with Satan – or even Baqash. How could he be the same as this sniveling demon? What comparison could truly be made?

Trent studied the demon, his long angular face, broad lips, strange eyes. "You claim you engineered my disgrace so I could empathize with you. But that wasn't your initial goal for me, was it? You intended that I rise within my denomination while spouting some meaningless drivel." Trent stepped toward the demon, the scenario formulating in his mind even as he spoke. "Clearly, you were attempting to please Helel. It wasn't until sometime later, after I had floundered, perhaps when you realized my brother was an archeologist, that you devised your little scheme." Trent turned, stepping to the left of Kim and Curt. "You'd secreted those documents away for centuries and never utilized them. But something changed. Perhaps Helel stopped trusting you. You couldn't find grace in him, so you decided to go home to Papa. But, Papa wouldn't have you, would he?"

"Ridiculous!" Baqash's face flickered, seeming to split into multiple features. "You have no means of knowing my heart!"

"Perhaps," shrugged Trent, attempting to appear calm, though his flesh had gone gold at the barely contained demonic image. "Convince me otherwise. Help us retrieve Ashley. Prove to me that there's still some honor in your dark soul."

"Your woman has supplied our adversary a hostage," sneered the demon. "What is it you expect me to do?"

Kim looked up from her father, tears staining her beautiful face, and Trent couldn't help but wonder if she'd ever really loved him or if their whole marriage had been a manipulation of Baqash. "I didn't," she squeaked. "I gave Ashley to Trent – to Sam." She shook her head, dug into her scalp with her nails. "Trent, you were there. You were Sam."

Trent knelt beside her, ignoring the leering demon, suppressing the growing revulsion toward the woman he'd loved. "Goober, tell me what happened. Someone took Ashley. Where did they take her?"

"She doesn't know that, Pastor. Pereh manipulated her."

Trent stared up at the demon who was clearly straining to maintain his human-like facade. "I was under the impression that you and Pereh were friends."

Wings appeared then disappeared as if under a strobe light. "Pastor, there are no friendships among the fallen. Alliances, yes, companions, occasionally. But friendship, loyalty, no. Pereh and I had a... parting of ways many centuries ago. He has since been assigned to monitor my activities. Apparently, Helel does not trust me."

"Apparently," muttered Trent. He rose, staring intently into the demon eyes, attempting to somehow seem formidable though his blood chilled at the proximity. His flesh tingled and burned as if in close proximity to a substantial electrical current. "And what will he do to my daughter?"

"Pereh has long known that I've been secreting these writings away, not destroying them as Helel had instructed. He did not inform the evil one. Now that I desire to use these pieces against Helel, Pereh seeks to destroy them and suppress my plot before Helel learns of his own disloyalty."

Trent's heart leapt, a small fabric of hope emerging. "So, you're up against one demon, not the full forces of Satan?"

"Correct."

"Satan is unaware of your schemes?"

"Assumedly."

"Case closed," said Trent. "Give Pereh the relics in return for my daughter."

"Never!" blared the demon, his voice, metal-on-metal, his face distorting into something hideous and deformed. Slithering wings appeared and then vanished. "You do not understand the life of the fallen. My existence is hollow, repugnant, my future grimmer yet. I will not forfeit this one chance at redemption, not for you, for your daughter, or any other creature, whether fleshly or spiritual!"

CHAPTER 37

Eldon downed his caffeinated slap-in-the-face, glanced briefly at the oozing sludge at the bottom of his mug, and then rose from his seat to pace
excitedly like a prancing pup at the sight of a juicy bone. "This is just too
much." He stared at the screen again, still pacing. "Nah." He moved toward
the coffee pot, thinking to add to his brew, then pivoted, picked up his
Blackberry from the table and punched a recently added number.

The phone rang, and rang, and rang, never kicking into voicemail.
"Come on, Trent. Where are ya?" After nearly twenty rings, Eldon disconnected.

Tossing the phone onto the table with a curse, Eldon reseated himself
and stared at the image on the computer screen. Could it be true? He'd found
the missing swatch to his undecipherable document. It'd been a perfect
match to the strange substance, a substance made of no known components,
with characteristics unlike anything he'd ever encountered. It was nearly as
thin as tissue, yet more durable than quarter-inch leather, silky smooth and
cold to the touch. He'd wrapped a thermometer in it and found it to be nearly
fifteen degrees below room temperature. How could that be? The writing was
peculiar, seeming to delve deep into the thin substance. He'd never found
another sample of its kind – until now.

After discovering the swatch, he'd opened each of the remaining crates.
Two contained similar specimens. The same light gray fabric, the same
unusual writing, the same temperature differential. They'd been packaged in
leather pouches, each labeled with a number that corresponded with the
supposed translations he'd been reading. These were the journals of Baqash
the demon and Michael the archangel, or so the translations claimed.

Skeptical, Eldon had seized the opportunity to decipher the writings, to
use these new pieces to interpret his specimen, and to determine if the
Baqash translations were accurate. Eldon, along with a former colleague – a
techie of great gifts – had developed a translation program. It enabled the
user to scan an original document and its translation into his computer. Then

a yet-to-be-deciphered document of the same language group could be entered. The program would utilize the known translation to interpret the unknown text. It was the same technique archaeologists had used since before there were archaeologists, but the computer allowed the process to be completed in a fraction of the time. Where it may have taken years – decades even – to decipher an unknown language, the computer could do it in hours, and with a higher degree of accuracy. Sure, there would be gaps and flaws where certain words in one document were not used in another, or when the same word had multiple meanings, but these problems were insignificant when weighed against the promise of near-instant translation.

Eldon had downloaded images of each original document and then scanned each translation into the program. The computer had done its thing, sifting through the images, cataloguing each written character, comparing these to the translations, building a lexicon of the strange language. With few minor exceptions the Baqash translations had proved accurate. Baqash may have translated the word "red" as scarlet, or "large" as huge or bulky, but there were no errors of substance. It appeared that these were accurate representations of these journals – the journals of supernatural beings.

Maybe the language was true, but the substance fictional. If an archaeologist from the future were to discover accurate translations of Tolkien's Lord of the Rings, it wouldn't make the tales any less fanciful.

Still…

Faith, they said, was the evidence of things unseen. Could he take that leap? Could he allow himself to open his mind to the possibility?

Did he have a choice?

Eldon gazed at the screen. The translation to his document, the one he'd secreted away from the dig, stared out at him:

Helel to *Baal*,

Dare not release this information, as its circulation could [not translated] *our strategies. Set quickly about your duties. Much* [not translated] *is needed, but the rewards, unimaginable…*

A message from Satan to Baal. Baal, who, according to the journals was a demon, one of Satan's lieutenants. And this was not an ancient tome like the journals of Baqash; this was a contemporary memo, listing places and names – prominent names, high level people, political and religious figures, as members of a demon-spawned race. This was part of a detailed plan, a major move of Satan set to occur within Eldon's lifetime.

Eldon grabbed his Blackhawks mug and marched over to the coffee maker, filling it. This had to be a fake. It had to. But it wasn't – none of it, not the journals, not this memo, not Baqash's involvement in it all. As crazy as it seemed, any other explanation was crazier yet. No one would dump millions of dollars' worth of archaeological treasures on Trent: the biblical writings, ancient pottery, golden statuettes, Egyptian idols, even a large brownish-gray fossilized egg (labeled "T-Rex"). If Trent had really been involved in some black market artifacts scheme the whole demon yarn would have been trashed before it was fully formulated. Why use a cover story that only a lunatic would believe? And what of these strange documents, on that strange substance, in an utterly alien language? Eldon had run his own specimen through every test imaginable. The fabric itself, the fibers, even the cellular components, none matched any known earthly substance. There wasn't even any carbon in it to use for dating. And what of that piece? How had he come to find it in that chamber, one small swatch missing? How had that missing piece come to be at the bottom of one of these crates?

This was all too much: too many coincidences, too much supporting evidence. Everything pointed to the existence of the supernatural. But could Eldon believe? Could Eldon really believe?

Setting his mug on the desk, Eldon made his way to a long counter at the north wall, opened a cabinet beneath, withdrew a large leather pouch, opened it, and withdrew the strange gray document he'd secreted from Turkey. Eldon pulled off his cap and ran a hand through his greasy and unkempt hair. Now what?

CHAPTER 38

"Give me back my daughter!" screamed Kim as if suddenly immerging from a cloud. She lunged at Baqash, fist flaying, screams and curses flowing from her lips. Baqash acted instinctively. The sophisticated facade fell away as the multi-winged creature with wide blazing eyes and four distorted faces struck out at Kim. There was a sharp sizzle and spark as his skeletal hand connected with her right cheek, the force of the blow lifting her from the floor and propelling her backward like a poorly thrown bean bag. Kim's head struck the pressboard end-piece to the bed with a loud *thok*!

"Kimmie!" screamed Trent, immediately scrambling to get a view of her head. "Kimmie, are you hurt?"

No. Not like this. She can't die like this. Pulling her into a sitting position, he moved his hand about the back of her head, searching for a bump, or worse: blood. "Kimmie, Goober, say something."

Kim's head lulled to one side, her lips contracting, forming words. "Where's Ashley?".

Thank goodness. She was alive, at least partially conscious, and there didn't seem to be any blood; though Trent could already feel a sizeable lump inflating like a balloon on the back of her head. "Open your eyes, Kimmie." She complied with a flourish of blinks.

"Demon, what have you done to my granddaughter?" croaked Curt Baldwin from the bed, still weak from his recent possession. Trent had nearly forgotten that the man was present.

"My apologies," cooed Baqash, once again eerily sophisticated and charming. "I do not respond well to confrontation. Is the woman well?"

Like he cared!

"The woman – my wife!" screamed Trent. "Is not well. There's a lump the size of an apple on her head and her daughter's missing – both as a result of your interference in our lives."

"Where's my Ashley?" Kim's voice was small, innocent, like a child asking for her favorite doll.

Trent cradled her in his long arms. "She'll be okay," he lied.

"We're going to have another baby, you know. Ashley's going to be a big sister.

If she lived. Ashley was the hostage of a demon. A demon! Who knew what unimaginable horrors she'd experienced, what life-altering trauma? Even if she somehow escaped physical harm, what emotional scares would she carry for years to come? Trent couldn't begin to imagine what his precious little girl might witness, what foul deeds might be perpetrated upon her. He was a grown man, and this whole thing taxed his sanity nearly to the breaking point, what could it do to a six year-old?

"Is Kimberly okay, Trent? Is she hurt?"

Trent ignored Baldwin and addressed Baqash. "My involvement in your little scheme is finished, demon. Until I have Ashley, I will refuse you everything. I'll destroy every piece of your precious collection."

"You tell him, boy," croaked Kim's father.

"Shut up, Baldwin." Trent had no patience for the man who'd housed this demon.

Baqash stared at Trent, a quizzical look on his smooth, shimmering face. "You are a complex person, Trent Troxel. You carry both the capacity for great devotion as well as the willingness to compromise for the sake of expediency." The demon stepped forward, gazing down upon him. Trent felt the air crackle at the proximity. "I propose such a compromise." Baqash held up his hand, staying Trent's objection. "I shall attempt to rescue your offspring, provided you release my documents to the public. Make a grand announcement. Use the funds I've granted you to promote the event. Utilize your brother's expertise, his credibility as an archaeologist, to ensure that this information is deemed credible. Let the world know that Satan is real. Let them loathe him and refuse him."

"And you hope through this to regain your position in heaven?"

"Precisely."

Trent shook his head. The whole thing was so bizarre. "You can't redeem yourself through blackmail, Baqash."

Baqash glared at Trent. "This is no joke, Pastor. I do not wish the child ill, but do as I bid or find her on your own."

"Tough choice. I'll take my chances." Trent's words had more conviction than his heart. How could he find Ashley on his own? Where did demons go when they weren't up to mischief? Where would Pereh hide Ashley? But still, he couldn't trust Baqash to work in his best interests. The beast could turn on him at any moment.

"No." It was Baldwin. He was rising unsteadily into a sitting position. "Don't take your chances."

"Curt, I really don't think you have any business…"

Baldwin cut him short. "Oh, but I do," he said, his shaky voice weak, yet firm. "Ashley is my granddaughter. We're talking about her safe return."

"And you're the one who housed Satan Junior here, allowed him to manipulate our lives."

"Yes, Trent, I'm the one who knows him most intimately." The man stared off into a corner of the room as if fearing the intimacy of eye contact. "For years I had no idea of his involvement in my life. And once I finally came to realize that there was something there, something not of me directing my actions, I…" He paused, lowering his head. "Trent I wasn't strong enough to defeat it."

"And this is supposed to increase my confidence in your advice?"

Baldwin sighed. "Listen, we know that Baqash desires redemption. This other demon, this Pereh, we know nothing of him, what he's capable of, or where to find him. What harm is there in aiding Baqash if it could mean the safe return of Ashley?"

"Uh, Curt, he's a demon."

"And Ashley's your daughter." The words were pleading yet forceful, obviously weakening the man. It was amazing the frailty of the real Curt Baldwin. His eyes were cloudy, his movements tentative, his posture bent. This was not the man who'd commanded every conversation, who'd dictated his family's every move. This was the real man, the one who had relinquished his life to one unworthy even to draw a breath. This was what was left of Curt Baldwin.

"I understand that, Curt," said Trent. "And I also understand that if I'd stood up to Baqash earlier, Ashley might not be where she is now."

"Trent, you can do this." It was Kimmie this time. She looked up at him, tears running down her cheeks.

"Kimmie, I can't."

"You can," she insisted. "You embezzled church funds so that we could take a vacation. And Gloria Rainey. Look at how you manipulated Gloria Rainey. I still don't think I have the full story on that one. And there were others too. Weren't there, Trent? Others that I'll never know about. You're not so pure. You're not untainted. You can give this Baqash what he wants in order to save your own daughter. It's in your makeup, Trent. Don't deny it."

"*It's in your make-up.*" Is that how Kimmie saw him? Did she really believe that those things displayed his inner being, who he really was at the core? Yes, he'd compromised himself. But the incidents were buried in the past. He'd walked staunchly away from those concessions. Even then, they'd ripped at his gut. He still couldn't believe he'd allowed himself to slip so far. And this? This was worse yet, an actual pact with a demon of Satan. He'd compromised in the past, made poor judgments, but to knowingly strike a bargain with a demon, could he really do that?

"Your decision, Pastor – now." It was Baqash, his voice soft, soothing, persuasive.

"Trent," said Kim. "It's our only hope."

CHAPTER 39

"Sorry, Trent. Can't do it."

Trent narrowed his eyes, and leaned toward Eldon, his lanky form towering over the smaller man. "Perhaps I haven't been clear. A demon has abducted my daughter." He paused, bit his lower lip, gazed at Eldon through moist eyes. "Eldon, my daughter. You know what happened to Reggie. How could you refuse me this?"

Eldon straightened, attempted to appear self-assured. "I get it, bro. Really. And Reg… I can't even get my mind around that. But, how do you know this Pereh character really has her? How do you know Baqash ain't spinning you a freakin' fairy tale? For the love of apple pie and Chevrolet, Trent, he's a demon. They're not exactly known for their honesty. Maybe if I do what you're askin', maybe that'll be the very thing to get Ashley killed." Eldon took a long sip of his coffee. His body was rebelling. It was now mid-afternoon and he'd still not slept. Trent, Kim, and Curt Baldwin had shown up just as Eldon was preparing to leave for a much-needed rest.

"We have no choice but to believe him," said Kim. She looked awful, her round, angelic face drawn, her eyes ringed in black, lips chapped and cracked, she continually pulled a sweater around her like a straight jacket despite the unseasonable heat.

"Listen," said Eldon after a pause and a swig. "There are a few things I need to tell you all." Glancing around the small circle of people before him, he caught Curt Baldwin's eye. There was a guy he could do without. He knew the man was Kim's father, but according to Trent, he'd been demon-possessed until a couple hours prior. How long before the demon returned? Or had it never left? It was hard enough grappling with the fact that he now actually believed in this crap, much less figuring out how to deal with someone potentially hosting an imp. "I've been doing some translating," he said. "And Trent, you have no idea what you have here." Eldon indicated the open crates. "But that's not the half of it. I've had a piece of this puzzle locked away in my safe for the last few years."

"I'm listening," said Trent.

"Brother, you're the proud owner of original, and I do mean original, New Testament writings. Epistles of Paul to be exact." Eldon paused, watching Trent's expression. He remained calm, but there was obvious surprise in his widened eyes and churning jaw. "But as astounding as that is," Eldon continued. "It's nothing compared to some of the other documents – angelic documents and demonic documents."

Eldon explained how he'd used the translations of Baqash to verify the authenticity of the strange language and of the various tests he'd run on a sample of the strange material.

Trent offered a somber grin. "Eldon, for an avowed agnostic, you sure sound like a man who believes in the supernatural."

Eldon shrugged. "Yeah, brother. Guess I was forced off of that bus at the last station. There's somethin' else I've gotta tell you, somethin' that scares the snot outta me." He strolled around the counter and placed his hands on the smudged and dusty glass, leaning toward his audience. "Trent, I never really told you why I left archaeology. At least I've never told you the truth about it."

"Mr. Troxel," said Kim's father, his voice weak, raspy. "I really think we should be discussing the issue of my granddaughter."

"Yeah, yeah. Be patient. This pertains to that issue." He paused again, wondering how to tell the tale. The abridged version, he supposed. Short, quick, to the point. "Nearly five years ago, during an archaeological dig in Turkey, I discovered a strange manuscript, like nothing I'd ever seen. The material was gray, and cold, much colder than the temperature surrounding it. The language was peculiar, not belonging to any known language group. The characters on the page seemed to penetrate the thin fabric. I don't know why, probably brain aneurysms or something, but instead of taking the thing to my associates, I lifted it."

"I'm familiar the substance," said Trent. "Baqash's journals are the same."

Eldon nodded. "And Michael's, yeah. Well, this one was written by Satan. Welcome to la-la land."

The room was quite. Trent appeared ready to say something, but paused, allowing Eldon to continue. "It's a plan," said Eldon. "It details a major move of Satan in the first half of the twenty-first century."

"Go on," prodded Trent.

"We'll leave the nuts n' bolts for later," said Eldon, again thinking of Baldwin. "Let's just say I won't be sleeping too soundly for the next several decades."

"Fine," snapped Kim. "What about Ashley?"

Eldon stared at her. What could he tell this woman? She'd given her own daughter to a demon, and now she wanted Eldon to bail her out. A demon! Eldon was still wrestling with the concept. He accepted it now, had come to terms with the reality of it all. But it was all so foreign to him. His mind kept fighting to discount everything he'd recently discovered.

"Kim," he said as gently as his tough Southside voice would allow. "I'll do anything I can do to get little Ashley back. Don't you ever doubt that. But we can't know this demon's real motivation or that he'd live up to his end of the bargain. By playing his game we may actually put Ashley in more danger." He paused, gazing into her tear-streaked face. "I'm sorry, Kim. I just can't do what you're asking."

*****

Kim had left weeping in her father's arms, furious at Eldon, and angry at Trent for not forcing his brother to comply. Eldon understood completely. She was a mother. Her daughter was in danger. 'Nuff said.

Trent had remained behind, pacing the cluttered room, mumbling about his daughter, about Reggie, and tossing out random and mostly flawed strategies for her safe return. Eldon needed to talk with Trent, tell him what he couldn't tell the whole group. But he was feeling claustrophobic and needed fresh air and a good stretch. More than that, he felt uneasy, like he needed to take his document and the memory stick containing its translation, and get outta Dodge. He was probably just being paranoid, spooked by this supernatural smack in the face, but he couldn't stay there a minute longer.

"Trent," he said, interrupting Trent mid-thought. "I need to talk with you, and we need to get some eats. Let's take a hike to Gino's East pizza – my treat."

The breeze off the lake was cool and fresh with the aroma of a spring rain. It was the only respite from the otherwise sticky and oppressive May air. Eldon hated Chicago summers with their ninety-plus degree temperatures and one hundred-plus percent humidity almost as much as he hated Chicago winters with their sub-arctic wind chill factors and snow-caked roadways. The only problem was, he loved Chicago: loved the scenic skyline, the rolling lake, the mountainous glass and iron skyscrapers; and he absolutely adored the city's mostly-disappointing sports franchises. For better or worse, he was a lifer.

The brothers weaved their way to Michigan Avenue, both nearly silent in deep contemplation. Eldon was tired, hungry, conflicted. They crossed at an intersection amidst a mob of twenty-some bustling cell phone equipped business people, over-loaded shoppers, and hip-hopping teens, then swept north up the crowded walkway and past the old water tower, the only surviving structure of the great Chicago fire.

"So," said Trent, breaking his uncharacteristic silence. "You are, of course, going to help locate Ashley. I can't imagine you'd deny me that."

"Anything I can do, yes."

"But…?" he prodded.

"But, there's more you need to hear before we can decide on how to get her back."

Trent cocked his head toward Eldon, his mismatched eyes narrow and piercing. "Okay, I'll bite. You somehow obtained Satan's day-timer. Fill me in."

"I found the piece during my last dig. We were near the end of the season, nearly ready to wrap up. Long story short, I…" Eldon hesitated, thinking of his bizarre dream that had led him to the find. "I got a strange feeling that this was something I needed to keep private, to hide away." He shook his head. "Don't ask me why, but like an ignoramus, I ran off with the thing, somehow made it back here without being caught, set up shop, and had at deciphering it."

"Apparently you were successful."

Eldon shook his head. "Nah. It wasn't till I had those transcripts from Baqash that I was able to decipher it. And I'm still nowhere on determining the physical composition of the thing."

Trent nodded. "And this document is what exactly?"

There was a key question. How could he really be standing here in the heart of a great metropolis, amidst the pushing and churning crowd, talking about Satan and his plans? Even days before, he would have discounted it all outright. But, now… Now things were different.

"It's a letter from Satan to Baal," he said, staring into his brother's blue and green eyes. "Detailing Satan's plans for the near future, naming prominent religious and political types that are either under his control or influence. Most, but not all, are already in place for some type of major move."

"Major move, are you referring to the apocalypse?"

"Armageddon, the antichrist, all that hoo-ha? I don't think so. But, for all I know, this could be a step down that road. That's more your field than mine. What I do know is that he's manipulating world events. Hand-picked a future US president, British Prime Minister, Russian and Ukrainian presidents, a Chinese chairman, several Arab hot-shots. He has names, strategies. A lotta these guys are already on the rise. All are to be in power by around 2020." Eldon glanced up at Trent, and added, "These people seem to have been bred specifically for Satan's purposes."

"Bred?"

Eldon nodded. "He refers to them as Nephilim: a race spawned of the union between fallen angles and human women. Satan wants to be god. He's breeding his own race to take control of the earth."

CHAPTER 40

Trent jogged the winding lakefront in a semi-delirious haze brought on by fear and confusion. Twice he'd broken into full-out sprints simply to scatter congregating gulls, before slowing, feeling like an idiot for his childish emotions. But his emotions weren't childish. They were quite valid. His brother was dead, slain before his eyes, his daughter was gone, abducted by a supernatural fiend, his wife estranged, nearly mad, and he and Eldon seemed to be the only human agents poised to resist a new and ambitious plan of Satan. Nephilim: the giants of Genesis chapter six reimagined. Could Satan really spawn his own race in order to rule earth once and for all?

But, Ashley. Poor, sweet Ashley. What unimaginable horror was she enduring at the hand of the demon? How much could her innocent mind comprehend? How much could she withstand? He had no real means of locating her. Where would a demon take a hostage? His only option was to follow Baqash down that wide and fiery road, hoping somehow he could retrieve Ashley and escape relatively unscathed.

Trent stopped running, realizing that he'd been charging ahead, nearly at a full sprint for several minutes. Wiping his brow and slowing his breathing, he gazed out over the dark lake, focusing on the rippled reflection of the huge Farris wheel at Navy Pier and spotting the occasional swish of a fish just below the surface. It was late, the multicolored sailboats were mostly all docked, and the beach deserted.

"Missing something?" It was the voice of an elderly man, gravely yet somehow smooth and melodic. Trent whirled, scanning the darkened beach. "I am quite sure that you are missing something," said the voice.

"Who's there? I don't see you."

Trent turned again. Cars sped by on Lake Shore Drive some five hundred yards from the water's edge, but the beach itself appeared barren save for a handful of gulls. It was amazing how solitary a man could feel in a city of three million people. Turning slowly, he strained at the sounds about him.

But there were no footsteps; there was no breathing, only the crash of waves, the hollow whistle of wind, and the frantic rush of distant traffic.

And then he was there. A short gray man of perhaps sixty-five stood puffing on a bowled pipe and wearing a heavy tweed jacket. "Missing something?" asked the man, his smoke wafting in Trent's direction.

"No," said Trent. "Just... I'm fine." The response was lame, awkward, but Trent was off guard and it was the best he could do.

"You're fine. Interesting. I'd thought you were missing something – or someone." The man smiled, displaying an uneven row of large and yellowed teeth below his red walrus mustache.

Trent felt his heart accelerate. "Who are you?"

"Who do you think I am?" The voice was hypnotic, soft yet firm, like worn leather.

Trent studied the man, short, frail, thin white hair tossed haphazardly over a balding head, with the thick loose skin of a pug, and flowing eyes such as he'd seen only on one other. "Pereh?"

"Oh, you are a perceptive one. Dear Kimmie never did quite catch on to that."

Trent glared at the small form. "Where's Ashley?" he nearly squeaked. "Is she..."

"Dead?" the demon asked with a slight lilt to the head. He drew long on his pipe. "What do you think? Is she dead or is she living? Dead or living, which one?"

Trent remained motionless, his eyes boring into the creature, studying it, seeking clues from within the facade.

"With the girl dead," said the demon. "You would have no reason to aid Baqash in his simplistic misadventure. Truly, you would oppose all that he did. It was he, after all, who brought you into this predicament." Pereh turned, ambling toward the feasting gulls. "That could be most helpful to me," he added. Casually, Pereh reached down, and collected one of the birds. Apparently the creature could not perceive his approach because it wasn't until Pereh snatched it up that it began cawing in fear and frustration causing the other birds to scatter. The demon silenced it with a quick twist of the neck. There was a sharp snap. The bird went silent. "Ah," he smiled. "Just like your brother." Pereh tossed the carcass at Trent's feet. Trent could do nothing but gape in horror as Pereh moved slowly toward him.

"The problem as I see it," continued the demon. "Is that you would have no desire to aid me either. None at all. You would hold me just as responsible as you would Baqash." Pereh smiled and puffed on his pipe. "That would not do at all."

Trent forced himself to breath. He glanced down at the dead bird, the head twisted at an unnatural angle, one sightless black eye staring up at him. "So, she is alive?"

"Oh yes, most certainly, most certainly. She is quite valuable, quite."

Trent nearly stepped forward to grab the creature but restrained himself. "I want her back."

"That you wish her returned is obvious." Pereh took a long drag on his pipe, exhaling slowly through his large nostrils, the blue/gray fumes dancing and swirling about his wrinkled head. "The question is what are you willing to do to retrieve her?"

Trent dropped his gaze once again to the still and silent gull, his hands closed tightly, nails digging into his own palms. When he spoke, his voice was dry, a near whisper. "Anything. I'll do absolutely anything."

"Of course you will," cooed the demon. The creature posing as a man seemed almost to dance in excitement.

Trent gazed into the demon. "You'll return Ashley?"

The hunched form leaned toward Trent with a broad skeletal grin. "You will have her before dawn."

Trent inhaled, focusing on the modulating eyes, searching for some semblance of humanity, but finding none. He turned, facing the waves. "You expect something of me, some task." Trent tossed his arms upward in frustration. "Of course you do. You're a demon. You live for this." He turned again, facing Pereh, his jaw churning, his eyes wet with emerging tears. "What is it you need?"

The beast held up one finger. "Just a moment. It's in here somewhere." He fished about in his pants pockets, producing a key. "Yes, yes, here it is.

Here it is" He held a gold-colored key before him, then squatted, placing the object on the sand and patting it affectionately. "The artifacts, they need to be eliminated. This key will get you in. After completing the task, return here for your daughter."

"You could destroy the documents yourself. Why do you need me?"

Pereh smiled and puffed. "If I do it, there is no consequence. But, you... Ah, another compromise." The demon turned to leave, and then paused. "Oh, and if you should decline my offer, little Ashley will still be here when you arrive, but she will be dead."

CHAPTER 41

Trent did as the demon had instructed. He took the key, entered Eldon's shop. There he found six five-gallon containers of gasoline and a box of kitchen matches. He didn't hesitate. He couldn't have. For if he'd taken time to think, if he'd taken even a moment to contemplate the greater implications of his actions, he may not have gone through with it. This place was Eldon's life, his livelihood, and though Trent's older brother could be opinionated, coarse, and outright cantankerous, he was still Trent's brother, and strangely enough, Trent was beginning to like the guy.

Trent hefted the closest container, unscrewed the cap, and began splashing the flammable liquid haphazardly about the place. *I'm History* was as it had always been: cluttered with relics, dusty, cramped, dimly lit, and difficult to navigate due to the numerous specimens littering the limited floor space.

Discarding the first canister and lifting another, Trent moved further into the building. Approaching the suit of armor that stood guard over the entrance to the back room, he gazed into the cold metallic face. It wore a Chicago Bears jersey, number 51. "Well, Butkus," he said, using Eldon's pet name for the thing. "I suppose this is it." Butkus didn't reply as Trent splashed gasoline over the thing, drenching the autographed jersey and causing liquid to dribble into the armor through the eye slits and air holes. It sounded like water pattering against a storm door at the conclusion of a spring shower, a sound that, until now, Trent had always loved.

He then moved to his right, dousing a terra-cotta jug dated 2000 B.C. On a previous visit he'd admired the gentle tan surface and apple-like curves, the simple yet attractive design of the piece. But none of that mattered. Only Ashley mattered. Only Ashley.

Next, he turned to a large brass Byzantine icon featuring the crucified Christ, two winged angels hovering above his head, and the skulls and serpents of hell beneath his feet. Trent gazed into the probing eyes, at the pained yet accepting face, the intelligent brow, the forgiving countenance. *Will you burn me as well?* it seemed to ask. *Will you burn even me?*

Only Ashley mattered. Only Ashley.

Disregarding the icon, Trent picked up another container, marched into the back room, and, with wide sweeps, splashed gasoline over the collection of Baqash. He then returned to the front room, snatching the box of matches, opening the red white and blue box, retrieving one small stick, and striking it against the coarse stripe on the container. The small flame danced before his sharp duel-colored eyes. He stared about the place, his breath held, his mind closed to any urgings of his conscience. Finally he tossed the gently glowing stick forward. Flames whooshed and bellowed behind him as Trent turned, wiped his moistened eyes with his forearm, and retreated through the nearby door.

*****

Kim had received the call a little before four AM. Trent's voice had been hushed, his tone sharp, edged with a slight quiver. He'd told her to meet him at the lakefront about halfway between Navy Pier and the Adler Planetarium, that with luck, he'd have Ashley by the time she arrived.

Now, nearly an hour later, she trudged down the near-deserted beach wishing Trent had been more specific concerning his location. "About halfway between Navy Pier and the Adler Planetarium" covered a lot of territory.

The city lights offered the only true illumination, and that hardly adequate. Clouds hung low obscuring the moon, wrapping around the city's towering edifices, and encasing the hot and moist lake air below an airborne blanket. She'd never find Trent here. With a muttered curse, Kim pivoted and began retracing her steps for the third time.

Two minutes later, she noticed a figure, slightly north of her, mostly a silhouette, but the shape, the mannerisms, were familiar. Kim recognized the long lanky form, the casual yet formidable stance. He was near the water, by himself, yet apparently in animated conversation.

*****

Pereh was no longer the little old man of hours before. No, this creature more resembled Baqash: tall, powerful, with long strangely off-golden hair. But unlike Baqash, there was no pretense of civility, no Armani suit or polished boots. The hair was bushy, unkempt, falling about the face in dull golden clumps; the countenance bore a hideous sneer, distorted and foul. Worse, the thing was naked, with blisters bubbling and popping, dribbling gray/green mucus about his form. The filthy body hopped and scampered like an agitated chimpanzee in a cage. Even the speech patterns had changed. Where the "old man" had been refined yet quirky, this creature merely babbled. Trent wondered how much of Baqash's civilized manner was a similar fabrication.

"My daughter, where is she?" demanded Trent.

"The child is not with me, not with me at all," blathered the creature, as its eyes darted about, seemingly focused on things unseen. "No, not here."

"Then where? I did as you instructed." Trent wanted to scream, to plead for Ashley's return, but he knew that if ever he hoped to see his daughter again he had to appear strong, in control.

Pereh glanced apprehensively to his left, and then scooted right. "You destroyed the writings. Destroyed the writings."

"Yes. As instructed." Trent's stomach tightened. He'd done what the creature had wanted – hadn't he? Could he have somehow misunderstood his instructions?

Pereh's eyes shifted apprehensively like those of a child facing a harsh spanking. "You burned the shop. Very little left, very little."

"The point, demon. Get to the point."

"Trent!" He heard Kim's voice calling from behind.

"You did not do as I instructed. Not as I instructed at all."

"I incinerated the place. That pretty much sums up my marching orders." Trent's tone was casual, but his entire form taut as a fan belt. Ashley was lost. He could feel it, sense it. The demon had lied. Ashley was dead.

"I would never give such a command!" roared the creature.

"Trent, what's going on? Where's Ashley?"

*****

Kim squinted. Who was Trent talking to? She could almost see a form before him, but not entirely, the image was hazy, flickering like a mirage on August pavement. She rushed to Trent's side, her heeled shoes kicking up sand, and almost causing her to stumble.

"What I desired," came a low, nearly familiar voice, "was that you re-trieve the precious writings, that I may present them as an offering to my lord."

"Excuse me," said Trent. "But you ordered those documents well-done. I complied."

"Sam?" asked Kim. It was Sam's voice, though smoother, breathy. She squinted, trying to focus on the illusive image.

"You destroyed the writings, the bible of Helel," said the Sam thing. "For that, the child will be sacrificed on the altar of Helel."

CHAPTER 42

There were five creatures, hideous things with multiple wings slithering at their backs like serpents, elongated fingers that seemed to bend in all the wrong places and elastic legs that belied no true knee joints. Two of the beings had multiple faces with features staring in every direction, eyes rolling, tongues darting. The wings were spotted and torn, some of them appearing to have eyes upon them, gazing malignantly at the scene before them.

One of the loathsome spectacles restrained Trent, not allowing him to reach his wife. Though Trent strained against it, his arms pressing forward, his feet digging into the shifting sand, he seemed not to understand that the beast was present. Two others held one of their own in crude iron shackles, though this creature, a tall being with multiple faces and a downward gaze, seemed resolved to the situation and did not struggle. A fifth brute bent toward Kim as she leaned forward to embrace it. Trent screamed, "Kimmie, no! Goober, you don't know what you're doing!" But the thing enveloped her, bursting into crust-colored mist like an exploding water balloon, dousing the woman, dissolving into the very pores of her being. Her form went taut, convulsed for nearly a minute, and then relaxed, shifting about, stretching at odd angles, head lulling to one side, eyes fixed and glassy.

Kim turned, the crusty brown glow of a demon pulsating about her form, vile liquid spilling from her twisted lips. Trent was released and stumbled toward her. Surprised by the sudden lack of resistance, he was unable to slow his fall. The attack was quick, fierce. Within seconds Trent was on the ground, his transformed wife straddling him, raking at his chest with curled nails.

"No!" screamed Eldon as he raced down the mildly sloping beach. "No!" he cried again as Trent and Kim tumbled into the rolling green swells of Lake Michigan.

"Do as you have been instructed," came a voice as much from within Eldon's head as from beside him. It was the voice from his dreams, the voice that had instructed him to locate and seize the strange manuscript in Turkey, to aid Trent in his dilemma, to come to this very beach. Eldon glanced up at the tall glowing figure now beside him, then immediately buried his face in his palms. The intensity of the sight was more than he could comprehend: the radiant light, the luminous eyes, the fine golden hair and subtle wings. Eldon trembled at the thing.

"Do not be afraid."

Eldon could think of nothing intelligent to say, so simply babbled, "You. You're the... You!"

"Yes," said the golden being, his voice carrying the underlying power of a tidal wave. "The one from your dreams, the one who has been directing you."

Eldon turned from the image. Truly, he must be mad. That was the only logical explanation.

"Do as you have been instructed." The voice originated somewhere within Eldon's cranium.

Eldon nodded, knowing his options were minimal. He was a pawn, and as such had little say in the matter. Attempting to steel himself, he took three rapid breaths and planted his quivering legs. Curiosity overriding fear, he ventured a quick glance to his right. Nothing. Eldon was losing his mind. He had to be losing his mind.

"*Heahyu*! *Yah-eh-ay*!" he screamed.

*****

The sandy water filled Trent's eyes, invaded his nostrils. His vision was red and splotchy. Blackness closed in about the periphery. Kim was atop him, thrusting his head into the cold, stinging water, rarely allowing him even a gasp. He fought against her, thrashed about, but couldn't overcome her insane strength. Pereh had enveloped Kim, oozed into her very being. Trent was wrestling the demon, but it was Kim who might be injured with each blow, bruised with every jab. He just couldn't bring himself to truly lash out. Not at Kimmie. Not like that.

Kim kneed him sharply in the groin. Involuntarily, his mouth opened allowing the murky liquid to rush into his mouth, down his throat. He hacked, but the fluid remained. His vision became darker, his thoughts panicked, unclear, all reservations about injury to Kim evaporated. Pure animalistic survival instinct was all that remained. He thrashed his arms about, but the pressure on his chest would not relent.

*****

It was Eldon's voice – but not his voice, not his words. The language – was that even a language – was strange, alien. The tone was firm, bold, authoritative. To his amazement the four creatures on the beach turned fearfully toward him, hissing and frothing, their eyes widening as they gazed in his direction. "*Iyha-weh-aieo! Euyeh-eh-ur!*" screamed Eldon.

The thing inhabiting Kim immediately jettisoned itself from her form, hovering above the lake, its tentacle-like wings slithering in the soft breeze. Kim had only a moment to appear confused and disoriented before Trent tossed her aside, bursting from the waves, hacking and vomiting seemingly gallons of green water from his lungs.

Eldon glanced about, confused and disoriented. He paused, stepped backward, fearful for his own sanity. The demons paused, scrutinizing him. What could he say now? The words were gone. They had been there, on his tongue, in his mind, but when he'd hesitated, when he'd allowed himself to focus on his own mortal fear they'd evaporated, slipping away like the final remnants of a summer shower. "You, uh, have no authority over Kim," he managed to stammer.

"Oh, but we do," hissed the largest of the creatures, a beast with huge pulsating eyes, a droopy nose, narrow lips, and greenish red teeth. "She is ours. From the beginning, she has always been ours. And not she alone." The thing may have smiled, may have cringed. Eldon really couldn't tell.

"But, the girl," ventured Eldon, though he could not say where he found the strength. "Ashley. She doesn't belong to you freaks of nature. Return her to Trent."

"They cannot comply," replied the chained demon, his voice high and warbling. "The idiot Pereh gave the girl to Helel the Satan. Apparently Helel had determined to use my journals in some sort of tribute to himself." The creature spat a foul brown and yellow substance upon the sand, displaying his feelings on the matter. "The master deceiver has manipulated me, allowing me to write and gather these pieces, encouraging me to think that I did so unobserved and against his will." He glanced toward the hovering demon, flitting over the lake, babbling to itself. "Unfortunately, the buffoon Pereh had not yet realized Helel's aspirations and so coerced your brother into destroying the writings. He now attempts to lay blame for their destruction on Trent. Pereh is a fool, and the devil will surely sacrifice the girl in anger."

"Baqash?" asked Eldon in sudden realization.

"Indeed," replied the demon.

*****

What was happening here? Baqash was in chains. Three other demons, hideous things resembling nothing of earth and certainly nothing of heaven, were confronting Eldon in some sort of debate. Trent crawled across the watery sand toward the bizarre convention, still hacking, his lungs feeling like they'd taken several good shots from the Hulk. He struggled to distinguish their words above the crashing waves. Had he heard correctly? Did Satan have Ashley?

Eldon spoke, the words nearly a whisper. "Then, Ashley's been killed?" he asked.

"Unlikely," replied Baqash. "But once Helel learns that the writings are gone…" the demon shrugged.

The writings gone! Trent had burned the writings, incinerated every last one of them. Had he destroyed Ashley's only hope? Had he killed his own daughter?

The writings. There was something about the writings, something he needed to remember. Trent tried to pull it from his muddled mind, but it flitted about like a butterfly eluding an anxious child's grasp. What was it? There was something else, something he was missing, something that had avoided the inferno.

Eldon's document. The memo from Satan.

Trent scampered toward the demons like an excited puppy dog, a mad plan already forming in his troubled mind. "But they're not!" he cried. "They're not all gone."

All eyes, human and demon alike focused on the dripping and bleeding Trent. "Explain," charged the largest creature.

"There's at least one document remaining. I shipped it elsewhere for safekeeping." Trent couldn't reveal that the thing was only a couple of miles away at Eldon's condominium. That would be the obvious place to look and he needed this bargaining position.

"And what exactly is this special writing?" pressed the towering being.

Trent rose, facing the demon. "A correspondence from Satan to Baal."

"Trent," urged Eldon. "You don't know what you're doing here." Trent simply glanced at his brother. What could Eldon possibly know about this?

The large demon glowered at Trent. "A letter to Baal?"

"Yes. It includes instructions, plans of Satan. It lists the new Nephilim, what their positions are to be, how they will be used to enhance Satan's influence in the coming years. It gives details, names, dates – everything."

The demon stepped forward, eyes boring into Trent. "Give me this letter," he demanded.

"Pastor, meet Baal," quipped Baqash. "Perhaps you prefer his company to mine." Trent ignored the demon. He cared little about Baqash's hurt feelings.

"I'll surrender the letter to Helel in return for my daughter. Otherwise, we will circulate its contents widely. Bear in mind, specific strategies and participants are detailed. Most people won't take it at face value, but it will cast doubt on your chosen ones. Enough doubt to disrupt the scheme, I'm sure. Satan would not be pleased."

What might have been a smile creased Baal's cruel, twisted lips. "Such an exchange will not be easy. Helel and the girl are in Pergamos."

Pergamos? How had they gotten Ashley all the way to Pergamos?

"Then I guess were headed to Pergamos," said Trent.

Eldon's face went ashen. "Nice goin' brother. You just set us an appointment with Satan."

CHAPTER 43

It was nine hours into the flight, the sky midnight black, the cabin nearly as dark. Trent's eyes lit on Kim. A huge purple knot adorned her forehead where she'd hammered Trent's head with her own; her hair was matted and unkempt, her eyes bore the leathery circles of prolonged insomnia. Like most passengers, she was nestled in an uneasy sleep, her head upon a tiny pillow. That was best. Kim had been distant, nearly silent since the beach. Trent didn't know how to relate to her now, and was relieved that he wasn't obligated to converse. Nearly a decade together and he couldn't think of a word to comfort her.

As for Trent, he hadn't bothered to accept the pillow. His sole focus was in retrieving his daughter. He could sleep later. He could patch things up with Kimmie later. Right now, his single purpose was to rescue Ashley. Nothing else mattered.

"Trent." It was Eldon, whispering from across the aisle. "Slide your tail over here. We've gotta talk."

Trent nodded, lifting himself out of his seat and plopping into one across the aisle and next to his brother. Eldon was becoming a nuisance. He'd been against the trip, but also insisted on coming. Doubtlessly, he was about to share more concerns.

"Trent, I've got a couple of concerns," said Eldon.

"Really?" asked Trent with a weak grin.

Eldon looked past Trent to Kim, making sure that she was asleep. "I'm worried about Kim," he said after swallowing a handful of peanuts. "She won't say a word; she's got that dreamy look in her eyes. I don't think we can trust her."

"She's my wife, El. Ashley's mother."

"And she handed her own daughter over to a demon, and later tried to kill you."

Trent shrugged, feigning unconcern at his wife's betrayal. He wasn't sure if he could ever love or trust Kim again. "That was the demon, not Kimmie," he said with little conviction. It wasn't even so much that she'd tried to kill him – though that certainly wasn't a plus – it was that she'd surrendered Ashley. Ashley! Their precious daughter, how could she have handed their little girl over to some supernatural fiend? And she did know what she had done, not completely, but enough. She'd known that it really wasn't Trent in her room that night, that it was someone called "Sam." Even if she hadn't known that Sam was a demon, how could she just give little Ashley to a near stranger?

"Uh-huh," nodded Eldon after a pause. "Did you happen to catch how that demon gained control of her on the beach? She reached out, hugged the slime-ball and invited him in. How do we know she won't do that again?" He leaned closer. "How do we know she hasn't already?"

Trent glanced across to his wife. He'd had the same concerns. How could he know that she was free of the demon? Still, what could he do, tell her that she couldn't come, that she'd been a bad girl and was grounded? She was an adult capable of purchasing her own ticket, of following them wherever they went. He couldn't force her to stay away. Besides, this was Kimmie. At least, at some level his wife.

"Trent, Kim is going to…"

"Kim is my wife," snapped Trent. "I'll deal with her."

"Like you did at the beach?"

"I subdued Kimmie at the beach. The demon fled."

Eldon stared at him as if he was gazing at an idiot. "Do you really think that demon fled you? Do you think you could have thrown Kim off if the demon was still there?"

An uneasy grin. "Hmmm, a mystery. Enlighten me."

Eldon lowered his eyes for a moment, apparently gathering his thoughts, then, with a sigh, leveled his gaze at Trent. "An angel was there. I think it was an angel, at least. Didn't look or act like any of those satanic types. He put words into my mouth, some whacked out language. The demons cowered. Strangest thing I've ever seen."

Trent tensed. This thing was traveling a path he just couldn't walk. He'd once believed that angels looked after him, that he was on the side of right.

That was before he'd learned that it had been a demon who'd guided him into the ministry, that whatever "faith" he'd held had been about as authentic as the Pillsbury Dough Boy. "I'm going back to my seat." Trent began to rise.

"Jeez, Trent, sit down."

Almost mechanically, Trent complied.

Eldon brushed some spilled peanuts from his lap. "Okay, so we put the Kim thing aside for now. But I gotta tell ya, she's gonna cause problems." Eldon paused, scrutinizing Trent with a look of love and puzzlement. "Brother, how well have you thought this thing through? What are we gonna do once we get there? Satan's temple is in the spiritual dimension so we can't exactly ask directions at the corner gas station."

Eldon held up a finger, halting Trent's ambiguous response. "Before you answer, I've got a couple a thoughts on that. Pergamos housed the temple of Zeus. Now a lotta scholarly types figure that's what the apostle John was talking about in the book of Revelation when he referred to 'the seat of Satan.' Maybe, maybe not. I say not." Eldon leaned forward and lifted a plastic cup from the tray before him, taking a sip of some anonymous foreign cola. "Anyway, the temple of Zeus is gone. It's been moved to a museum in Berlin."

Trent offered a tight grin. "I'm guessing you're eventually leading to a point."

"I think I've already been there."

"Excuse me?"

"To Satan's digs. I think it's where I found his letter to Baal."

Trent cupped his chin between thumb and index finger. "Why do I suddenly get the sense you've been holding out on me?"

Eldon took another sip of flat cola and then waved his free hand dismissively. "Minor stuff. The real issue is what do we do once we get there – waltz right up to Satan and exchange this memo for Ashley? I'm hoping you have a better plan than that, 'cause I just don't see the devil keeping his end of the deal."

Trent scratched his nose, nodded and sighed. "Nope. No better plan. Any suggestions?"

Eldon shrugged.

Trent dropped his head.

A tiny grin flitted across Kim's lips.

CHAPTER 44

The outdoor restaurant was nearly empty. It was late evening, a pleasant 72 degrees Fahrenheit, and Istanbul was still bustling, though many of the locals were turning in for the day leaving the nightlife to the scoundrels and the tourists. Some considered the two groups to be one and the same. Trent made his way through the narrow row of tables, each adorned with white lace tablecloths and fine silverware. Eldon and Kim sat at the far end of the pier-like patio which jutted out over the waters of the Bosporus Strait. Being the world traveler of the bunch, Eldon ordered meals for the three as Trent squeezed past the waiter, a small dark-haired lad of about nineteen, and sat down next to his wife and across from his brother. Kim was silent, brooding. Trent felt a chill scamper up his spine as he glanced into those hollow eyes he'd so adored.

"*Tamam*," said Eldon to the young man. "*Tesekkur ederim*."

"You're welcome," replied the waiter in broken English. "Your Turkish, it is very well spoken."

Eldon shrugged and smiled. "Yeah, well, I've spent a lotta time here."

"You are Americans. I wish to attend school in United States of America next season, Harvard. We speak English, you and I. I practice."

"No problem, kid, but I don't think mine's the kinda English they'll be jawin' at Harvard."

"Oh! You are uneducated?"

"He's highly educated," injected Trent. "He just likes to talk like an illiterate oaf so that nobody catches on to it."

The waiter smiled and nodded, probably wondering what the strange American had said. "I will return with your order," he said before leaving.

"I'm assuming those weren't hamburgers you just ordered."

"Don't worry, Trent. Nothin' scary, just kebabs. Meat and vegetables cooked on a wood fire. There'll probably be some pretty hot peppers though."

"Sounds intriguing. Though we'll need to put it on inhale mode. We're due back at the airport in an hour and fifteen minutes." Trent picked up a piece of dark bread and leaned forward gazing past Eldon at the black and subtly rolling strait. "I virtually accosted six different airliners. No change. There are still no planes leaving for Izmir until 6 AM." He paused to sip some water. "But someone that overheard me on the phone said his uncle was a pilot, flew against Cyprus in 1974. He dialed the number, we procured a plane."

*****

Osman proved to be a competent pilot. The takeoff was smooth, he handled turbulence well enough, though the small – and quite elderly – plane creaked and groaned with increasing volume throughout the trip. The Turk's only reaction to the racket was to yell even louder as he jabbered about everything from politics to gardening.

Seated in the copilot's seat to the right of the pilot, Trent handled the brunt of this impromptu filibuster while Eldon shared the increasingly uncomfortable back seats with Kim. The lump on her forehead seemed to swell and pulse, and with her wide bloodshot eyes and tumbling locks she looked like a demonic unicorn on crack. Worse, she sat staring at Eldon, rocking forward and back on her seat and mumbling something that sounded like "little red cots" over and over.

Eldon pondered Kim without looking at her. He'd never known the real Kim; the one Trent had fallen in love with. His first sight of her had been as she'd walked through the door, disoriented, and soon to be ranting. Trent had discovered drugs in her purse that night, but Eldon had suspected, even then, even before the supernatural reality of it all had slammed into him like a NFL linebacker, that something more was happening with Kim, that something was deeply wrong with the woman. Something that drove her, manipulated her, influenced her thoughts. He wondered if Trent had ever really known her for who she was, or if she'd somehow fooled him, even unknowingly, from the beginning.

Subtly, almost without Eldon noticing it, Kim's mumblings changed. It was the rhythm he noticed first, not the words. She'd been repeating the phrase "little red cots" for over half an hour and the cadence had become as familiar to him as the *clack clack clack* of a train to an Amtrak rider. But it was different now. Instead of the slow monotonous drone, her rhythm had sped up, her voice rising in pitch, sounding like a male falsetto. What was it she was saying?

Eldon caught her reflection in the window; she'd leaned further in his direction. Tightening his grip on the leather case containing the satanic document – it hadn't left his possession since Chicago – he turned to face her, trying to comprehend the words. Her wild blue eyes focused on him. Well, maybe not focused. He really couldn't be sure that she perceived him.

"Idoniadauwer. Idoniadauwer." She seemed to chant. What could that mean?

"Idoniadauwer. Idoniadauwer."

Eldon glanced at Trent. Between Osman's perpetual run of the mouth and the creaky craft, he could hear none of this.

"Idoniadauwer. Idoniadauwer," she chanted in that high ethereal voice.

"What do you mean by that?" hissed Eldon, a strange fear crawling in his belly. Was this some demonic tongue?

"Idoniadauwer. Idoniadauwer."

No. They were separate words run together, not one foreign word. The plane bucked, and Eldon leaned forward, attempting to hear her more clearly.

"Idoniadauwer. Idoniadauwer."

"I done killed my daughter?" Eldon gasped as he tried to pry the sentence into something comprehensible. "I done killed my daughter."

"Idoniadauwer. Idoniadauwer."

"Kim, your daughter's not dead. We're going to her. She'll be okay."

"Idoniadauwer. Idoniadauwer."

"Kim, really. We'll get little Ashley back." He had no way of knowing if this was true, but Eldon felt a need to calm the woman. Besides, Ashley was a hostage. Eldon had something Satan needed. As long as he still held the document Ashley should be safe, probably not well treated, the poor girl would likely need psychological help for years to come, but alive at least.

Kim squinted, rearing her head back, almost like a cobra preparing to strike. "Idoniadauwer. Idoniadauwer." The chant was slower this time, allowing Eldon to finally grasp the true meaning.

"Eldon is a goner. Eldon is a goner."

Eldon gasped. The plane bucked.

"Eldon is a goner. Eldon is a goner."

"Why? What's going to happen to me?"

"Eldon is a goner. Eldon is a goner."

Eldon drew back into his seat, and stared out through the window, clutching the leather case in his lap, and attempting vainly to ignore Kim's continuous mantra.

"Eldon is a goner. Eldon is a goner."

It would be a long flight.

*****

The landing was rough but welcome. Osman, the jabbering pilot, had spotted a flat area perhaps a quarter of a mile from the ancient city of Bergama. He'd circled four times, flying low and scanning for obstacles.

Finally, the pilot dropped the left wing sharply, angling east and swooping in low and much faster than Trent felt necessary. A loud creak emerged from the rear left, but Osman seemed unconcerned as he rolled the steering column back to the right. Trent could hear Kim talking throughout the descent, but could make out none of the words as the desert land grew large in the windshield before him. The plane bounced once, twice, and then seemed to skid slightly to the left before finally righting.

The small craft came to a mildly jolting stop about thirty yards before a large jutting stone about half the size of the plane. "Well, I'm for disembarking," sighed Trent who'd been unconsciously gripping the arm rests like a weightlifter clutching a three hundred-pound barbell. Without another word, he unlatched his safety belt and rose, making his way past his wife and brother, and moving toward the hatch.

Eldon caught up with him about fifteen yards from the plane. "Trent, we gotta talk 'bout Kim."

Trent kept walking. "Haven't we been through this?" Trent understood his brother's concern. Heck, he shared it. He was, after all, the one she'd almost drowned. But what could he do about it? No matter how much he longed to, he simply couldn't leave her behind, couldn't simply walk away from the woman he'd loved for all those years. Not Kimmie, not in her present state. At least this way he knew where she was, what she was doing. Hard telling what she'd do on her own.

Strangely, or maybe not so strangely, Trent was no longer thinking of Kim the way a man thinks of a wife. He regarded her more like a beloved family pet gone rabid. He still had emotions for her, sure, a tangled mess of them, but he had to hold the wellbeing of Ashley and the unborn baby above that of Kim. Trent felt very small for feeling this way, but wasn't inclined to change his attitude. Kim had betrayed him. Not just recently, but from the beginning. The Kim Trent loved had never really existed. He thought he might just hate her for that.

Eldon grabbed Trent's arm, stopping him and forcing him to turn. "She's possessed, Trent. Right now. This minute. I'm sure of it."

Trent raised an eyebrow and glanced toward the plane. Kim was descending the rickety steps. She looked shaken, disheveled, her eyes wide and glassy. "Curious," said Trent. "You may be right." He smoothed his hair with a palm and gazed at his brother. "Listen, I'm fully aware of the danger in bringing Kimmie. She needs help – that's obvious. And I'm going to get it for her, but Ashley comes first."

"Help? Trent, you make it sound like Sigmund Freud and a bottle of Prozac will turn her into June Cleaver. She's possessed, brother – possessed. You should have heard her on the plane, chanting over and over, 'Eldon is a goner, Eldon is a goner.'" Eldon took a step closer, invading Trent's space. "I'm with you on rescuing Ashley – that's the priority. And that's exactly why we can't bring Kim with us. Think about it, Trent. You know what she's capable of doing."

Trent glanced toward Kim again. She was now only some twenty feet distant. "And I'm supposed to do what? Leave her here by herself? Put her back on the plane? She's my wife, El. At least, that's who I always thought her to be."

"Hello, Trent, Eldon," said Kim as she approached the brothers. "Holding another secret conference? Trying to figure out what to do with nutty old Kim?" She smiled and inclined her head toward Eldon. "Pleasant flight, wasn't it?"

*****

Eldon marched up the shaky metal stairs and back into the cramped plane. He had no reason for this other than the need to be free of Kim Troxel. Plopping into his seat, he turned, staring through the dark and dusty window at the barren landscape.

"Not going with your companions?" asked the pilot, his voice low, halting, not nearly as animated as during the flight. Probably just tired, thought Eldon. After all, Trent had awakened him from a sound sleep. His second wind was sure to be faltering.

"Just taking a break," said Eldon. "I needed a little space."

"I suppose we all need that," agreed Osman with an odd twist of his head. "But there is something I need to tell you."

That was weird. What could the pilot need to tell him? Maybe he wanted to hit Eldon up for more money. No luck there. Trent was the one with the big bucks. "Yeah," said Eldon. "Whaddaya need?"

The man shifted slowly, awkwardly, then turned to face Eldon, his expression blank, his eyes glazed. "Eldon is a goner," he said. "Eldon is a goner."

CHAPTER 45

The vast chamber was familiar to Trent – frighteningly so. No, he'd never been there before. But he knew this structure just the same. It was the place described in the journals of Baqash, the palace of Satan, though Trent had never imagined its awesome magnitude. This hall alone had to be the size of three pro football stadiums, perhaps larger. The ceiling seemed to reach for heaven itself. Trent could only guess, but five hundred feet seemed a fair estimate of its height.

Tattered and bloodstained remnants of once fine tapestries hung about the walls. They were nothing more than rags really, and without prior knowledge Trent would not have recognized them for what they'd been. Great columns of marble lay pulverized about the cracked and crumbling floor causing him to wonder how the huge structure had remained standing. An immense fire burned in the center of the room, spitting and crackling, reaching for the lofty ceiling and smelling of rotted meat. The thing seemed more to be fueled by bones than wood, for that was what spilled from the flames. Skulls, femurs, whole skeletons of creatures great and small, of lions and dogs, of apes and of humans shifted and tumbled as the flames devoured them, reducing them to ash.

Scattered demons flittered about, chattering mindlessly, scrapping with one another and picking at pus-filled sores on naked bodies, their imbecilic noise creating a kind of staccato buzz, their stinking forms causing the air to smell stale and old.

But how was it that he could see this place, this door to hell? It should have been invisible to his fleshly eyes. How had it been made visible to him – to any of them?

The structure had not been far from the airplane, perhaps a half-mile to the west, adjacent the crumbling remains of some nameless structure. Nearly as soon as the threesome had begun walking, Trent striding purposely, Kim following, and Eldon ambling strangely silent behind, Baqash had appeared, sullen and filthy, motioning them toward the palace which suddenly loomed in the distance as if it had always been there. Trent supposed, in a way it had. Baqash had simply somehow enabled his fleshly eyes to perceive what should never be perceived. The demon had hissed, locking eyes with Eldon before addressing Trent. "You are a fool, Pastor," he'd said in a low voice. "You have one document with which to bargain. And that one is already lost to your cause. You could have had hundreds."

Trent had ignored him, thinking nothing of this, nor of the structure before him. He supposed he'd been too preoccupied, too focused, to worry about such mundane details.

Now, as Trent gazed about the vast chamber, his attention focused on a particular demon, one seated on the golden throne, his right leg thrown casually over the armrest as he gnawed on what appeared to be a human arm. The human arm of a small child!

Trent stopped breathing. "No," he choked. They couldn't have come this far only to find that this beast had already destroyed his little Ashley. But there were the tiny fingers curled ever so slightly as if still fighting, even in death, to form a fist with which to fend off the monster. The skin that remained seemed smooth, soft, childlike, glinting in the shimmering light. But it was dark skin, a deep, rich brown; the skin of a Mexican, an Arab, a Turk. It was not an arm that could have belonged to the fair-skinned Ashley. Trent exhaled, feeling both relief and shame. He was thankful that the limb belonged to someone else's child. Thankful that some other father was weeping and searching, never knowing what had become of his little girl, never guessing the evil that had consumed her. Despicable as it might be, he was thankful. Ashley might still be alive. And if that little relief made him unsympathetic to the pain of others, so be it.

The demon rose as Trent, Eldon, and Kim were escorted by a muttering and cowed Baqash to before the towering platform. The beast was tall, perhaps six foot seven, his hair long and fine, darker than that of Baqash, but still seemingly golden. His skin was smooth, pale, yet glittering with shades of precious metals, not marked by boils and sores like that of so many of his underlings. His body was naked and firm, showing no signs of infirmity. And his eyes! Not only did they flow, one color rolling into another, one shape relenting to a newer more hideous form, but they were luminous, glowing with a beautiful color which Trent had never before seen. It could have been a distant cousin to green, but at once seemed more of the orange family. Truly it was a shade foreign to this world, at least to the physical plane of this world, a color normally not visible to the natural eye.

This was Satan himself. The father of lies, prince of darkness, the serpent. This was the creature who had first conceived evil, who had, whether directly or indirectly, influenced every atrocity ever committed by mankind. No, Satan hadn't directed each degenerate act, every despicable deed. He hadn't personally started every war, committed every act of rape or murder. And neither had his demons. Men were perfectly capable of devising evil within their own hearts, of walking away from what was good and right in favor of things lusty and tantalizing. But the fallen one had initiated the concept of evil, nurtured it like a loving gardener, watering it, spreading fertilizer, pruning it, watching it grow into a festering vine encircling the globe, squeezing, suffocating, inhibiting all that is good and worthy.

This was Satan, the beast. This was the devil that held his daughter.

"So," said the monster, his voice tinkling like wind chimes on a summer breeze. "You have arrived." He casually tossed the partially devoured limb into the blaze. "I will see this supposed memo now."

Trent did not respond immediately. His mind seemed to move in slow motion, like he was swimming in a sea of mashed potatoes. He glanced past Kim toward the still silent Eldon. Somehow he had expected his brother to defy the devil, to spit and curse him; maybe to even threaten the destruction of his prize should the beast not comply.

He had not.

In fact, what Eldon did was so startling as to cause Trent's knees to weaken and his chest to tighten. Slowly, with no change in expression, Eldon knelt, tore open the satchel, and produced the cool gray document. Without hesitation, not even glancing at Trent, he marched toward the devil.

"Eldon, what are you doing? We don't have Ashley yet," said Trent as Eldon continued marching. "Eldon, no!"

Trent acted reflexively, bolting forward, grabbing Eldon about the shoulders, twirling him in his direction. But it was not Eldon that faced him. It was the towering, repulsive form of Pereh, eyes swimming, drooling mouth pulling into a Jack-o-lantern grin.

"How... Where's Eldon?" sputtered Trent, as he stumbled back in shock. The demon did not reply, but thrust Trent harshly back with the casual flip of a tentacle-like wing. The world spun and seemed to flash from light to dark as Trent skittered across the bloodstained floor like a lopsided bowling ball, his head repeatedly slapping against the hard cold marble. He halted only a few feet before the blaze, close enough for the heat to singe the fine hairs on his arms. By the time Trent had righted himself, Pereh had flown up to the platform and was handing Satan the manuscript.

Trent had lost his leverage.

Scrambling to his feet, ignoring the growing mound on the back of his head, Trent marched to the foot of the platform. "It seems my end of the bargain is complete. I'll take my daughter now," he said with far more bluster than he felt.

Satan cocked his head, neither smiling nor frowning, his glittering face a plastic mask, still and lifeless. "Why should I comply?" he asked.

"I brought you that letter, fulfilled our arrangement."

"This?" He held up the scroll. "You think this important?" Without unrolling the document, he casually tossed it into the flames, not even caring to watch as it entered the blaze, erupting into spiraling fragments of red and green that looped and flitted about the flames before finally evaporating within the fire.

"Do you not see?" smiled Satan. "You are merely an entertainment. That trifle meant nothing." Satan pivoted, pacing to his left. "Oh, surly you could have released its contents to the public. The National Enquirer or the Weekly Globe would gladly have printed the story right next to the photograph of a three-headed alien chimpanzee that resembles Elvis Presley." Satan leered. "My plans are secure, human, the new Nephilim dispatched. The industrialized world no longer believes in my existence, and the less sophisticated lands still worship my servants."

Satan stared at Trent directly. "But, it's not too late for you," he said, his voice melodic, tantalizing, inviting. "You have great abilities, staggering potential. It is not your fault that Baqash failed to nurture you properly, to establish you in a proper position, to make sure that your loyalties became true." Satan glanced at Baqash who cowered with a hiss. "You were to be placed in a large metropolitan ministry, a place from which you could rise among the ranks of your denomination, influence decisions and doctrines; not in some small, backward rural church." The devil lowered his voice, the tone sweet, beckoning. "It is not too late. These things may still be accomplished. Join our ranks, Trent Troxel. Embrace your destiny. You do not belong to humanity. You never have. You never will."

Trent gaped at the beautiful creature, its silken skin gleaming, its tingling voice tickling his ears. Was it true? Was it all true? Had he ever truly belonged to God? Had he ever really been a true believer? It had all seemed so real, his faith a near tangible element. But that had been a lifetime past. Everything had changed. God had abandoned him, allowing Baqash to run rampant in his life. Trent had fallen, never to return. And if he was already lost, destined to this life of demons and Satan, why not embrace his destiny, why not make the best of the lot he'd been given?

Ashley!

Whatever he was, whatever fate awaited him, he would not sacrifice his daughter to Satan, to an eternity in hell. He may be lost, but she need not be.

"Give me my daughter!" screamed Trent as he rushed the ten-foot high platform. Realizing that there were no steps to climb, he began jumping like an excited puppy, trying to grasp the top, to pull himself up and face the beast eye-to-eye. "Where is she? What have you done with her?" he bellowed, still jumping, attaining the ledge several times, but never gaining a grip.

There was a tug on his right shoulder, then another about the waist and two about his legs. Trent was pulled forcefully to the unyielding floor as several chattering demons pulled and jabbed at him. He felt the cool moist touch of their forms against his skin, felt razor-like talons trace cutting lines through his pants and into his thighs. He screamed as he saw a greenish gold arm actually reach through his flesh and into his belly. The sensation was as if he'd been on a rapidly descending roller coaster while being simultaneously trampled by the Chicago Bears defensive line. Judging by the result of this invasion, the demon had literally reached in and squeezed his bladder – a great demon party trick.

"Cease!" he heard the devil's voice echo about the great hall. Immediately the grotesque tormenters scattered, scampering off silent and fearful like roaches fleeing a sudden light. "I believe the young lady has something to say."

Young lady?

It was then that Trent noticed Kim. In truth he'd nearly forgotten her. She'd been so silent, so distant. But now he saw that she stood no more than five feet away from him, gazing up at the leering beast, her hands tightly clenched before her waist, her body taut and quivering. "Ask something of us," she said. "Give us another task. Allow us to win Ashley's freedom."

Trent attempted to rise, but a sudden rush of vertigo sent him back to the floor. "No, Kimmie. Don't."

"I will do anything. Trent will do anything. Ashley means much more to us than she can to you. Let us earn her freedom." She seemed resolute, in control, but terrified. Trent now noticed the glint of tears upon her reddened cheeks. Was this a demon talking? He didn't think so. This was Kim, the real Kim, if there was still such a person.

"Kim, please," pleaded Trent. "A second pact with the devil will be no more useful than the first."

Satan paced the platform, apparently pondering the proposal, his movements swift, graceful, feline. Trent knew the devil would accept the offer, he also knew that Satan would not keep his end of the deal, and that whatever this beast concocted would be diabolical.

"Woman," said Satan. "I believe you may be correct. Some sport is in order."

Suddenly the devil was on the floor, standing before Trent, those glimmering eyes twirling and rolling, one color folding in upon another. "It seems fitting to me," said Satan, "that those most directly involved in this debacle participate. The woman has already done her part." The beast glowered down upon Trent, causing him to scoot backward on the cold marble floor. "A contest then. Should the male win, the girl will be returned. And for the idiot Baqash," he turned to face the skulking demon. "Should you be victorious, treacherous one, you will only be chained and tortured for, oh," he paused, staring at the cowering demon. "Two-hundred years. A very mild sentence considering your blatant betrayal. And should you lose, I believe a millennia chained beneath the dark, cold ground should temper your ambitions." He turned as if preparing to leave, and then paused, obviously for dramatic effect. "Oh, and demon, you may bring me a sacrifice of thanksgiving after you have won the contest."

"What type of contest?" asked Trent, fearing he already knew the answer. He had, after all, read the journals of Baqash.

Satan smiled. "A fight to the death, of course."

CHAPTER 46

Trent kicked through the bone-littered floor, inspecting the varied and plentiful specimens before finally selecting a large rib, broken and jagged at one end. He hefted it, testing it for balance and strength. The broad curve made it awkward to manipulate, but it was heavy and large, perhaps four feet from one end to another. He supposed it had belonged to an elephant or at least a rhinoceros. Trent tossed it from one hand to the other, and then held it horizontally, with the ends facing out like bull horns. He tried to flip the bone vertically as if to swing it down like a hatchet, but clumsily dropped it while executing the simple maneuver. The vertigo had left him; he had no excuse for such awkward movements. But he'd been a quarterback, not some crazy gladiator swinging swords and hatchets about, facing death every time he walked onto the coliseum floor. His chances of surviving this encounter were next to nil.

He could pray, he supposed, call on the devil's oldest adversary, the God he had sworn to serve, and whose name he hadn't uttered in seemingly a lifetime. A strange thought to even consider this. It had been so long. Even during his years of ministry, praying had never come easily. He could preach about it, of course, but in truth, he'd rarely exercised the practice in private. At the time this had bothered him. Now, he understood his limitations better. His call had not come from God, but from the other. So, why now? Why even entertain the idea? Foxhole conversion, he supposed. Even the stoutest atheist tended to second-guess his assertions when facing eternity. But Trent would not pray. Who was he to call on God? His former peers in the ministry would argue that anyone, even the worst of criminals, could still find salvation, that no one was beyond redemption. Maybe so. But… There was something stopping him. Something holding him back. His own pride perhaps. Maybe this place. Trent was unsettled, questioning his every thought. He needed to free himself of these doubts, these contemplations. Now was not the time. Later, perhaps.

If not now, when?

There may very well never be a later.

Trent shook his head violently and walked away from the fiery grave-yard, the bone hanging loosely in his right hand. He caught Kim's gaze. She was staring at him, hugging herself tightly with her own arms and crying. "I love you," she said as he passed within ten feet of her. Though his very being longed to run to her, to cradle her in his arms, to share the agony, he did not respond. Nor did he slow. Kim had become a non-entity, a dangerous non-entity, nearly as dangerous and deceitful as Baqash. There was such sorrow in her eyes. Deceitful to the end, he supposed.

Baqash was before him now; a large black gorilla crouched beside him innocently picking at pests in its fur. Where did they get these creatures? Did demons fly off to some African jungle and carry the beasts back? Did they impersonate zoo representatives and have them shipped to some non-existent Bergama zoo? No matter. The gorilla was here and Trent would be forced to battle it to the death. No, not battle the gorilla, but battle Baqash within the body of the gorilla. It would be no animal he fought; it would be a cunning, intelligent, battle-tested demon housed within the strong and brutal form of the ape.

Baqash stared across the space to him. There was no sly smile, no superior gloat, not even the intense gaze of a focused athlete. If anything there was simply weary resignation. His scheme, centuries in implementation, had come to disaster. His nemesis, the devil, had long known of his actions, and had even planned to use Baqash's collection of writings for his own gain. Baqash was a beaten soul now alienated not only from God but from Satan as well. There was no place in heaven, hell, or on earth for the demon. All he could hope for would be a minor victory which might save him a few hundred years of physical torment from the devil.

Baqash stepped into the ape, or perhaps, evaporated into it, simply turn-ing toward the creature, bending slightly at the waste, and vanishing amidst a sparkling gray and gold vapor which encircled the beast, swirling like water down a sink, and fading swiftly into the creature's pores. The gorilla shut-tered and spun with frantic panic-stricken movements, like a wild horse trying to buck a 400 pound rider. It fell to the ground pounding furiously at its own rolling head with thick black hands, squealing like a pig in a slaughterhouse while its feet drummed against the floor in uncontrolled frenzy.

Then, as if a switch had been thrown, it relaxed, sprawled limply on the ground, its eyes blinking as if trying to focus in a new and brighter light. It rose calmly to face Trent, its expression neutral, unconcerned. The whole thing had taken no more than ten seconds.

"Baqash?" asked Trent wondering if the demon would be capable of speech.

"It-is-I," replied the thing, its voice coarse and halting, the vocal chords unaccustomed to such use.

"Wait," said Trent, holding up a hand in the gorilla's direction. Then, turning toward the throne of Satan, he hollered. "I want to see my daughter."

The devil smiled. "Did I mislead you into believing you have options?"

"We always have options," said Trent. "They're just not always favorable." He threw the large bone to the floor with a clatter. "But I'm going to take this option anyway. Show me my daughter right now, alive, or I refuse to fight."

Satan stared down at him, a look of contempt upon his luminous face. Trent wondered if he was about to receive a personal attack from the devil; if he'd be slain right here and now, the whole thing over without him ever seeing his little girl again. That thought struck him harder than the thought of death itself. Never see Ashley again. Could that really be? What would happen to her if he was gone? What kind of life would she have? Would she even have a life, or would Satan simply kill her? No, he could not let that happen. Not to Ashley. Not to his little girl.

"If I order the fallen one to slay you," said the beast, "He will do so, whether you defend yourself or not."

Trent inhaled sharply. He knew this and dreaded it. But he also knew this was his last chance to rescue Ashley. Maybe if he could see her. Maybe if he could get close to her, he could cause some sort of diversion, swing some deal. "I understand that," he said through a tense jaw. "I'll take my chances." Trent was betting that the beast's appetite was whetted for sport and Satan would concede this minor battle. But he'd never been that great at reading people and wasn't sure if he was quite up to psychoanalyzing the devil.

He wasn't.

Satan shrugged. "Baqash, kill him."

The gorilla glanced wearily at the devil, then padded forward on its knuckles. There was no enthusiasm, no verve. Baqash was simply doing as he'd been told.

The buzz of chattering demons from above increased to a deafening roar. Somewhere in the background Kim screamed. The gorilla rose onto two feet, raising its massive arms high above its head, preparing to crash them down upon Trent's skull. Demons whooped and howled as Trent dropped to the floor, rolling into the apes legs and toppling it as Baqash thrust its arms down to where Trent's head had been a moment before.

"Imbecile!" grunted Baqash as he righted the beast. Trent was already on his feet, the long jagged bone once again in his grasp. He probably was an imbecile. There was no way he was going to win a fight with a demonized gorilla. But good old survival instinct had kicked in. He simply could not remain still for the quick and relatively painless death.

"Why, Past-or?" barked the ape as it lunged forward, then retreated at a swipe of the jagged point. "Had-you-trusted-me, I-could-have-been-re-deemed!"

Trent ran to his right, putting some distance between he and the demon-thing. "Demon, do you really think God wants you back?"

The gorilla ambled forward standing upright. "I-could-be-re-deemed."

"Have you ever known any demon to successfully return to paradise?"

Not waiting for a reply, Trent charged the ape. Weapon raised, he swung at the gorilla, missing the head but striking the right shoulder. The jagged end of the bone pierced the thick hide, penetrating perhaps four inches into the tissue. The ape howled and twisted, pounding Trent's back with its left fist, then grabbing Trent's arm and tossing him away. Still, Trent held firm to the bone even as he was thrust backward. The resulting tension caused the bone to snap. A six-inch piece remained imbedded, jutting from the black fur.

Still screeching in fury and pain with a voice amazingly human, the ape charged, its now useless right arm dragging beside, bouncing against the marble floor. Trent had lost his weapon as he'd hit the unrelenting floor. Now he flipped from side to side attempting to locate it. Where had it gone? Trent rolled yet again. There! About ten feet to his right. Scrambling to his feet, Trent bolted toward the broken bone. Just as his fingers flitted against the crude weapon, the bone soared skyward. Tent caught sight of a looping and cackling demon fluttering away with his only defense as the massive arm of the gorilla smashed against his back. The world went momentarily black before bursting into a sea of pulsating color.

Trent struck the ground and instinctively rolled. Vision clearing, he attempted to rise, to race toward the blaze, find another weapon. The ape slammed into his back, knocking the wind from him, and sending him back to the floor. Trent shot an elbow backward, connecting with the gorilla's gut as it bent toward him for the kill. Trent rolled and desperately kicked at its groin. Seemingly unperturbed, the ape continued the assault. Still, Trent hammered the thing with his feet, like two pile drivers on concrete.

Lowering itself, the beast pressed a knee into Trent's belly, its weight compressing his innards, pinning him to the cold unrelenting floor. Then, with a curious, almost hurt expression, it reached out with its good hand – the other remained limp and twitching, the bone still protruding from the fur – and placed it loosely about Trent's neck. His thoughts went to his daughter. Ashley would be sacrificed. She would never grow up. Never have a crush on a boy, marry, have children. She wouldn't even be granted a full childhood, a trip to Disneyland, a case of the chicken pox. Her life would end only six years after it had begun. Six years, barely a chance to appreciate the changing seasons, barely a chance to ride a two-wheel bicycle or have a best friend.

"God," Trent gasped, knowing he had no business, no right to call on him. "Ashley, please, Ashley. Save her. Save her."

"Still, you-do-not-petition-on-my-account," said the ape.

"It would do no good," replied the fallen pastor. "You're already lost, Baqash. You have been since the day you were cast from heaven."

"You-too-walked-with-God-then-turned-away. You-are-as-lost-as-I. If-you-can-be-re-deemed. I-can-be-re-deemed."

"No," The ape was putting pressure on his throat making it difficult to speak, but was not yet squeezing so tightly as to strangle him. "It's too late for you."

"Fallen-humans-are redeemed," insisted the demon.

Trent gasped, attempting to fill his lungs, which seemed to be collapsing in upon themselves like parachutes after landing. "Only the living ones, Baqash. After death is judgment. You've already been judged. You're already dead."

The thick black fingers tightened about his neck. "If-this-is-so, why-do-you-not-pray-for-your-wife, for-your-self?"

Trent took one last gasp of air. "I think," he said as his vision closed into penetrating darkness, "that perhaps we too are already dead."

Baqash squeezed.

Demons cheered.

CHAPTER 47

Kim stood, wrapped in her own arms, trying to comprehend the insanity about her. Having not read the journals of Baqash, she had trouble understanding what this place was, how it was that it could exist unseen by the outside world, how Trent could be fighting a talking gorilla. It was talking wasn't it? The gorilla actually spoke. She shook her head and shuttered, wishing she had a cigarette, even better, some little-red-hots. She just couldn't deal with all of this, couldn't handle the stress.

Glancing about, she wished the fluttering and chattering demons would shut up. The constant sound hurt her head, confused her, made her want to scream. Where was Sam? Maybe Sam was here. Maybe he could make them stop. She turned in a full circle scanning the bizarre yammering faces, and looked for the familiar folds of Sam's aged features, for the tell-tale pipe, the tweed jacket, the red mustache.

But the only face she recognized was Trent's, and he'd rejected her, barely spoken a word to her since that night on the beach. When was that: yesterday, the day before, a month ago? She really didn't know, couldn't really remember what had happened at all. But Trent had changed. He'd already seemed cold and distant to her, but since then he'd become stone: hard, inflexible. She believed he truly hated her, and for what, she didn't know.

But, Trent was in pain now, dying. The ape was on top of him, strangling him, stealing his life's breath. He probably deserved to die. Pretending to be so holy when all along he was a lying thief, dragging Kim and Ashley into his little demon thing. The man could not be trusted. She gazed at Trent, his eyes were fluttering, his skin becoming blue, and she hated him for all he'd done, hated him for who he'd become, who he'd forced her to become. She wished she could be the one on top of him, that she could be the one with her fingers about his neck, that she could feel the pulse slow, the skin grow cold, the rising and falling chest wane and finally cease its movement.

Kim shook her head, trying to clear her mind. Could she really be thinking these things, these awful violent things?

Trent was her husband.

Trent was a beast.

He'd been her lover, the father of her child.

He'd betrayed her, belittled her, even struck her.

Trent had tended to her when she'd been ill.

He'd turned his back, rejected her when her world turned upside down and everything stopped making sense. He'd hated Sam when all Sam had done was to try to help her through a difficult time. He'd let their precious little daughter be taken away by horrible monsters, and then treated her as if it was all her fault.

Kim's right foot bumped against something as she took an unconscious step forward. The something was hard, rolling away with gentle clatter. A bone. Not a huge curved thing such as Trent had used, but long and straight. Something from the leg of some animal, perhaps a horse or a zebra. Kim looked toward her spiteful husband, then back at the bone. She bent, her knees cracking as she reached down and slipped her fingers about the smooth white femur.

Again, she wished Sam was here. He'd help her. He'd give her the strength for what must be done, for what she knew only she could do. Marching toward the ape and the man, the bone held tight in her fist, she glared into the fluttering eyes of her husband, the man who had caused her such pain, the man who'd ruined her life and was yet oblivious to any fault of his own.

Kim approached them from the ape's right, Trent's left. "May I?" she asked as she raised the bone above her head, preparing to bring it crashing down. She stared once again into Trent's uncomprehending eyes as the gorilla leaned back and glanced in her direction, a perplexed frown upon its muzzle.

Trent, the deceiver.

Trent, the fallen.

Trent, the source of all her tragedy.

The bone came down hard, propelled by years of confusion and frustration. Kim could feel the brittle cartilage of the nose give way, the cheekbones crumble, and the soft tissue behind recede, surrendering to the crash of the raging swing. Blood splattered Kim's face, soaking her knotted yellow hair, striking her eyes, blinding her so that she couldn't see the limp form of the ape tumble back, its already fractured skull striking the cold marble, and the body convulsing in the spasms of death.

Trent was her husband.

CHAPTER 48

Something was above the ape, behind it, a shadow, vaguely human in form. Trent's vision was dark, indistinct; blackness closed in from the peripheries. The rhythmic thump of his heart was slowing, nearly halting, like a tape recorder running on low batteries. He attempted to focus, but his eyes simply fluttered as the ape's thumbs pressed deeper into the soft flesh of his neck, its stale breath dominating what little air he could steal.

Then there was a voice: Kimmie's voice, hard, cold, doused in hate. "May I?" she asked. There was a pause, and then the grip loosened, the creature pulled back, no longer bearing down. Trent gasped, attempting to force glorious air down his enflamed throat. He blinked and squinted. Balloon-like spots of green and yellow danced before his eyes. There was Kim, above the ape, glaring down at Trent in contempt and revulsion, a long straight bone held above her head. Realization collided with relief. She meant to kill him herself.

"Kim," he tried to say, but only his lips moved; no sound escaped his larynx. The bone swung downward, quickly, lethally. He was powerless to move. Still, he retained eye-contact in that strange slow-motion reality which proceeded death, staring into her cool blue eyes, seeking elusive understanding. It was over. The devil had won. Ashley was the prize.

But the blow never came. Just as Trent braced for contact, the bone arched away, catching the gorilla in the muzzle. The face folded in upon itself like an empty Halloween mask, crumpling and inverting. Blood erupted from the creature, spraying Trent as the beast tumbled to his left. Trent rolled to his right, coughing and gasping, straining to breathe.

He heard the thump and crack of the ape striking the marble just as he heard a clatter from behind him, the sound of a bone dropping. He turned, his body protesting, and stared at Kim, her eyes glassy, her hair disheveled, the horn-like lump on her forehead purple and red, nearly glowing as adrenaline-propelled blood raced through her veins. "Thank you," he croaked, before spitting something thick and pink from his lungs.

The excited buzz of demon chatter rose in Trent's ears as foul creatures cackled and taunted. But even through this cacophony, one voice dominated: a piercing scream, a howl of the insane. Baqash. The demon had exited the lifeless ape and rolled about the floor twittering and crying, chattering in incomprehensible sentences of multiple tongues. His eyes were wide, yet unseeing, his fingers opening, closing, opening, grasping for nonexistent phantoms. He rolled from side to side, then, flipping onto his belly, began licking the floor with his long narrow tongue as his fingertips drummed staccato rhythms on the marble.

Trent knew what was happening. He'd read about it in the journals. Demons that inhabited fleshly creatures at the time of their demise were often driven insane, unable to cope with the physical act of death. The condition could be short-lived or last for centuries. Trent silently wished the latter upon his hated nemesis.

It was then that Kim knelt beside him, her eyes clear, her cheeks glinting with rolling tears. She hesitated, but only for a moment, and then leaned forward, kissing him solidly on the lips, lingering there for several seconds as if hoping to capture the sensation. And when finally she pulled free, Trent had tears on his face as well. "I tried to hate you, Goober. I…"

"Shhh," said Kim placing an index finger on his lips. "Whatever it is, I'd rather not hear." And then she rose to her feet, her eyes locked with his. "It wasn't all a lie, Trent. Don't ever think that it was."

She turned then, hesitated only momentarily, and then marched purposefully toward the devil. "Kim, no!" Trent put both hands on the cold floor, attempting to steady the swaying room. Taking three deep breaths, he rose on rubber legs. "Kim! Get back!"

But Kim continued forward. "Your gorilla lost the dual," she said. "Give me back my Ashley." Her voice was strong yet tight, demanding yet almost questioning. "Give me back my Ashley," she repeated.

Trent took one step forward then hit the floor hard, barely extending his arms in time to break the fall. An imp, covered in festering soars, its golden hair clumped and spilling across its face, was seated cross-legged on the marble surface grasping Trent's shin and cackling wildly. "Let go of me, you beast!" he screamed while kicking and shaking. The demon responded with exaggerated fits of hysterics.

"Yes," said Satan as he strolled to the edge of his golden platform. "The pathetic Baqash was not successful. That is no great surprise."

"I need my Ashley," repeated Kim.

"Yes," smiled Satan. "You do. And for your service to me, you shall be rewarded." Satan gestured toward the roaring and cracking blaze. "Behold, your daughter."

*****

The sea was endless, stretching out in dark rolling waves, crimson foam topping thirty-foot swells. Kim was waist deep in the blood-red water gazing out at the moonlit horizon. There was a speck, something floating in the distance, rising and falling with the breath of the sea. It was of wood, perhaps a piece of a ship, or… Something else, something more familiar.

A chest of drawers. Yes, a chest of drawers: dark, walnut, with a deep purple stain atop where Ashley had once spilled dye. It was the chest her mother had given her soon after she and Trent had been married, the one she'd given to Ashley for her school clothes. That was strange. Why would her chest be in the water?

The ocean swelled and then dove. The chest disappeared behind a dark rolling wave, and then reappeared atop an even greater surge. Now there was something on the dark walnut surface, something small, white. Perhaps it was a gull snacking on a fish, taking a break from the swirling winds. But it seemed too big for that, too ill-at-ease, too frightened.

"Aren't you going to rescue your daughter?" asked Sam. He was standing beside her in the hot rolling sea. "Can't you see that she needs you?"

Yes. Yes, she did. That was Ashley out there, on the chest. Naked and cold, screaming for her mommy. Another wave surged forward attempting to toss the child from her precarious perch. But Ashley hugged the thing as if it was the dog she always wanted but had never received. She sank down again, out of sight, and this time when the chest rose she was no longer atop, but beside it, clinging to an open drawer. Her long golden hair hung drenched before her face, covering it, cutting off her air supply. But still she screamed, "Mommy, Mommy, help!"

Sam lit his pipe. "She needs you now, Kimmie. She really won't last much longer."

"Ashley. Ashley needs me." Kim stepped into the deepening water, her skin becoming hot, pink, her eyes dry and stingy. "I'm coming Ashley!" She dove into a crackling wave, the hair of her arms singeing, her lips parching. She took a stroke, then another. A surge tossed her back, but she righted herself, swimming forward again, her arms pulling feverishly against the hot red liquid even as her skin began to peel.

"Mommy!" cried little Ashley, but the voice seemed more distant.

"I'm coming, sweetie," cried Kim as water shot into her mouth, burning the taste buds from her tongue, causing her to scream involuntarily. Kim stroked furiously, moving further and further into the blood-red sea. She could see the skin on her arms peeling back, curling, revealing the taut blackened muscle beneath.

There was Ashley, just ahead. She was free of the chest, going under, sinking, drowning.

Kim dove, following the descending form, the pale spot with the wide blue eyes and the flowing blond hair, the little hands reaching for her mommy, the one person who could help her, the one person who would risk it all to save her.

Kim's skin screamed, her body seemingly erupting into flames; but she pushed forward, stroking, pushing, reaching. Her lungs were to the point of bursting, forcing her to open her mouth, to suck in the stifling hot liquid, but she was almost there, almost to her Ashley. She could see the little round face, the dimpled chin, the pleading eyes. Kim reached, just another couple feet, she could get her, she could save Ashley. There! Ashley's hand was right there, her little fingers, clutching, opening and closing, reaching.

And then, just as Kim extended her hand to clasp Ashley, to finally hold her daughter again, to regain all that she'd lost, everything was gone: Ashley, the sea, Sam, the entire world.

*****

"Kimmie, no!" Trent kicked at the restraining demon, attempting to free himself, to stop Kim before it was too late. "Kimmie, don't! He tricked you! Kimmie, you'll die!" But Kim did not respond. She was trance-like, staring into the great pulsating blaze, edging closer, closer. Pereh stood beside her, whispering, coaxing, deceiving.

And then he was free, the demon cackling and drooling as Trent scrambled to his feet, racing toward his wife, screaming her name. But she was moving now, stepping into the fire, her arms rotating as if she meant to swim. "No!" he screamed as his wife's golden hair burst into red and yellow flames, her skin peeling from her back and arms as she silently dove into the heart of the blaze. "Kimmie! I still love you!"

But she never heard these words.

She was gone.

Dead.

Beyond recovery.

Trent would never again gaze into Kim's laughing blue eyes, never stroke her fine shimmering hair, never kiss her soft teasing lips, never make amends, never forgive and be forgiven. Kim was gone, and nothing would ever change that. And the baby! The unborn child, it was dead as well, never to be born, never to taste a single breath or receive a loving hug.

"No!" he screamed as his body trembled in fury and loss. "No!"

And he raced toward the throne of evil. Charging the devil, hurling curses at the author of all such oaths. His intent was to dismember, to punish, to kill the evil which could never be killed; to tear the creature apart, to toss the arms, the legs, the smug condescending face into the hellish blaze which had claimed his precious wife and unborn child. But he would not reach the golden platform, could not even get close. For a long thin arm reached out, narrow golden fingers closing about his forearm, halting him with a jolt. "Pretty pastor," said the insane Baqash, brown and green ooze dripping from his quivering lips. His eyes stared off in opposing directions. His voice was sing-song and moronic. "Pretty, putrid, pastor."

"Let go of me, you beast!" screamed Trent as he pummeled the uncomprehending demon with his free fist.

"Pretty, putrid, pastor," Baqash repeated. Trent kicked the thing, connecting sharply at its groin. "Pretty, putrid, pastor." He spit in Baqash's face. "Pretty, putrid, pastor." Frantic, Trent lunged forward, catching the demon's ear in his mouth, biting down, pulling, tearing. "Pretty, putrid, pastor."

And then Satan ended it all.

"Enough," he said. "Allow your failure to join his wife."

The buzz of a dozen demons engulfed Trent, wrenching him from Baqash's grasp and lifting him skyward. "Pretty, putrid, pastor?" he heard Baqash say one last time as he hovered perhaps seventy feet above ground. Demon claws sank into his flesh, pawing, tugging, pulling, causing his innards to twist and recoil. He kicked and screamed, clawing at the things, beating his fist against their snarling heads and clawing at their insane eyes.

It occurred to Trent that he was about to die – to really die. His earthly life was at an end, only seconds remaining. This was it – the end. And Trent had failed in all that had mattered. Kim was gone, Ashley lost or dead. Even Eldon was unaccounted for, probably murdered by some hideous demon. Trent had failed in all he'd hoped to do.

"Daddy!"

The voice was distant, surely a hallucination.

"Daddy!"

Trent struggled to turn, to arch his head in the direction of the faint familiar voice. He saw the blaze bellow, the fluttering demons, the scattered bones and ruins.

"Trent!" This time it was Eldon's Southside baritone. "Trent!"

"Eldon!" he hollered. "Where are y…" A demon hand clamped across Trent's mouth, stifling his question mid-sentence, even as he caught sight of Eldon, Ashley held firm in his arms, their eyes raised to meet his.

"Trent!" cried Eldon as demon hands released Trent. He was in free fall, rushing straight into the fiery mouth of the consuming blaze, the hungry flames leaping eagerly to receive him.

CHAPTER 49

The flames did not engulf Trent. Their dancing and cackling tentacles, stretching, reaching though they may, never grasped his flesh, never seared his being. Instead, they pulled away, became distant, inconsequential, even as they reached for him with lapping tongues of torment. Trent slowly realized that he wasn't about to die; that he was being held, carried by strong darkly golden arms. "Pretty, putrid, pastor," came a quivering voice. "Pretty, putrid… progeny."

Baqash dipped, twirled, avoiding the swipes and jabs of his fellow imps.

"What did you say?" managed Trent through impending nausea. "What did you call me?"

Baqash hissed, slashing at a charging spirit. As they dipped and swooped yet again, Trent managed a glance at the demon. The eyes of Baqash rolled in madness; his mouth drooped like that of a stroke victim.

"What did you call me?" Trent nearly screamed. Progeny! He'd called him Progeny – as in offspring!

Baqash seemed to concentrate, perhaps attempting to retrieve evasive lucidity just long enough to answer the twice-asked question. "I… may be beyond redemption," he said with much effort. "But, not so my son. Not so my son."

Before Trent could respond, a demon, green and red with four hawk-like wings of tattered flesh, descended on Baqash from above. Baqash used one of his own wings to snatch it from the air, pull it close, where he then bit the beast's nose, tearing and shredding. The demon howled in protest as Baqash kicked it free, still chewing on the nose like a wad of bubble gum as his foe tumbled toward the hard marble surface. His eyes were vacant, his expression, the dim smile of a sleeping imbecile.

Baqash swooped to nearly ground level and dropped Trent perhaps ten feet behind Eldon and Ashley. "Pretty, putrid, parasite," he said as he fluttered away with the rustle of uncoordinated wings. "Pretty putrid – dead!"

Trent glanced upward at the space filled with circling demons. Baqash was engaged with three of them already, attempting to fight them off, to give Trent a thin chance at escape. "Helel!" Baqash bellowed. "Helel, I am, was, maybe!" His mind seemed to slip in and out of reason. "You, me, you have me. Have me already – ARGOONAH! – Have my soul. Nothing else can you do to me."

And then the swarm smothered his words amidst a flurry of cackles and screams.

There was a sharp tug at Trent's arm. Eldon. "Trent, this way. We gotta go."

Trent turned one last time, but Baqash was obscured in a flurry of demonic frenzy. Had his words been true, or simply the ravings of an infirm mind? He had to be lying – had to!

Didn't he?

*****

Trent sat on a large stone cradling the silent Ashley in his arms as the sun peeked over the horizon at his back. The palace of Satan was gone, or at least gone from his view. It had faded away as Eldon led him through a narrow crevasse. Even the fire had disappeared, though Trent had found a couple of bones sticking out of the hard ground where it had been. He was certain that if he were to dig, he'd find the bones of lions, elephants, gorillas – and of his wife. The temple yet existed in the spiritual plane. It had not risen as the earth had collected dirt and dust through the centuries. It was still where it had been in the beginning, now deep beneath the surface.

Eldon approached Trent from his right, having respected his grief and given the father and daughter some time alone, some time to come to grips with it all – as if that would ever be possible. Still, Trent appreciated the consideration.

"You okay?" Eldon asked as he seated himself beside Trent on the rock.

"No. You?"

"Nah." He gazed toward the horizon. "Nothing a lobotomy and a life-long prescription of Prozac won't cure."

Trent nodded and embraced his daughter. She had not uttered a word since screaming "Daddy!" in the palace, but clung to her father like a drowning victim would cling to a lifeguard, squeezing him, wrapping her small form about him, nearly pressing the breath from him. It was a wonderful and precious feeling.

Trent had not yet told her about her mother. One day he would; the conversation was unavoidable. He would tell her of Kimmie's courage, of how she'd sacrificed herself for Ashley. But not now. Not for a long while. Trent glanced at Eldon. The man's hair was matted with blood. Stripes of red streaked his face.

"The pilot attacked you?"

"Yeah, with a wrench. Well," he corrected. "A demon attacked me. It just used the pilot. Poor guy probably had a whale of a headache when he woke up. I bopped him a good one before passing out." Eldon kicked at the dirt and rubbed his forehead. "When I woke up you and Kim were gone. I couldn't see the temple."

"Obviously, you found the place."

"That crazy voice in my head again. An angel, I guess. Wacky stuff. All of a sudden I could see that ugly abomination Satan calls a palace. And it was like when I was here years ago, on that dig; I knew just where to find that document. Somehow, I knew where to find Ashley, and then you."

Trent angled his head toward his brother. "What are you, some kind of prophet now?"

Eldon scoffed. "Yeah, I'm a prophet for a god I never believed in. And you, you're..." he let it go, not finishing the sentence.

But Trent finished it for him. "And I'm the son of a demon."

Could that be? Could it be true? Was it possible that he was a Nephilim? Or had Baqash deceived him yet again? Perhaps he'd simply rambled in his fading lucidity. But Trent knew the answer. He knew it deep down. In truth, all he had to do was look at his own family. All of them: Eldon, Reggie, both of his parents, all short, all dark-haired with brown eyes. Each, a bit on the stocky side. But Trent, a lean six foot six, red hair, one blue eye and one green. And his mother. Oh, his poor mother. She'd had a breakdown after Trent's birth, had never been quite right, not ever in his lifetime. Now, she resided at the Elgin mental facility. Oh, the poor woman. He didn't know the details of his conception, but he could imagine.

Trent stroked Ashley's head. She'd fallen asleep. Who knew how long it had been since she'd had opportunity to do so? He couldn't begin to imagine what his poor little girl had experienced, what terrible things she'd seen and heard, what horrible things demons could conceive.

Eldon rose and walked toward the sun, his back to Trent. "There's more," he said.

Trent looked up, but didn't turn to face his brother. "I'm listening." But he didn't want to listen. He never wanted to think of any of this again. A fallacy, he knew, but an attractive one. Anything Eldon could add would be too much too soon.

"Why did Baqash save you?" asked Eldon.

"Excuse me?"

Eldon sighed. "Think about it, Trent. Baqash is a freakin' demon. I kinda doubt his motives were pure. Maybe he's still trying to manipulate. You've made it through this whole thing intact. The fire didn't get you; you faced a swarm of wasps without a single sting. Kim's dead, Reggie's dead, little Ashley seems nearly catatonic, and here sits Trent, sound mind and body. Maybe Satan still has plans for you, brother."

Trent glared at his brother… Half-brother, he supposed. The blood tie wasn't quite so strong as he'd always assumed. "I'm of no use to them, El. You've uncovered their schemes. I can no longer be duped into becoming their pawn."

Eldon dropped his head, staring at the ground. "Are you sure, Trent? Are you really Satan's enemy? 'Cause it doesn't seem like you've been doin' too much to help the good guys lately."

Trent muttered a curse under his breath. "Enough, Eldon. I'm done with all of this."

Eldon shook his head. He was silent for several moments. Trent even began to think that perhaps the conversation was over. Finally Eldon turned, half facing his half-brother. "The memo, Trent, the one Satan wanted. I made a copy of it. It's on a memory stick." Eldon turned and walked back toward Trent, standing before him. "I still have the names of the Nephilim, the one's he's positioning for world control. You're some kind of demon-spawn, I've got some wacky angel whispering in my ear. You really think we're done with this? Because to me, this all seems like some sort of crazy calling, some whacked-out mission."

Trent didn't answer. He didn't want to lie to Eldon, but he wasn't ready to accept the brutal truth of his life as it now was. Quite likely, he'd never be done with this. Not ever. And this was something he didn't truly think he could live with. He cradled his daughter, kissed her on the top of her head. And then Trent wept, a deep, gut-wrenching weep. He could never be done with this.

EPILOGUE

From the journal of Baqash, the eternally fallen

I am evil.

Entirely so. Eternally so.

Such a great folly is mine. There is nothing good that yet resides within my being. None. My goals, my grand scheme, my plans of redemption, these were motivated only by a love of self, a loathing of my circumstances, a fear of what must come. I have had no pure thought, not one, since the fall. No glimmer of light, no momentary goodness, I have performed no unselfish deed.

Acts of kindness, of sympathy, of goodness, these are alien things. At best, vague memories of another being, a being of great potential, great love, great hope. That being shared the name Baqash, shared the same skin, saw with the same eternal eyes.

That being is no more.

My son, the putrid pastor, is right. I am dead, beyond redemption.

And now the madness has come. It is only in this moment of fragile lucidity that I pen these final words. I do not know if I shall ever have the capacity or the desire to do so again. Even now, mad images flit about my mind, taunting me, coaxing me, enticing me to join them. They are foul things, my imaginings, but they are mine. And I shall soon join them.

Imaginings. Perhaps, as you believe this tale to be such. You think it to be the fancy of an over-active mind, a simple diversion from the rigors of life. Nonsense, you say. Fiction. Perhaps it's best that you believe such. At the very least, it might give you comfort at night. For I'm sure you would not sleep so well if you should recognize that I have spent time with you – so many hours – that it was I that directed you through these pages. That it is I that sits beside you even now as you ponder these, my final words. You doubt me, of course. I can see it in your eyes, in the subtle twist of your mouth, the slight arch of the brow. This is good. This is as it should be. Take comfort in your unbelief. Embrace it. You and I, we have time, dear reader. We have so much time.

VISIT

SPEAKING VOLUMES ONLINE

HUGO, NEBULA, EDGAR,

SHAMUS, ANTHONY MACAVITY,

AGATHA, CARL SANDBERG,

ELLERY QUEEN, OWEN WISTER,

SPUR & BRAM STOKER

AWARD-WINNING

USA TODAY & NEW YORK TIMES

BEST-SELLING AUTHORS

www.speakingvolumes.us